MAGE
OF THE
BREWIN

MAGE OF THE BREWIN

E.J EATON

MAGE OF THE BREWIN

Copyright © 2022 Elliot Eaton

All rights reserved.

ISBN: 9798442985474

FOR MY FAMILY, THANK YOU FOR YOUR HELP AND SUPPORT. THIS BOOK IS HERE BECAUSE OF YOU!

CONTENTS

	Acknowledgments	i
1	The Deadly Ritual	Pg 1
2	**Chapter 1** - Heena	Pg 15
3	Jack	Pg 30
4	Jon	Pg 45
5	Jack	Pg 59
6	**Chapter 2** - Jack	Pg 72
7	Agent Lo	Pg 82
8	Thearon	Pg 89
9	Jack	Pg 99
10	Jon	Pg 107
11	Jack	Pg 113
12	**Chapter 3** - Atton	Pg 121
14	Agent Lo	Pg 128
15	Jack	Pg 136
16	Spence	Pg 152
17	Agent Lo	Pg 161
18	**Chapter 4** - Jack	Pg 168

19	Thearon	Pg 180
20	Jack	Pg 190
21	**Chapter 5** – Agent Lo	Pg 203
22	Sophia	Pg 208
23	Jack	Pg 219
24	Thearon	Pg 230
25	Agent Lo	Pg 239
26	**Chapter 6** - Jack	Pg 246
27	Sophia	Pg 245
28	Jack	Pg 265
29	Agent Lo	Pg 281
30	Thearon	Pg 290
31	Jack	Pg 314
32	Thearon	Pg 339
33	Jack	Pg 354

THE DEADLY RITUAL

As far as Androne temples go, the Arastone temple was still in good shape. Jon Skies made it his priority to make sure his son could be introduced to Androne in the right way. This is no religion, it's a cause to fight for a better, safer way of life. Well, this was what his father used to tell him.

Jack was too young to know what was about to happen. He had made it out of the forest which was a scary mission for a young boy. But still it had its enjoyment. Especially when his first sight after leaving the forest was an old temple, covered in cracks and overgrowth.

The forest had a calming feel for Jack. The sound of the birds singing to each other sent his thoughts to some strange places, but he is only a six-year-old boy after all. Every step he took excited him as the mist that covers his path moved around his feet allowing bright illuminous flowers to appear. Jack's mother had told him stories about the poisonous flowers that are in the wildlife. This didn't stop him from inspecting the colours and small intricate parts. His parents were rushing him out away from the forest, he didn't understand the rush and how they couldn't enjoy what was around them.

The closer Jack got to the mysterious building the more intrigued he got with the markings on the walls. These markings amazed Jack who started to get frustrated at his father for taking the flaming torch away which lit the walls up in the dark night. Jack admired his father so much, to a stage where he didn't know anything his father could not do. He was the strongest, most fierce man he knew. The door to the temple was heavy, too heavy for even Jon to manage. After several attempts and aid from Nash, his most trusted guard. A deep sound of concrete scraping across rock started to scare Jack, until his mother took him by his hand which calmed him down like a mother's hand should. The huge door opened as Jon and Nash put all their weight against it.

Fear started to grow on Jack. Heena, his mother, still holding on to his hand pulled him in with her.

Heena was quiet and looked very scared, she tried not to show it for Jack's sake, but he recognised it very early on even when they were back in the forest. As they entered the room, Jacks grip on Heena's hand tightened,

"Jack." she said in her soft voice, as she removed her hood, allowing her long brown hair to fall past her shoulders. "You will be fine, we won't be here for a minute longer than we need to, I promise." Jack calmed after a kiss from his mother and seeing her face that was no longer hidden.

Jack stroked his shivering fingers across markings that filled the wall. The markings were not clear to him as most of them fell into shadow as Jon moved the torch. The markings told a story, one Jack couldn't understand. The smell of the pine benches distracted him as it reminded him of the forest he had left.

Jon stepped around the side of the room, careful not to hit anything. He lifted his torch to find a lamp hanging off the wall by a chain. He touched the lamp with the tip of the flame causing the room light up, as flames rushed around the walls making everyone turn away closing their eyes.

"Nash, there should be a large stone with Androne's mark on, help me find it." Nash nodded and helped Jon brush dust and debris off everything in the room.

"It must be here, once we find it-" Jon turned to talk to Jack, but he wasn't there.

"Jack!" he shouted as he spun on his heel, he found him sitting in front of a stone with markings on it like a gravestone shaped rock. But this was no grave. It was a one-thousand-year-old relic of Androne, one of a few that remained.

Visible engravings on the stone were a large star with three triangular shapes pointing into it. Jon sat next to his son who had his eyes closed. Although he was still, Jon felt that Jack was in pain. Under no circumstances should you wake anyone who appears to have a connection with Androne. Jack's face was turning a deep red and a visible vein started appearing.

"Jon please!" Heena groaned, "look at him." all Jon could do was to hold her close, trying to comfort her.

"We will hurt him more by waking him" Jon said but he couldn't make Heena appreciate or understand. He knew this was the first time his wife had experienced this ritual.

"He needs to make the full connection, or he will never be able to fulfil the role he has-".

Jack fell forward saving himself with his hands, but he was still in his dream. Jack closed his hands around the dirt and little chips of rock on the ground. He groaned in pain which made it harder for his parents. For a ritual to be complete, a connection with Androne must be secure or memory loss and nightmares will occur.

"My Lord!" Nash yelled as he came running into the room tripping on broken planks of wood sticking out all around the room. He pulled Jon's arm, "you need to see this, come outside with me now".

Jon followed Nash as a mighty crash of thunder vibrated the whole building. Jon managed to keep his footing, turning his head to see Jack still in the same position as he was when he left his side. As they exited, the sky had turned a dark grey as furious clouds rolled towards the temple.

"He's here" Jon said to Nash, "we must

leave now!"

They both ran back into the temple to see Jack still meditating holding on to his mother's hand. The peacefulness of the scene stopped Jon in his tracks as this is what he promised Heena it would be like for Jack. Jon shook himself back to his senses, he knew he had to break the ritual, or they would all perish, and the temple would become their tomb.

"Jack come on son; we need to go now." Jon said, shaking his arm as his grip tightened.

"What are you doing, you said we can't wake him." Heena pushed Jon away and held her arms around Jack.

"I have seen in you what this ritual can do to someone when completed, so it won't be my son who has to go through a worse life." Jon knew she was right, it was a risk, but he also knew the imminent danger they were all in was more severe.

"He will die if we stay, we all will" Jon said as he threw Jack over his shoulders. "Nash get Heena out of here, keep her safe. If we split up, he can't follow us all, I'll meet you back at the boat".

The roof and walls around them began to crumble, rocks fell from above them. Jon fled the temple hearing calls from Heena for him getting quieter.

Nash was pulling her away in the opposite direction as he headed back to the forest.

Rolling clouds followed him, lighting up the sky with fire as if two dragons were battling. As he entered the forest he looked back at the temple as it crumbled to nothing. He continued into the forest knowing if he was to stop, the pursuit would end with him killed.

Jack began to move around in Jon's arms slowing him down, making him loosen his grip. Jon found a small cave-like opening, where he could calm Jack down from the awakening. Jon didn't know what real damage this could cause to Jack, or the pain he may have to endure ending the ritual prematurely. Inside the cave overgrown moss covered the rocks, making it a soft place to lay Jack down. Jack's skin was burning up to the state where it would scold you to touch. Jon poured what water he had left over Jack's head in hope that it would cool him off.

As the water ran off Jack's forehead, his eyelids tightened to stop the droplets of water stinging his eyes. Once the water had passed, his auburn eyes opened, to see his son open his eyes made Jon smile gave him optimism. He held Jack close and began to move forward with a new intent. He had to get back to the boat and meet up with his wife. Is she alive? Did she make it? Jon had to push on, these thoughts would only slow him down and put Jack's life at risk. Jon's pace got quicker; he was moving as if he was skating on ice, pushing branches and other wildlife aside. He then hit a wall of rocks and had to stop.

The cliffs surrounded them, he knew he had to get over them to get to the coast where his boat and his wife awaited, or so he hoped. His head began to hurt as ideas of how to get there were coming and going but none of them good enough for his brain to accept. He knew he had to climb, climb with a six-year-old on his back.

Jon started to make his way up, eyeing his every possible foot placement, any wrong move and they would both fall.

The thunderous clouds crashed and banged ever closer. The noise was deafening, the lightning flashed sharper, and the rain felt like little stones hitting him. Jon lifted his arm up for his next move, but every finger felt like a weight of its own, until to his relief, his head peaked over the top, he made it. He rolled Jack on to the surface and pulled himself up and lay down exhausted.

The rain stopped. The lightning was the only form of light, which only gave Jon seconds at a time to find his route ahead of him. After a couple of flashes all Jon could gaze into was a figure of a man no more than a shadow. Two small white eyes stared straight back at him, there was no other feature no mouth or nose, no emotion,

"You're not here, get out of my head, you're dead" the shadow replied only with a cackle that echoed around Jon. The words were not clear. The shadow then said something that he did understand.

"Jon Skies, revenge." it was almost inaudible. Jon heard it loud and clear, he held his son close and whispered into his ear, keeping his arms wrapped around him,

"I'm sorry son."

As the noises got louder it was echoing like a stampede rushing past them.

"This is it." Jon muttered under his breath.

Time seemed to stand still, years of fighting and running from this poison and it would all come to an end. Jon had always fought back but now he felt defeated, on his knees. The figure now towered over Jon, who prepared himself like he knew what was about to happen. Jon held Jack's head to his chest as the shadow now stood above him, leaving smoke like trails behind him.

Any light soon disappeared as the shadow surrounded them both like a large blanket that had fell over them. Jon met his eyes as they got closer, he could feel the evil pouring out of them as it attempted to enter his soul. If he had any facial features, Jon imagined there to be a grin so large full of victory and death. Horrified, he closed his eyes, turned his head towards Jack and waited.

The sound of thunder stopped and the ground around him shook. Vibrations got so big Jon had to cover his and Jack's ears from the deadliest screech. A pack of Armstrong hounds pounced over their heads towards the figure. The shadow rose into the storm which didn't go away and looked more threatening than it did before. Jon pulled Jack back to his feet who seemed to have recovered from his black out. They got ready to move but then saw that the Armstrong hounds were surrounding them. The wolf-like creatures were deadly. They had teeth like hunters' knives and claws like a hack saw. All Jon could do was hold his hands out and hope that the hounds knew they meant no harm and wanted to leave. All but one growled with clenched teeth, saliva dripped from each jaw. Jon looked into the calm hound's eye's ahead of him, which he assumed was the leader,

"Please." he whispered in a weak, tired voice, but that was all he could muster. After what seemed like a short standoff, the leader of the pack edged towards Jon and inspected them both. Then, to Jon's surprise they left them alone. The rainfall once again had become so strong a large puddle had emerged around them.

As they moved forwards, they spotted the route to get to the boat in front of them. Although they were no longer in a chase, they knew they were not safe yet.

The river was finally in sight. Jack could see the figures of his mother and Nash. His excitement of seeing his mother showed as he dashed off in front of Jon to reach them as quick as possible. Jon had to remind himself of Jack's age in these situations. His speed and the difficulty he faced in keeping up with a six-year-old with no fear was not ideal in a dark forest.

"My lady! Look!" said Nash as he pointed towards her son running towards them with Jon close behind. Heena ran out to meet Jack and threw her arms around him, almost smothering him.

"Oh, Jack you're OK," Heena ran her hand through his hair and then around his cheek. Jon slowed a little but finally reached his family and put his arms around Heena.

"We must go." said Jon, but Heena still held on to Jack patting him down making sure he was ok. "Heena please!" Jon shouted.

Heena kept hold of Jack as she climbed into the small boat.

"Mother why did you leave us alone, we couldn't find you." Said Jack in his small voice. Heena looked up at Jon and then back into Jack's eyes,

"I'm sorry Jack, you needed to be with your father, he could protect you better than I could." Jon froze whilst listening to Heena as he knew these words would get him in a lot of trouble in the future. Instead of waiting for the conflict that was about to happen, he turned to Nash,

"Nash, I need you to go back to Ando, we're going to have to go and start a new life for the safety of my family. I can no longer put them at risk, he will hunt me forever, he won't stop," said Jon. He turned to step into the boat, "this is the last order I give you my friend, stay safe". He climbed in next to Heena and pushed away with the ore.

"My lord what message must I give Ando." Nash stood and watched them sail away,

"Tell them we perished in the storm." Jon shouted back to Nash who nodded, and turned, and ran off into the forest,

"This needs to stop, Jon, I mean it no more, did you know what we were about to go through? Was that an Ando initiation? I don't want to hear any more about Ando, Androne or anything, wherever we land we start a new life do you understand. Or I take Jack and go by myself," Heena said in a demanding yet sobbing state, "If we even make it to shore alive."

The waves hit the boat hard, and the route ahead looked even harder for them to pass.

"It's over, it's too late now. That was our last chance. Like us he will be on the run for the rest of his life." Jon said looking at Jack with tears starting to form in both of his eyes. "All we can do is try and give him a chance of life while hiding from everything. I know somewhere we can go; we will be cared for, and we can all have our new life" he turned and looked at Heena "I have failed."

CHAPTER ONE

12 years later 1020 AGW

HEENA

Dust, mud, burtings, farming was never on Heena's life plan. But when your family must run and hide changing your life, selling burting meat and milk will have to do. It was never going to make them rich, but it was keeping a roof over their heads and food on their table.

   The Beachdale residents relied on Heena and her milk supplies, and the whole town came to her. Heena needed people to come to her stall as this was the only attention she got. Jon had risen to commander within the Dale Guard. Meaning he was roaming the streets which felt like twenty-four hours a day.

As for Jack, well he was all for his father, and he wanted to get to where he was as soon as possible. Heena knew it wouldn't be long until they took him from her, but she knew it is what he would want. At eighteen years old he had become a strong fighter like his father before him. He spent hours with his father training. As soon as Jon walked in from duty, he was in the yard helping Jack. Heena felt jealous of this bond, but his strength and ability would save him, protect him, or kill him.

Heena had never seen this shadow that Jon tried to tell her about as Jack only mentioned him as a nightmare. She knew her trust and even her love for Jon was shrinking year by year, day by day. He loved her and Jack, but she feared that the history of their family and the threats that seemed to surround them would consume them. She was fearful and living afraid of something that wasn't her doing.

It was a burden she may no longer be able to live with. This had improved since Jon stepped down from the guard. He was at home more and the community of Beachdale showed a huge respect towards the family for his service.

But what life would Heena be able to live without Jon? These were the thoughts that flew around her mind. Jack wouldn't stay with her, why would he? With his father he could achieve power, with her, well she was close to the mayor of Beachdale who could get him into politics.

Unfortunately, that didn't have the same attraction. Not compared to power, respect and being feared by most other troops from local towns.

Her daily routine very rarely changed, after she woke, she would head down to the pens that were full of burtings that varied in size. Some of the young burtings were only two feet tall, with the wool making up for half a foot of that. But the burtings she looked after were female. The Skies farmed the burtings for milk and meat. The meat from the males was the most popular, but Heena left them to Jon as they could grow to be the same size as a person and well-built muscles to boot.

Afterwards, she would take the milk to the local market where she sold it to the stall that gave her the best price in an auction. This would guarantee sales for the stall so the auction could get very heated. This didn't bother Heena as it meant more money in her pocket and for her family. Heena couldn't wait to leave as she hated the smell of meat, herbs, perfume. As well as the amount of sweaty, dirty people crowded and enclosed under a huge marque held up by rope.

No visit to the town centre would be complete for Heena without harassment from the town Governor Louis Biggs.

"Heena Skies how are you on this beautiful morning." It wasn't a beautiful morning. In fact, Heena felt it was a depressing morning as she shivered and squinted when hit by piercings of sunlight. But Biggs was an optimist for the most part, until Heena replied.

"Beautiful? in your mind Biggs." Heena replied.

"When are you going to give up this farming nonsense and join my team? You would fit in wonderfully." Biggs said trying to keep up with Heena as she was walking away at some speed.

"Biggs, as a farmer I will get more respect than if I join your office."

"But your boy, Jack, I could find a place for him. Think of the future he could have, safe from harm," Biggs pleaded. "He is as fierce as Jon and he has your intelligence, you never know he could rise as far as Governor one day,"

"There is more chance of the Malkav rising from the underworld than any of us joining your corrupt office." Heena sneered.

"Fine, er, I'll let you sleep on it." said Biggs.

As he scurried away looking over his shoulder as if the Malkav, the beast of death, had risen from the underworld.

Heena missed her parents and sisters. She left them when she left with Jon. His stories of past adventures seemed so much more exciting than anything that she had experienced at her hometown of Brid. Her parents still live there, she assumed. She hadn't seen them since she had left, something she knew her sisters would never forgive her for. She was the youngest of three which always put her in the position of the lonely sister.

As her older sisters had a friendship group that she wasn't invited to, she was too young. So, when she came home one day with a strong, handsome young foreign boy, it didn't help her popularity within the family. Her parents also didn't approve as she was to follow tradition and marry a local boy. The baker's son who had been trying to get her attention for years but looked awkward all the time. No, making her sisters jealous was much more appealing to her.

The old town was very picturesque, it attracted many travellers. Heena's brunette curls had caught Jon's attention and once he made eye contact with her, they bonded. Jon could offer exactly what she wanted, escape. When that day came, she always remembered sitting with him looking out to sea. He seemed nervous, and this wasn't a trait she had seen in him before. The sun had started to set on the horizon creating a shimmering purple reflection off the water.

"Heena," said Jon. "it's time for me to go, my friends and mentor are moving on, given a new mission to complete."

"Why can't you stay here, with me!" Heena pleaded with him, "you can stay with my parents, and my sisters."

"I can't, it's not safe for me here and I will put your family in danger." said Jon trying to comfort Heena. "I am now an important part of this mission; I have to go."

"Well then I will go with you" said Heena immediately, "I will go and pack up a few things, I won't be any trouble." She turned and ran back to her house before Jon could argue with her.

Heena lived on the coast, her bedroom looked out over the endless horizon. When she made it up there, she looked out to the calm ocean waves rolling over the sandy beach. This was her favourite thing to do when stressed, it took her into another world of peace, where she had no worries.

"So, you're going then?"

"Caroline!" Heena jumped as one of her older sisters walked into her room. "What do you mean?"

"What do you think mother and father will say, when their youngest, perfect daughter, runs away with a foreign boy" Caroline said. "You don't need to leave to find happiness, Heena, what can he offer you, excitement? Adventure? Please." Caroline strode around Heena's room with purpose. She picked up her possessions and dropping them down like she was above Heena by more than her age.

"Why wouldn't I want to go and explore? There isn't anything here for me."

"There's family Heena, one day, you might learn that!" Caroline picked up Heena's hairbrush and used it on her long brown hair. Like many things it was identical to Heena's, only height and age separated them.

"Father isn't from Brid! If he didn't travel here, he wouldn't have met mother." Heena sputtered. placing clothing into her case.

"That was because of war Heena, he fled from Mitchler, because of war! You're leaving because you're selfish, and you're ungrateful for hat you have here." The sisters' voices both became venomous.

"You're selfish, actually you're jealous that I have found something or someone that's more exciting than your own boring existence."
Both sisters fell silent. Heena shocked herself in what she said. Caroline couldn't believe what words were coming out of Heena's mouth. The sisters didn't share the closest of relationship, but they rarely argued or fell out,

"My life is not boring, not anymore anyway."

"What do you mean?" Heena asked.

"Why do you care? You're leaving! What happens in Brid isn't enough for you" Caroline said, waving at Heena as she turned towards the door.

"What, Caroline? Is it a boy?" said Heena. Her brown eyes widened with interest.

"A boy?" Caroline chortled. "No Heena, I'm not like you, I would rather work hard to achieve something rather than putting my future on a boy."

Heena was leaning from side to side to try and see Caroline's face, who was still facing the door, for, in fact, she was smiling. Caroline turned back to Heena with her arms crossed and her smile still etched on her face.

"I'll make a deal with you." Caroline said. Heena stared Caroline in her eyes waiting for Caroline's offer. "I will tell you what I have been up to and share it with you, if, you forget about the boy and you stay here."

Heena gulped and struggled with the urge to find out what the secret was. She then turned to look back at the perfect ruby horizon that she would be about to explore with Jon.

"Fine." Heena breathed. "I'll stay."

"Really?" Caroline asked rather surprised she came around as quick as she did.

"Yes." Heena said deflated.

"OK wait here, I will be back."

Caroline ran out of the room with gusto.

Heena, picked at her nails waiting for Caroline to return. But before Heena had chance to turn back to the horizon, Caroline was back holding a small beaten-up book.

"What is that?" Heena asked.

"I will show you, look." Caroline sat next to Heena on her bed.

"Mage of the Brewin?" Heena said, confused, reading the title on the cover.

"What is it?"

"I have had this for a while, it has spells in it that you can learn."

'Who is Filheart?' Heena asked.

"He was the first Mage of the Brewin!" Heena shrugged her shoulders still as confused as before.

"Look it says here, 'Filheart the Great, became the first person to use Brewin magic. He created the common spells we use now and to this very day. Filheart or Filheart the Great, created Brewin magic for street entertainment which then followed with huge success. Selling out theatres entertaining everybody. But, after teaching his assistant all he knew, she started using Brewin magic as a weapon."

"Brewin is magic?" Heena asked.

"Yes, I have been learning it too, it's very

hard, and takes a lot of practice but look what I can do."

Caroline turned to her chest of drawers that had four long lit candles, she closed her eyes and held her hand out towards them. A few seconds past with nothing happening.

"Caroline, what are you showing me?" Heena asked.

"Wait, I'll try again" this time, Heena felt a gust of wind propelled from Caroline, blowing the candles out.

"Yes, it worked!" Carline shouted.

"That's brilliant!" Heena said rather impressed.

"We can learn this together and become famous." Caroline said.

Heena picked up the book and started flicking through the pages,

"I told you it was better than some boy."

"WHAT BOY!" scowled a towering figure standing at the door.

"Father!" Caroline gasped. Making Heena drop the book on the floor sprawling pages around them. Eder, the girls' father, ran the household with a strict and powerful ideology. To talk about running away or Brewin magic with the door open with him in the house would not be a smart move.   Eder strode into the room with a scornful look, his two bushy eyebrows sat curled, over his small grey eyes.

"What is this?" Eder said in his low coarse voice, as he picked up a handful of loose pages.

"BREWIN MAGIC!" Heena stood shocked the windows did not shatter at the sound of his voice. Heena and Caroline held on to each other as they cowered in the corner of the small room. Looking up at Eder when he was in this mood is so imposing, to the state where they couldn't see anything in their peripherals. Only Eder towering over them.

"I will not have anybody practising this in my house, do you know the danger you could get us in? If the Dominion were to find out they would come and kill us all assuming you haven't already blown us up. And this boy! Anyone going to tell me about him?" The sisters stayed silent and passed a few glances towards each other.

"I met him father" Heena said.

"Local boy?"

Heena shook her head looking at the ground.

"A foreigner!?" Eder exploded. "Not only are you trying to learn illegal magic in my house you're breaking all traditions we have brought you up with and running away with a strange boy. I am disgusted, I will deal with this later, but for now, who's responsible for this?" Eder held three pages scrunched up in his hand.

"It's mine, I was showing Caroline." Heena lied. Caroline stared at Heena in disbelief.

"Come with me now!!" Eder clenched his fist around Heena's scruff and pulled her out of the room, and finally let go when they arrived at the front door. "Who is he? You tell me now, this boy has got you into this hasn't he, HASN'T HE!" Eder exploded again. Heena stepped back, resting up against the door.

"What are you going to do?" Heena asked sobbing, deep down she knew/

"I'm going to make sure this boy knows who he's dealing with so you can take me to him."

"No, father please don't!"

"You tell me now or you can get out of my house."

"You don't mean it" said Heena.

"Tell me where he is" Heena knew he was serious.

"I can't!"

"Why? Are you telling me, you care more for his safety than your own?"

"No, I'm protecting you, he's well protected, you won't be able to hurt him."

"Don't question what I'm capable of!"

"I know what you're capable of, that's why I'm telling you to stay here!" Heena had never raised her voice at her father before. "Stop protecting him, in fact, if you care more for him, then go, go to him."

"No." Heena pleaded.

"Go now!" Eder kicked the door open and pushed her out. Once Heena hit the floor Eder slammed the door shut.

As Heena lay on her back staring at the locked door of her home, flickering candlelight caught her attention from her bedroom window. Inside, looking out was Caroline with distress etched on her face. Heena wondered why she took the blame for possessing the book, especially whilst dealing with her father's questions about Jon. She knew deep down she couldn't go back, and although she made the promise to her sister to stay, she knew it was the end. Heena picked herself up and gave Caroline a desolate look and walked away from her childhood home, never to return.

"Heena, you came." Jon said as he spotted her approaching from the distance.

"I'm staying with you; I can't come back." Heena said through heavy tears.

"I understand." Jon said wrapping his hands around her. He knew this was never going to happen peacefully and that he had to do what he could to comfort her.

The sailing away from Brid was hard for Heena. The boat had many people who knew Jon, who she had never seen before, many were unfriendly and rude to her. Not to mention the filthy surroundings she found herself in, it was a stark difference to the life she had lived back at home.

Heena wanted to leave with Jon because of how life at home with her family. Especially as her sisters weren't enough for her compared to the exciting life, she thought Jon would give her. Yet today, even though she had got what she had wanted all those years ago, she found herself wanting to escape back to the life she once had.

JACK

Finally, it was dawn. Jack would always start the day dressed in his training clothing, swinging his practice sword around like a dance. It was very impressive for an eighteen-year-old to move like he did. Ever since Jon had stepped down from service and been at home, Jack had started to surpass his skill in training, knocking him down on a regular basis.

Jon stepped out of the house into the rear garden of their farmland and watched his son train. He was very proud of what Jack had become and his ambition. Jon knew Jack could be very cocky when in the garden, spending hours swinging his training sword at the planks of wood standing up as if they were the enemy. Jack spotted Jon, seeing him in the corner of his eye. This was the opportunity to show off to show his father what he could do, but it never impressed him.

Jon stood by the gate of the pen of the burtings. Burtings were a delicious meat to eat which made them very valuable to them. But if you upset a male, they could do some serious damage to a human. not only did they have long pointed horns, if they hit you with a good shot by their long thin tail it could snap your spine. Jon had wanted to challenge Jack for some time, and he finally looked ready,

"So, you think you're a fighter, and ready for the Dale Guard?" challenged Jon, Jack turned with his training sword in attack position.

"I'm ready when you are father."

"You know the burtings well, you have looked after them since you were little. You have also slaughtered some for their meat, but can you protect yourself against their revenge?"

Jon opened the pen and a huge burting stepped out. Burtings range from the size of a small child up to the size of an adult human, they were pure muscle on four legs. The biggest were usually looked up at as the leader whether they were wild or farmed and they knew when you were taking them for meat.

"Remember Jack, you won't win with strength." Jack looked back at Jon and smiled. The burting started to charge, dust flew up from its hoofs. Jack stood his ground but then at the last minute jumped to the side to avoid the beast. Jack couldn't believe the speed of the thing.

"Come on! You can't dodge it forever." Jack grumbled under his breath trying to encourage himself. Jack decided to stand his ground and face it one on one. Jon watched anxiously at his son's decision as the burting charged at Jack.

He swung his sword at the head of the burting which got caught between the animal's horns. It held for mere seconds before the sword shattered sending Jack hurtling back from the follow through.

"She is not going to be happy with this," Jon mumbled to himself. "Jack you will never be stronger than a burting, especially an adult male, use your brain, think! That is the one advantage you have in this fight." Jack picked himself up.

"I have no weapon." Jack shouted looking

at his sword laying in pieces on the floor.

"Find one!"

Jack looked around and saw the farming store, but the burting prepared for his next charge. Jack ran in the opposite direction to the store encouraging the burting to follow in a charge. Jack used a barrel to springboard himself over the on-charging beast, who continued through the side of the outbuilding. Jon sighed looking at the damage.

"I am definitely in trouble." Jon sighed. although impressed with his move. Jack rushed over to the open store building which was full of different pieces of equipment covered in silvery cobwebs. He chose to pull out a metal prod staff.

"You have got this Jack." He muttered to himself to assure himself he could do it. Jack ran towards the burting swinging the prod towards the burting's head causing the beast to swing its deadly tail around his body. The shot aimed for Jack, who managed to dodge it at the last second. Jack then hit the burting's shins on its front legs, tripping it over. He knew this was his chance but couldn't keep himself on his feet. He stumbled and hit the floor.

Jack's face was a scarlet red and had sweat dripping from his forehead.

"It's not over Jack, come on, get up," Jon shouted from the other side of the yard. The burting made it to its feet long before Jack, who shocked him with its stamina. This time the burting ran at Jack and made a sharp turned a few feet before him. It swung its tail towards his face, which twisted around his prod. But Jack managed to keep control of it whilst spinning round and then lodged the tip through the skull of the burting. After swaying from side to side the burting fell forward face first to the ground taking Jack with him.

Jack pulled himself up and pulled his prod from the burting's head with a proud smile on his face.

"Impressive son, very impressive. I did think for a moment it had you there, that would have been it for your mother." Jon joked but then turned serious.

"But how would you fare against a fully trained captain?" Jon picked up his sword and started to walk towards Jack. He had bettered his father several times but not when he was at his best with a metal sword.

"Are you sure about this, did you not see

how the burting turned out?" Jack had waited a long time for this and awaited his father's attack.

"I'm sure son, there's still plenty of life in me yet." Jon swung his sword towards Jack who blocked each strike using both ends of the prod. Jon could feel that, despite what he had said to Jack, he could no longer fight at the pace he used to. Each blow from Jack vibrated through his sword almost making him drop it.
"Are you done father?" Jon ignored the question, thrusting his sword towards Jack's arm, but Jack bettered every swing and attack. Jon knew this wouldn't last long. Before he even decided his next move Jack crouched swinging his prod round, taking Jon off his feet, pointing the end towards his father's face.

"Are you done father?"

"I'm done," Jon replied taking Jack's hand as he lifted him up "that was very impressive. In fact, there is very little now that I can teach you." this was a huge compliment to Jack as he was very aware of his father's abilities in his prime.

"Do you think I'm ready for the guard?" Jack asked. This was a question he had wanted to ask for some time but knew Jon wouldn't give him the answer he thought he deserved, but now he had beaten him in combat.

"The Dale Guard would be lucky to have you son. Come with me, I have something I want to give you." Jack felt a strange feeling of excitement but nerves at the same time.

They headed into the house passing Heena who did not even turn to acknowledge them. Jack felt a little confused as she had never ignored him before. This thought soon passed as his excitement of what his father might be giving him clouded over everything else and they entered the basement.

The basement had always been off limits to Jack although his father spent many an hour down there in there, but never shared with him or his mother to why. It was dark, cold, and small, Jack started to wonder what could be down here that his father had to give to him. Jon pushed a pile of papers off the top of a small case. It looked old and worn, brown in colour with leather seals on the corners. He opened the case and inside sat a forearm shield. It was a charcoal black colour but still a thing of beauty, the star like emblem engraved into it gave it its uniqueness.

"I made this when I was younger when I was on my adventures. It's made of vendel, it's stronger than any other metal. It's not indestructible but it will take many hits with a sword to give you extra defence." Jon placed the shield on Jack's forearm "I want you to have it, as it served me well during my time on the guard."

"It's so light, I can't feel it." Jack couldn't help but to wave his arm around and was still amazed by the weight.

"Vendel is expensive so if people see you with it, they will challenge you for it or try and take it. Especially pirates." As Jon started tidying the space up, he noticed Jack's eyes were getting closer to the bigger chest that was next to them. "That chest is for another time Jack, prove yourself in the guard first."

The following day, Jon took Jack to the Beachdale Barracks, where he was once captain of the Dale Guard. They passed under a sandstone archway into an open ground with soldiers training with wooden swords. They were being splinted from speed and power that they were being struck. Behind the soldiers, there were archers aiming at targets dotted around the boundary wall.

"Take this in Jack, this will be your second home." Jon said.

"Where do I sign?" Jack responded turning his head in every direction, trying to see everything around him. "This is incredible." He had never seen where these soldiers trained. The soldiers that he admired so much and had worked so hard to emulate.

The training area was a huge space within a circular wall. Enclosed within was many disciplines, archery, sword fighting and a stamina course full of obstacles for the trainees to overcome. In the middle of all the areas was the barracks themselves. A building that wasn't large, but a marvel of architecture with stone pillars surrounded the building. Each one holding a banner with the symbol of each team of the Dale Guard. For archers there was a black banner with a gold arrow within a gold circle. Infantry was a scarlet red banner, with two swords clashing and trainees was a dark green banner with a silver flame inside a triangle.

Jon opened the heavy doors and the sight made Jack's jaw drop and freeze on the spot. In the centre of the room was a statue of two soldiers sparring, standing on a plinth, it was a grand sight to behold. A glimmer of light from the candles that were lit around the room shone off the pure gold surface. The room was busy, with people moving from place to place, without making eye contact.

"This is amazing," Jack said as he stepped towards the statue, "let me guess this is you right?"

"No," said Jon amused, "this statue has been here long before we arrived but look at this." Jon took Jack closer to the statue and pointed to the six-foot-high black marble plinth.

"There, look" Jack read what was engraved on a golden plaque.

"To honour the service and bravery of the captain and his men, Jon Skies, Jack read with pride. "Wow."

"He didn't do too bad, I suppose." they both turned round to see a huge man with short orange hair, topping his round head.

"Morton Grice." Jon said shaking his hand, "I see your still captain."

"Who else would do it better than me Skies, hey?" Morton said back in his low coarse voice, "no need to tell me who this young lad is, you must be Jack?"

"Yes sir." Jack said, standing as straight as a board.

"Ha, at ease, my boy, now I can only assume I know why you have brought him here Jon."

"There is very little he can learn from me Morton." Jon said, Jacks eyes hadn't left Morton's until he let out another laugh.

"OK so where are we putting you young Skies, you will of course start as a trainee, but you need to choose a path." Morton returned his gaze into Jack's eyes, leaning closer as if I he could read Jack's thoughts. "Are you brave and strong enough to be a soldier in our infantry? or do you have the patience and eye to be an archer? Many young boys come to me Master Skies, and your father before me thinking they are ready to join the Dale Guard, BUT!" Morton roared. now centimetres from Jack's face.

"They drop during training Jack, they run at the first sight of conflict. We will push you to your limits and remember this." he paused as he raised back up to look towards Jon and then back to Jack.

"You may think because your father is Jon Skies, you're invincible. It doesn't mean the sight of a Hajobe Dragon won't strike fear down your spine, do you understand boy?" Jack was still a little in shock at what was going on and didn't realise he was stood in silence with his eyes wide open, still staring at Morton.

"Well err... Morton thank you, for that. Expect his application in the coming days." Jon stepped in front of Jack, trying to take the attention of his inexperience of being in front of Morton Grice.

Jack was quiet for most of the walk home. He thought being able to see the barracks was an amazing thing, although he didn't have to admit that he found Morton's introduction very intimidating.

"He's right you know." Jon said stopping outside their farm, "you do need to pick your path, and beating me in a duel is not the same as coming up against an army in a war. Which is why you can't learn anymore from me, I stepped down to be with my family Jack, my fighting days are gone. War is coming, I can feel it, I don't want to send you to your death. What I'm trying to say Jack, is that beating me does not make you invincible." Jack looking at the ground and nodded.

"So do you see yourself as an archer?" Jon

said finally.

"No, I'm a fighter, I'm not going to hide behind a bow and arrow."

"Jack, one day, a bow and arrow might save your life, remember that."

"OK, I'll join which ever one gets me to captain the quickest."

"Well, that depends on you Jack, not your weapon, your blade may well be the sharpest on the battlefield. That doesn't mean you're going to win the battle. There's more to it than that, there needs to be more to you as a person and a leader. Arrogance will get you killed Jack; you need to be confident. But in my experience, and from the people who have fought by my side, under my command anybody can kill anyone when it comes to the time."

"Morton can't be beat that easy, can he?" said Jack.

"Morton? He was my second in command, he wanted to prove himself for so long. I beat him every time, yet he always towered over me, he's stronger than me, faster than you think. But he is bloody useless with a sword though." Jon laughed as he placed his arm around Jack leading him into the yard.

"Now, let's keep the visit to the barracks

between you and me for now, let your mother get over the destroyed yard first!"

The following day, as they guessed. Jon was fixing the fences and shed walls, following his sparring with his father and his fight with the burting. Jack had to help his mother butcher the burting.

"Jack come on; its blood didn't bother you when you stuck the prod through its skull." Heena said exhaling with frustration. "What was your father thinking, I'm worried about soldiers trying to kill you, yet your father is encouraging the livestock to do it for them."

Jack stayed silent and listened to his mother's rant. He had never watched the burtings butchered for their meat, now he knew why. Every time Heena's knife went through flesh, Jack had to turn away. His face turned a murky yellow.

"You want to join the Guard and your scared of a bit of blood, oh Jack," Heena teased.

Jack gulped and took a deep breathe, the smell of raw meat was enough to make him want to leave.

"Hang on, you're helping me, spend some time with me for once in your life. What would you do if your father left hey, don't say go with him?" Heena looked down and flinched once she realised, she was pointing the sharp knife towards Jack. The knife fell out of Heena's hand making Jack step away.

"Oh my, I'm sorry Jack, I know you're going to be leaving soon, and I have watched you with your father fighting, why wouldn't they want you. They always thought so much of him, and I am sure they will of you too. I'm scared Jack, I'm scared of losing you. I left my home, when I was your age and haven't been back since, I have no idea how they are, if they are even still alive." Heena leaned into hug Jack.

"No... please, the blood." Jack pleaded. Heena stepped away with a small smile.

"When they call for you, I know you will make us proud, but please, don't be a stranger to me, losing you, well I don't know what I would do. Now go before you vomit all over the place, if you think blood alone is bad, try cleaning them both."
Jack accepted and rushed away towards the house; the sooner he could clean himself up the better.

JON

Jon's adventures and experiences were something to be envious of to any stranger to whom he tells the tales. But to him it was painful, he was an orphan picked up by some strangers who claimed him to be of special importance. Of course, as a child you can only go along with what you're told.

Yes, he learned more as he grew more knowledgeable, but he never understood what was happening. Every day seemed to be a constant battle against people who were chasing him and his companions. Through his travels and the people, he went along with the situations that he found himself in, he became a fierce fighter. His obsession with his abilities took him away from even trying to find his real parents or any family members for that fact, he felt it would make him weak. He didn't know or worry about them then so why should he now.

Of course, the time came where his heart felt different, and he fell for Heena. This was new territory for him as he could not ignore how he felt. He chose to take Heena with him against advice from close friends. His mentor told him it would put both in danger and it would be his fault if Heena was killed. So, Jon married her. Then had a child, Jon matured over night at this point he had a son, he knew he had to protect this child with his life. They ran to Beachdale because of the town's well-known Dale Guard who could protect them better than any other number of swords.

Beachdale didn't give land and a home to any strangers who walked in. But once Jon showed his ability with a sword, they gave him a home in return for service within the Guard. This was ideal for Jon as he could use their intelligence on planned attacks. He could also fight alongside the best fighters in the land who were being used to protect his family.

Moving up the ranks of the Dale Guard was inevitable; it was the small amount of ambition that was still inside him trying to come out. Although it wasn't long until he stood down, he had to serve six years at least which he surpassed. But when he found, he was working to protect more people as the leader of the Guard he knew he had to focus on his family again. Ten and a half years in the guard, six of them as captain made him very well respected. It made him very proud, but he knew his relationship with Heena was suffering. He became somewhat of a celebrity to some of the townsfolk, especially the children who could only dream to be able to fight like he could. As a husband, he tried to give Heena what she needed. But when you had a son who was so ambitious and wanted to be with you every minute of the day it was difficult. He knew Heena wanted more.

After giving Jack his old forearm shield, he felt he had let go of some of his past. By doing this, he was on the road to giving Heena more and save the relationship and their family.

Days later, he watched Jack training again in the field sporting his new shield. He could see it suited him well. After he watched for some time, he went inside looking for Heena.

You never told me what they said at the barracks" said Heena.

"He has a lot to learn yet Heena, they won't

take him until he's ready."

"Biggs has offered to take him on at his office." Heena said.

"Politics? He would eat Biggs alive, besides, Biggs isn't interested in Jack."

"What is that supposed to mean?" Heena snapped back.

"That man is a creep, Heena, a snake, he puts his head down and walks past me when he sees me and a good job, I would take his head off if he gave me the chance."

"Jon! he is the Councillor, if they heard you say that they will…"

"What would they do?" Jon interrupted "The town agrees with me, Morton agrees with me, he would do anything to take you away from me."

"I knew it!" Heena said through gritted teeth. "I knew you were accusing me of something!" Heena squared up to Jon pointing her finger in his face. "I have been nothing but loyal to you, and all your, your family history, you never appreciated it, I left my home for you."

"Heena, I'm sorry. I wasn't accusing you of anything." Jon said trying to put his arms around her as she tried to push his hands away. "You're right you have sacrificed a lot for me and our family. I will be forever grateful, I love you" Heena stopped fighting and allowed him to embrace her.

"What's this?" Jon said, after noticing a purple mark on Heena's back.

"Oh nothing, I'm fine. The burting must have had a spasm in its tail as I started to butcher it and its tail caught my back." Said Heena.

"Spasms?" Jon said. "I have never known burtings' tails to spasm. Are you sure there isn't anything else you want to tell me?"

"No" Heena whispered shaking her head cowering.

"Who..." a strong vibration in the earth stopped Jon mid-sentence. He ran outside to see what could be happening and stood by Jack who was also trying to investigate. Another explosion in the distance drew their attention.

A cloud of dust grew into the sky and continued out over the town. The sun could no longer break through the black cover. Jon grabbed Jack by the scruff of the neck and pulled him inside covering their heads from the falling debris. Jack dug his heels in to the dirt, but Jon pulled harder knowing full well he would not go willingly.

"Father I can help!" Jon ignored him, he

opened the basement door and threw Jack in, locking it after him. Shouting started to echo through the door.

"Father please! I can fight!" Jon turned to the door.

"Not in this war!" Jack didn't understand. "Heena, you need to get in too."

"No, I'm coming, I can help get people to safety." Heena protested.

"I don't know who is attacking but, what I do know is that was one powerful explosive, I can't lose you."

"I'm coming to help the people; you are not locking me in the basement Jon."

They left the house after Jon grabbed the first thing he could use as a weapon which happened to be the prod that Jack had beat him with.

As they turned the corner of the street, they saw soldiers pulling villagers out of their homes and even killing the ones that resisted. As strong as he was, Jon knew he couldn't take them all alone.

"Jon, they need help, the villagers, they will kill them all."

"You help them, leave the soldiers to us."

"Us?" asked Heena. Then from behind him stepped his predecessor, Morton Grice. The rest of the Guard appeared all wearing white with silver breastplates and helms.

"Glad you could join us Jon." said Morton.

"I wouldn't want to see you take all the credit Grice." they smirked at each other and marched on. Heena picked up some villagers and tried to help who she could. Already, she could see that the street had become a warzone as the people started to fight back. the villagers used knives and whatever they had in their homes that they could use as a weapon. They fought bravely but they were out matched by the well organised soldiers.

"It's the Dominion" shouted a villager as they ran for his safety past the onward marching Guard.

"Dale Guard! Let's clear these Dominion scum bags out of our town!" Morton raised his sword, and they charged towards the soldiers. Jon and Morton lead the attack into the soldiers with a clash of their swords. The townsfolk rushed to get away from the battle with Heena trying her best to get as many people as possible away.

Every soldier who gets into the eyesight of Jon only manages a few deflections of his prod before he knocks them down and kills them. The Guard started to take control back from the Dominion soldiers, with every clash of swords, a Dominion soldier seemed to fall. Outside the main battle, one Guard defender called Meer Drake started to help pull some trapped civilians from under a damaged wall. He was a qualified guard but was not experienced in battle and this showed as he let his guard down whilst helping the children out of the house. After getting the third and final child out he felt a sharp pain on his back, he commanded the children to run. Heena found them and put her arms round them but could only watch as Drake had his throat slit by a Dominion soldier.

Jon battled on alongside Morton and started to see the end of the street by clearing the Dominion soldiers. They entered the town square and the Guard gathered around the Dale Guard memorial that the town built in memory of the fallen and past members. The Dominion soldiers backed off as a rumbling noise appeared to get closer and closer.

The Guard stood their ground as they tried to see what it was coming towards them. In front of their eyes appeared a transport that rolled along on tracks and pulled along by soldiers on horseback. These weren't any horses; their muscle wasn't like anything Jon had seen before.

It finally stopped. The dust was everywhere; it was as if clouds had descended on the town. As it cleared all that anyone could see was two shiny black boots standing in the fog. His figure started to show as his dark blue coat showed through. "Kill them all." the figure ordered, a huge soldier stepped out from behind him, out of what looked like a barracks on tracks. Each man had a staff with a sharp knife on one end and a curved hook on the other.

"The Knights of the Dominion," Jon whispered to Morton. "Deadly well-trained killers, I had only heard rumours, get ready." The Guard prepared for them as these soldiers were much superior fighters to those they had fought. They clashed in the centre of the square. Instead of being able to kill a man after a couple of blocks, each swing of Jon's prod seemed to get deflected every time. One of the Dale Guard tried to manoeuvre around the oncoming soldiers and go for the leader. But these guards were well trained and before he could get close the hooked end of one's staff grabbed the soldier round the neck and slit it from ear to ear.

Jon could feel himself start to tire, as he hadn't fought anyone for this long before and his total concentration started to waiver. He looked around and could see the men starting to fall until there was only him and Morton left.

"Morton, where are your archers?" Jon asked as they both stood waiting.

"I err... don't know, Jon."

"Loose!" screamed a soldier from a rooftop. "Take cover!"

Morton pulled Jon to the floor as arrows rained down around killing many of the Dominion soldiers.

"Get up there, now!" the same mysterious voice hissed as a line of troops scrambled to get to the roof tops. A new battle started as archers fought against the Dominion soldiers, but to no avail as they soon had to retreat after they were overwhelmed.

"Well, it almost worked, Morton." Jon said as they both looked around at the circle of men surrounding them.

"Captain Morton!" sounded from behind the ring of guards, "it's over my friend, stop your resistance and no more will die."

"More will come from further out once they get our message." Morton said standing up to the leader. "We do not fear you, another captain of the Dominion who will be tossed aside once you're shown to be weak."

"Sure." he replied curling his lips into a sharp smile. "Sure, Agent Lo of the Dominion takes down the Dale Guard with one swift move, yet I'm weak, remember where you are Morton."

"You can kill me here Lo, but Beachdale will get revenge it always does!" Morton threatened.

"Chain them up." Lo ordered stroking back his slick black hair. "I have no interest in killing you Morton, I'm not here for you or your precious town."

"Then why are you here?" said Morton giving little resistance as guards cuffed them both.

"Well, I have been informed of someone more valuable to me, and rumour has it he lives in your very town, in fact! I'm feeling lucky today, Morton, so lucky that that man is standing in chains behind you" both Lo and Morton turned to Jon.

"Ha! This one" Morton said pointing at Jon. "Corporal Neal? Really? Agent Lo he's no more important to you than he is me, I don't know how he's still alive, look at him, you have the wrong town." Lo shook his head at Morton.

"In fact, you're right Morton. He is very important to you, as he is to me." Lo turned away towards his men. "Can someone please take Captain Morton and chain him somewhere out of my way." Two soldiers stepped forward and dragged Morton away.

"So, it's just you and me, Corporal Neal." Lo let out a chilling laugh, "He's a joke, that Captain, no wonder the town fell so easy. Anyway, back to it, you have been very quiet. Let me start a fresh here and explain myself. I'm here searching out the infamous Ando Captain Jon Skies, perhaps you could help?"

Silence.

"OK, let's do this a different way, bring her," Lo shouted, waving his gloved hand in the air. The circle of guards stepped out as one pulled a chained up Heena to her knees next to Jon. Jon kept his composure and tried not to look at Heena. Knowing that to show any signs of compassion would give him away.

"OK, oh what to do now, you are making this difficult. I'm not here to kill Captain Skies, I want to talk, if would you like to share his location if, indeed, you are not him," Lo asked.

Jon continued to say nothing, Lo exhaled, then pulled out his sword and swung, stopping it as it touched Heena's neck.

"No!" Jon screamed, that was it, he knew now, any cover that he had was now gone.

"Well now." Lo said, his smile returning. "Luckily for you I don't know who this woman is but that was an interesting reaction. Jon Skies has a wife and a son here in Beachdale, you match the description so does she. The fact that you are being stubborn towards helping me is making me think my suspicions are correct. Or ironically you are Corporal Neal and very brave, or stupid, either one." Lo glanced from Jon to Heena and back to Jon.

"You're not making this easy, I'll give you that." Lo sheathed his sword and stepped away from Heena, "I'm a patient man, you know, I can wait because it will come to light soon enough. Or I can go into your town and kill and threaten as many families as possible I need to before someone will confirm to me, you are who you say you are. In which case I don't need you and you would be considered as a common criminal working against the Dominion and be killed anyway.

I will find Jon Skies, mark my words."

JACK

Jack could only stand at the little window that had a barred opening which let in the only light into the dark room which felt like a prison cell. All he could see was chaos descending on Beachdale and he felt like a prisoned animal watching his kind be slaughtered. Jack had faith that his father alongside the Dale Guard would protect the town and push back and attack those that had broken through. Two more earth trembling explosions shook the basement. Rubble starting to fall from the ceiling and Jack tried to save items rolling off the shelves.

The building felt like it was going to collapse. Jack had never disobeyed his father but in an event like this, he thought he had no choice but to try and find a way out.

"You search this one I'll take across the street!" shouted a Dominion soldier as they filled the street. Jack didn't know much about the Dominion, but he knew these were not the Dale Guard and he knew now he had to get out. For Jack going into a battle like this excited him but leaving the basement unarmed was going to be a mistake. He searched the basement for anything he could use to defend himself and do as much damage as he could whilst getting away.

Everything he found was all garbage or at least to him it was, to his father it was all keepsakes'. He then looked over at the chest he saw earlier. After the response his father gave him, he was sure it contained something that could be useful.

The chest was well sealed, he tried with any loose object that he could find to open it. Jack soon lost his patience, he wanted and needed to get out of this basement to help his parents. The more frustrated he got the rougher he got with chest to the extent of picking up the nearest hard item and hitting the chest until it broke open.   Jack opened the lid carefully like it was a prize possession although there was not much left of it. Inside was something wrapped up in soft silk. He started to unravel the fabric with care, until a sword in its sheath showed through. The rage turned to excitement as he lifted his new possession, he took hold of the grip and pulled the blade out. It was a matt black colour, like his shield, is it vendel as well? It looked like it. He questioned himself and after he had the whole blade out, he held it up and it was as light as a handful of pebbles.

Soldiers thumped the front door; Jack knew now something was wrong and his parents were not ok. He clipped his weapon to his belt and started to beat the basement door to get out. Vendel was stronger than other materials like it, these were his father's words. Jack pulled his new sword out and in one swing it smashed straight through the lock.

"Hey, did you hear that? Someone's here!" one of the soldiers said, "I'm sure Hi-Pec said this was the Skies farm."

"I bet you that's one of the family, let's go!" The soldiers moved around the house trying to find from where the bang originated.

Jack crawled out of the basement and straight into a corner in a shadow. The soldiers joked about Jon and how they believed that they had captured him and his bitch of a wife. Jack felt the anger reappear throughout his body. With his sword still out, he waited as a soldier came close, he struck. The blade went straight through any armour the man was wearing and killed him instantly.

One down, he knew this tactic could get him out of the house, so he found his next shadow. He crouched down under a window in a room towards the back of his house. The only beam of light shone an inch over the top of his head covering him in complete darkness. The Dominion soldier walked in completely unaware of the danger he was walking into. Jack waited for the footsteps to go past and pounced; the soldiers throat was slit before he knew he wasn't alone.

Once Jack saw a gap in the troops walking through the streets, he made his way out. It was quiet. If a family had not been taking away by the Dominion, they were hiding in the attic of their homes. The curtains pulled shut in every home, candles all extinguished. He didn't understand, it was like the fighting had ceased in a second.

Daylight was lessening so Jack knew he had to find his parents or at least try and save them. Jack came to the end of his road and saw a gathering. At first, he knew it would be suicide to try and take them on. But what if his parents were there and they were being tortured. Or his father was using his experience and laying low somewhere waiting to strike. His questions were finally answered after looking closer towards the gathering. There through the crowd, he saw the slick black hair of his father. But that's all he could see, was he hurt, was he held down, dying? He didn't wait to find out. He was gone. Never had Jack run as quick as he was now. Any form of tactics was no longer in his mind.

His speed was picking up by so much, that the soldiers only noticed that there was anything out of place because of the clouds of dust rising around him. The soldiers started walking towards the sandstorm which was getting stronger. Jack's figure came out of the cloud, and he then struck against the first of the soldiers. He was angry, and his fighting style showed. He went through the soldiers like a hot knife through butter. Anxiety started to show within the ranks even more so than when Jon and the Guard stood before them.

Jack's dominance would not last long as the Knights pushed through the Dominion soldiers. Their gold metal plates shone through the crowd and before Jack knew it, they were in front of him. Hi-Pec was the leader, this captain was a mountain of a man, he looked brutal, but Jack felt like he could beat anyone.

"Stand down boy! We don't want to get hurt today now do we!" Hi- Pec's deep voice echoed through the street.

"I won't." replied Jack,

Hi-Pec gave a little smirk. He turned to the knight beside him and with a nod of the head, the knight stepped out to meet him. Jack swung his sword towards him. The knight's blade deflected it. Jack shifted to the side and caught the knight on the shoulder making him lose grip of his sword. Hi-Pec moved in grabbing Jack's blade with his hand and his elbow barged into Jack's nose knocking him to the floor. Hi-Pec still had hold of Jack's sword by the blade, he noticed blood start to trickle down the burnt like metal.

"Vendel? That's an impressive weapon you have." Hi-Pec passed the sword to the knight next to him and stared at his hand. "You know it's a good job that's not my bow hand." Jack ignored the comment and tried to get back to his feet. "Chain him up, take him to Agent Lo." The Knights dragged Jack to the centre of the square, where Dominion soldiers surrounded him.

The chains were uncomfortable, heavy, and close to the floor stopping Jack from standing up straight. Jack felt a thump on the back of his head which knocked him back down to the dirt.

Jack opened his eyes seeing raindrops appear one by one. He picked his head up to feel them on his face, but his attention was caught by the sight of his father and mother on their knees with two blades to their necks. Heena had a look of absolute fear on her face, and his father, well he looked disappointed. Jack had never disobeyed his father so not staying in the basement would have upset him and to be honest Jack started to wish he had stayed. A figure stepped in front of Jack, his long coat fell all the way to the top of his boots, it had badges on the front. They were like the badges his father had when he was captain of the guard so this man must be important.

"Agent Lo sir! We caught this one trying to

break through our ranks." Hi-Pec lifted Jack's head up pulling his hair. "He is a skilled fighter sir and was carrying this." Hi-Pec held up Jack's sword to show Lo.

"A rescue attempt you think?" Lo's voice was soft but terrifying. Hi-Pec, nodded in agreement.

"I have had to put a leash on your dog captain." He turned to face Jon. "who is he?" Jon looked at the ground, how could he get his son out of this one? He had protected him all this life one way or another but now felt a little helpless.

"He's just a boy, who shouldn't be here." Jack felt from Jon's body language that the last part was meant for him.

"He didn't fight like a just a boy corporal, look at my men lying dead down the street... I don't believe you; he is something of importance to you." Lo stopped for a minute with a look on his face like he had achieved something quite amazing.

"Corporal Neal!" Lo shouted, making Jack look around for who he was referring to.

"We are going to try something new!" they both moved away from Jack, Lo stepped towards Jon. "I'm going to ask you one more time, are you the Ando General Jon

Skies?" Jack looked at Jon, he had heard of the Andos but only in the stories his friends told him. Other members of the Beachdale community made Andos sound like the enemy. Is his father the enemy?

"I'm a corporal with the Dale Guard!" Jon said as he lifted his head.

"Liar! Hi-Pec!" Lo turned and waved towards HI-Pec who picked up his huge bow. Then he pulled an arrow the size of a small log from the huge barrel that was next to him, placed it on his bow and pulled back.

"WAIT!" As soon as Jon saw the arrow aimed towards Jack, he couldn't control himself.

"Yes? Corporal, what have you got to say." the words exploded from inside him.

"I am Jon Skies of the Andos!" Jack hadn't taken his eyes off his father and now he didn't know what to think.

"Good, I knew you would help me eventually. Although it now makes me wonder who this young man is. As you soon broke as he arrived here." Lo turned his attention back to Jack. "So, who are you boy? What is your name?"

"I'm not someone who you can play with!" Jack replied. Lo made quick glance at Hi-Pec who picked up the arrow for the second time.

"Jon, I'm going to continue to assume this boy is an acquaintance of some sort, or family member, nephew or even your son?" Lo got as close to Jon's face as he could, watching as it started to look like every bit of blood was gathering under Jon's skin.

"As it stands, the question is whether I believe this boy will be an asset to me. I have an arrow ready with Hi-Pec, don't give me a reason to use it. So, who is he?" Lo yelled turning back to Jack.

"Do you know why I spend most my life tracking down Ando rebels? No? because they threaten everything the Dominion has worked so hard to build! They are terrorists! Jon over there is in fact a terrorist, are you?" the intensity increased.

Jack was now looking at the dirty ground that he was kneeling on. His father a terrorist? no he didn't believe it. Jack found it hard to see how the Dominion could even consider themselves the good guys after today's chaos. But they are the government, well they are the most powerful, but people would argue who are in charge.

"I'm getting tired, Ando. I'm glad I found you Jon, but if this boy is who I think he may be, he is somewhat of importance as well. Not on the same scale as you but he may be a valuable tool for me." Lo announced after a short silence.

A piercing pain struck Jack's whole body, making him collapse to the floor. The pain wasn't from a strike from Lo or an arrow from Hi-Pec, it was inside of him. Jack held both hands on top of his head as he crouched over.

"Jack," Jon whispered under his breath, he looked away as he couldn't do anything to help him.

"Aagghh! What is this?" Jack screamed "my head!"

Jack's vision went blurry, in and out of focus every couple of seconds. Agent Lo put his hand on his shoulder.

"What's the matter boy?" Lo said, but the small touch seemed to increase the pain for Jack. All he could see was blackness. Flashes of a location came and went but it didn't stay long enough for him to recognise where it was. He felt like he had seen it before.

Agent Lo stepped back from Jack as he continued to crouch forward pulling on the chains that were holding his hands behind his back.

"Jon Skies, what is going on?" Lo asked.

Jon shrugged his shoulders, still looking at the floor. Jack fell silent, but he was screwing up his face in pain.

"Curious." Lo said looking Jack up and down.

"Curious? My lord?" Hi-Pec said.

"Yes, this isn't the first time, I have had this reaction to my touch or even my presence." Lo confronted Jon once again.

"Jon," Lo sighed, is there something else you need to tell me? About yourself? the boy? Now is the time because I'm ready to move on. Is it worth keeping this boy around? Or should I keep him alive?"

"Keep him alive he's just a boy!" Jon pleaded.

"Many young people have died here today, what makes him special?... General Skies?"

"He is special."

"No Jon!" Heena snapped.

"No carry-on Jon, I'm interested. This could after all save all your lives, by being honest. I have a friend interested in you Jon, and well, three prisoners are better than two. But I still have questions I need you to answer, and his safety seems to determine whether you give me an honest answer. So, Hi-Pec, prepare another arrow will you, now."

Lo leant back in towards Jon's face who then finally lifted his head back up, his eyes were scarlet red. Almost like they were about to bleed.

"Come on now Jon." he whispered, in his ear. "I know there is a descendant in this town, who is it?" No answer. Lo shot back to his feet.

"Come on Jon, last chance, help me here." Jon looked around the town centre, he looked at Heena who was shivering next to him. Tears ran down her face. He could see market stalls burning down the street and bodies of Beachdale townsfolk lying on the paths. He then looked at Jack, who stared straight back into his eyes and then he looked at Lo.

"No! Take your army and go back to where you came from!"

"Hi-Pec!" On the other side of the square Hi-Pec picked up his bow and reattached his arrow, turned to face Jack and then THWAK!

CHAPTER 2

JACK

Everything was dark, it's like he was living out a dream that he would soon wake up from. Pick up his leathers and his wooden sword and head out to the yard to practice. These were his dreams most nights, fighting and becoming the most powerful warrior in Beachdale. He could remember the burting running towards him and defeating it to his father's surprise.

His bed felt comfortable and for once he didn't want to get up. When he opened his eyes, he saw a solid brick wall. He had seen this wall before, the symbol on the wall was a star and above three triangles pointing into it. What did it mean? His mother was sitting next to him holding his hand. Then she was pulling on his arm as the wall started to crumble.

"Mother, what's happening?" Jack said tugging on Heena, but she didn't move, "the room is collapsing! mother! Let's go!" it was no use he couldn't move her, "where's father?" the two walls left fell in, making Jack cover Heena like a human shield.

"Father!" Jack shouted. But Jon didn't answer, and he couldn't see anyone. The ground beneath Jack split in two. Dust filled the wreck of the building as he fell holding on to an overhanging slab.

"MOTHER PLEASE!" he screamed. He could see the top of her head still stuck in the same position as if she was frozen solid. Jack looked down to see the bottomless canyon below. Another hand grabbed his, digging sharp nails into his wrist, making him flinch. But as he looked up, it was his mother's body that was holding him, but her face was not hers. It was no longer a soft looking face, it was gaunt and white, her nose had become hooked, and eyes were pure black. Her hair was now like rats' tails hanging down the side of her head, this wasn't Heena at all.

"Jack Skies!" it hissed. Piercing the air with a sharp, high-pitched crackle.

"Who are you? Where's my mother?" Jack shouted through gritted teeth.

The pain from his wrist felt like daggers were being hammered into his bones. His grip let go and Jack fell, and fell, it felt like he was never going to hit the bottom. He closed his eyes and prepared for the inevitable crash, but then it all stopped.

Jack opened his eyes and he saw a bright light as if he had never opened his eyes before. Dust was floating everywhere. He couldn't see his father or his mother, in fact he couldn't see a hand in front of him. As his eyesight sharpened, he saw a figure on the floor but who was it? Then another crouched over him, he had a scar right through the middle of his face, it glowed like a red flash. It was Hi-Pec!

The size of him gave it away and it was Agent Lo on the floor, what had happened? The last thing he could remember was Lo shouting Hi-Pec's name, then Hi-Pec closed his eyes as he lifted his bow arm.

The ground around him started to move. His vision was improving by the minute, but he felt like his body was uncontrollable. The monument in the middle of the square to which Jack was chained, started to slide away from him. His chains lay on the floor, broken up. The buildings around him were sliding past him like they were on a cart pulled by some horses. This must be another dream; had he been killed by Hi-Pec and his soul has been taken away to some sort of afterlife. Jack had never believed in any afterlife but maybe, it was true. What happened to the others? Why was Lo laying on the floor and how did Hi-Pec get that nasty gash on his face? Hi-Pec was not the most attractive person in the world and an extra scar would not help. He wouldn't care, he looked like he was used to a battle wound or two.

By this point the grand archway had passed and Beachdale itself was going into the distance. Jack felt like he was getting higher and higher, was he going on to the afterlife? Maybe he would meet some of his father's old relatives. Jon always told Jack stories of his father, Jack's grandfather and how knowledgeable he was and strong. He must have been such a good fighter and taught father everything he knew, Jack thought to himself. But Jon never took Jack to meet him. He always spoke about him, but Jack assumed that he was dead because his father had never introduced him.

Reality then hit Jack with a thump. Once again Jack was laying on the floor, but this time a grassy floor. Well, it was better than the muddy, dusty floor of Beachdale Square. As Jack looked up it then occurred to him how he had made it up the hill. A huge man, similar size to Hi-Pec sat down in a heap next to him, he was out of breath.

"Did you carry me up here?" Jack asked.

The man turned his bald round head towards him and gave him a little nod. The man was strong, his muscles were like the burtings that he had fought. But they were all over the man's body, in fact the trousers and top he was wearing didn't kept them inside.

"Who?" Jack stopped himself from asking another question as he could see the man had tired. His face was sweating like a fountain. The man opened his satchel and took a cloth wrapped around something. As he opened it a cracker appeared underneath, and Jack's mouth started to water. The man picked it up and handed it to Jack.

"Hungry lad? I bet you are, here." he had a growl-like voice. The cracker felt a bit stale, but Jack was grateful all the same as he hadn't eaten for some time. After finishing his cracker and dusting of the crumbs from his shirt he felt his vendel shield on his arm.

"Ah thank God!" Jack said out loud making the man turn and look, he didn't seem that impressed. After seeing the charcoal colour of his shield, he then remembered his sword, but he couldn't find it. That sword was his father's which he took and now had lost. He imagined seeing his father's face, raging with anger, that he had once again lost something because of his incompetence. Jack wanted to know what had happened and how he went from being chained up to hitting his head on the top of the hill.

"Who are you and how did you get me out of there?" Jack asked.

"I'm Maddox. I knew your father when I was younger, he wouldn't remember me, it was a long time ago but non the less. He was in trouble, and we were in the area, so we knew we had to do something." Maddox replied whilst still crunching on a cracker.

"You knew my father? but if you knew my father why I am sitting here and not him."

"It is what he would have wanted lad, besides Thearon will explain more when he gets back." Thearon? He knew that name, he was sure his mother and father had mentioned him before, but he couldn't remember why.

"Are we going to help my father, we can't leave them down there to be kept hostage by that Dominion slug." Jack said to a half-interested Maddox.

"We had to get you out, that was our mission ok. We used one of the Dominion's explosives that they had created, along with all the other things they are making in their base. It has given us time to get you out and get up here out of the way. Once they are ready, they will look for us, so once Thearon returns, we will move on. Agent Lo won't kill your father yet he's too valuable you see." Jack assumed that he was supposed to feel better about it, but he didn't.

"Your mission? So, you knew the Dominion were coming to Beachdale?"

"We were in Mitchler, you know the capital, where the Dominion have their headquarters. The base of their self-proclaimed government. Anyway, we were on a bit of a spy mission, and we overheard that this Agent Lo was heading to Beachdale, so we followed."

"Could you not have sent some sort of

warning? Crows can fly here quicker than boats."

"We did, several in fact, Biggs should have had 'em, I bet he ignored the lot of 'em, bloody useless that man."

"Yea, he wanted me to join his office as some sort of apprentice." Jack said, which made Maddox choked on his crackers.

"The son of Jon Skies in politics? Not a chance, now listen Jack. They care about one thing these politicians, and that's themselves and their own pockets. Your father was a fighter, he could have held his own against most of them Dominion soldiers in his prime, and I'm confident you will grow to be the same."

"My father hated the idea, so did my mother, but Biggs is obsessed with her. I think he felt that getting me to join gave him a chance with her, father hated him, if he weren't Councillor, I imagine his head would have been off by now. I'm joining the Dale Guard like father did, that's if it still exists."

Maddox lifted himself up and then held his hand out to Jack.

"Come on son, we better go meet Thearon, as those Dominion things will be here soon no doubt." Jack grabbed his hand and got whiplash from the speed Maddox pulled him up. "at least you can walk now, give me back a rest, you weigh a ton for a small'un".

"Are you an Ando Maddox?" Jack asked.

"I'm not from Ando, but I fight for the same cause."

"Which is?"

"To fight back at the Dominion, they try to control by killing folk. You saw them at Beachdale, the Andos fight against them, try to keep people safe. Trouble is nobody trusts anybody these days, if you're an Ando, you're a traitor, if you're Dominion you're a weak-minded fool. People think they know better than everybody else, Jack, I don't think you're gonna get this option, but I wish I could keep me 'ead down."

"What do you mean I won't get that option?" Jack asked.

"Well, you're destined to have a bigger part in this fight than me, unfortunate really."

Jack followed Maddox for what felt like hours, but they didn't seem to get anywhere. Beachdale was still visible in the distance, making Jack keep looking towards it to see any evidence of Agent Lo and his army leaving town.

"Maddox, what happened to Agent Lo and

Hi-Pec?" Jack asked.

"Well, we saw the big man aim the arrow at you so before he had chance to fire it, we let an explosive off and I hit him with an arrow, didn't kill him though."

"What happened to his face?"

"Well, he didn't stay down, so when I came to release you, he tried to stop me. So, I swung me sword and gashed his face, ha, he stayed down then Jack."

"And Agent Lo?"

"He was dazed after the explosion, so I gave him a punch and he fell like a sack of spuds." Jack asked a lot of questions of Maddox, who he could see was starting to get tired of answering them by sighing before each answer.

"My parents, were they hurt?"
"They are fine, well health wise, we will help them if we can Jack, but now we need to find Thearon."

AGENT LO

The dust had finally settled around the Beachdale square. Hi-Pec helped Agent Lo up to his feet by which wasn't very appreciated. It was rare for the Dominion soldiers to see Lo knocked down. Lo pushed Hi-Pec away from him as he dusted himself off.

"Who were they? someone must have seen them!" Lo stumbled around in anger, finally sticking his gaze on Jon and Heena. "Get those two on the transport before we have anymore interference!" Lo had such anger in his voice the soldiers soon made sure his wishes were their commands.

"My lord, what about the boy?" asked one of his men with a slight nervous tone to his voice.

"Search the perimeter of the town there must be some signs of how they got in."

The two men scurried off. Lo turned to Hi-Pec who was nursing his scar with some cloth he had ripped off one of the fallen soldiers.

"If you find them or discover where they were heading, take some men and bring me the boy, kill the rest."

"Yes, my lord." Hi-Pec bowed and roused his men as they followed him. Agent Lo headed into the transport.

The big wooden transport had a room for his men, himself and of course a small prison at the back in which he watched Jon and Heena had been placed. It wasn't much bigger than a small cupboard under a staircase, but they made sure the prisoners fit in through any means as necessary. Lo made a point of walking past Jon on his way to his quarters.

"He won't be gone for long. If Hi-Pec doesn't find him tonight, then I'm confident we will have him visit us in some sort of rescue attempt with his new friends. That's if my men haven't already killed them. You look uncomfortable miss Heena, there is plenty of room here with my men." Lo finished with a grin. "I will come back to you once we have the boy to continue our little chat."

Agent Lo made his way to his room which had armed guards watching day and night if he was on board or not. Behind his bed was a picture that was floor to the ceiling of him the day he became Agent. Before then he was known as Maraj Lo. This was the name his mother gave him. Still to this day his closest friends and his higher ranked officers would still call him by his name but there wasn't many of them left. Most called him 'my Lord.' He had trained them into doing this as he was not one to be disrespected and not react. After his cloak was destroyed by the blast, he changed it for a new fresh one, from his vast wardrobe.

He walked over to his desk which was covered by a brown coloured sheet. He inspected it, it was a world map and had been marked with the journey that he was currently taking. Lo was a fierce fighter and leader, but his knowledge of geography was not up to much. The map was essential to him to get to where he needed to be as he would not accept being informed by a mere soldier.

Hi-Pec returned to the transport and climbed the steps in a hurry to speak to Lo.

"My Lord! We have two men found dead southeast of the town, that is where they got in." Hi-Pec informed Lo with a proud confident voice. "Must I take the garrison?" Lo turned and looked down at his world map. Hi-Pec stood waiting with a surprised look; He didn't think it was going to be a hard decision for him.

"No, send the Gindar squad." Lo replied.

"The Gindar Squad my lord? it will be a suicide mission for the Gindar, they are not ready." Hi-Pec could not believe the response, the Gindar Squad were soldiers who were new recruits. They were not yet good enough to make the main soldier group. On an assignment, they shadow the well-trained soldiers until they showed they could make the grade.

"Whoever it is who took the boy is very clever and will kill with ease. If I send you and everyone else, I could lose too much and gain very little. I don't know who this boy is yet, he came after Jon before and I'm betting he will again. For the time being we continue heading for Woodale and deliver what we promised."

"I doubt they will be able to track down and find them my Lord." Hi-Pec suggested in a quiet voice.

"Give them one hound, but nothing else, I'm only sending them to make the boy think we're still interested so he follows us!" Lo instructed.

"So, it is a suicide mission." Hi-Pec was getting brave by this point and red mist started rising in Lo's face.

"They would die anyway Hi-Pec! now stop questioning my orders or you can go with them! now go!" Hi-Pec turned and headed down the steps. Agent Lo very rarely had any kind of resistance from his men. So, Hi-Pec's reaction came as a surprise, but it would soon leave his mind and chose to return to Jon and Heena in the prison.

"You're not going to tell me who broke him out are you? Wait of time asking I suppose." said Lo pulling a stool up to the jail bars.

"It wasn't anyone at Beachdale." Jon replied, sitting up alongside the bars whilst Heena curled up in the corner.

"Why would I believe that, or can you tell me who?"

"No, I can't, other than I know Beachdale doesn't have that kind of weapon in its armoury. Which you should know Lo, it's a Dominion explosive, the last time I saw one was fighting in the last war."

"So, you're suggesting it was one of my own that broke him out?"

"No, I can't imagine anyone brave enough to do that." Lo smiled at that comment.

"I think you're right, but unfortunately, you're wrong. Because someone is brave enough or stupid enough." said Lo as he poured himself a whiskey plus one for Jon.

"I don't want you to get hurt, I definitely don't want to kill you." Lo held out the glass of whiskey to Jon, who shook his head gently, "suit yourself." Lo poured it into his own glass and sat back down, "I remember the war you're talking about, I didn't fight in it though, in fact Jon you may not know this, but I haven't always been in the Dominion, actually, for many years I travelled around most of the world searching..." Lo stopped to take a sip of whiskey and changed the subject.

"I was asked to join the Dominion after they threatened me one day on a road in the outskirts of Mitchler. The Typhone desert, don't suppose you have ever been Jon, have you?" Jon listened but didn't give any reply.

"Not a place an Ando would travel to these days. I was searching for Typhone relics and anything that I could learn about the man. But the Dominion turned up and seemed offended by my meddling in their leader's historic sites. Useless their leader. So, I agreed I would stop if they beat me in combat, me versus their strongest. Well let's just say I hope he wasn't the Dominion's strongest or we're in trouble!" Lo chuckled and took another sip of whiskey.

"The leader happened to be one of the big boys within the Dominion and talked me into joining as an Agent. So long story short Jon, I'm not in this to kill you so think about it. Do as I ask, and you will leave my side unharmed, if you don't, I can't promise that you and your family won't get hurt." Having had no response from Jon, Lo became tired of his one-way conversation. He finished his whiskey and went back to his quarters.

THEARON

Jack continued to follow Maddox. To him it was fields of nothing, a couple of hills and rocks and Maddox repeating the same thing over again.

"We're meeting Thearon, we can't be late, we're meeting Thearon we can't be late." Jack tried interrupting him at one point to ask where he was taking him. But he got a glare which soon put Jack's eyes back down to the floor.

They arrived at what can only be described as a castle ruin. Jack stopped and stared at the sight of the building. There was something about this place that made Jack feel uncomfortable. His head started to ache but kept going until Maddox told him to sit on a rock outside of the gate to the ruins.

"Sit here kid, Thearon will be here soon." Maddox said as he sat down next to Jack.

"Who is he, this Thearon?" Jack asked Maddox.

"He knew your father, they travelled around the world together from what I know. He's as close a friend to your father than anyone could be. He let me come along with him when everybody else saw me as an outcast. You see in this world you must show what you're made of, or others will walk all over you. I needed Thearon to teach me this or I would be in a gutter in Hajobe somewhere." People always seemed to know his father or travelled with his father.

"Maddox? Did you see a sword when you saved me?" Jack was desperate for any good news; he couldn't believe he had lost something so amazing as his sword. He felt sick that he only wielded it for about ten minutes before he lost it.

"You mean this sword?" a rough voice came from behind Jack which made him jump round as quick as he could. "it's a nice sword this, I can remember helping your father make it. He wouldn't have wanted you to find it. But to know that you have it now will warm his heart." A figure stepped into Jack's eyesight holding his sword.

"Ah Thearon, you made it, I started to

think they had got you for a minute!" Maddox said with a smile.

"The Dominion guard seems to be moving on." The three of them moved to the edge of the cliff to see. From this position you could see most of Beachdale. Lo's transport could be seen moving off into the distance.

"Are they going to let me go that easily?" Jack asked.

"Easily! Pah! Speak for yourself, you're not light you know!" Maddox joked at Jack.

He held his lower back to help support his statement but got very little sympathy from Thearon.

"No, I don't think they are, you're going to need this, Jack." Thearon handed Jack his sword. Although he had seen it in Thearon's hands, to have it back in his felt even better.

"Thank you, Thearon," Jack said as he clipped it back on his belt, "are we going to help my father?" Jack asked.

"Yes Jack, but we need to take you somewhere first as there is something I need to know." Thearon put his arm around Jack and turned around to head up the hill side.

"Maddox says, you knew my father?" enquired Jack.

"Yes, I did. Your father and I did a lot of

travelling together, in fact we met when he was very young. He had a lot to learn but had huge potential, and he grew more wise and powerful than I could have dreamed. To see him on his knees in front of Agent Lo troubled me." Thearon answered.

"But why help me when it's my father you were friends with?"

"We had to make a choice as we knew we couldn't save everyone, and we felt that your mother and father would be stronger together. If I could have asked, the Jon that I knew would have wanted me to save his son. You have huge potential as well you know Jack and we will teach you as much as we can while we travel as it could be a long trip."

Thearon walked up to a very old and fragile brick wall. The bricks were grey stone but now covered in moss and overgrown with climbing weeds. As he pushed some of the overgrowth aside, there was a hole big enough for them to fit through. Until Maddox tried and he seemed to take a layer of bricks with him as he pushed himself through. They entered a small room that had deteriorated some time ago as the brick was no longer its original colour. The dirt was so thick you could mistake it for bricks. Jack didn't understand why Thearon had taken them inside, was it for cover whilst they were resting? Or some other reason. Jack turned to find Thearon looking at a cracked slab lying flat on the floor. Jack was a bit unsure about the two strangers that had saved him, not knowing whether to trust them or not. Thearon tried lifting the slab which was the size of a small bed. Jack looked around to see if Maddox was around to help him, but he had gone back outside.

"Jack, come and help an old man out, would you?" Thearon asked, Jack walked over to Thearon and tried to find a way to get his fingers under the slab. "On three," said Thearon "one, two, threeee!" They both strained. Putting all their strength into lifting the slab and finally with a crash it hit the wall and sent dust and dirt flying, filling the area.

"What is it?" Jack asked. Thearon held his hand up at Jack and then began rubbing at the stone, trying to remove all the dirt and moss covering it. Finally, he cleared the stone and he looked up at Jack who had all his attention on the engravings that had appeared. Thearon stepped back.

"I've seen this before." said Jack, it was a symbol, a star with three triangles pointing into it.

"You have, it's the star of Androne. You saw it when you were, let's think about this, six I would say, your father took you to a similar temple." Thearon replied.

"Androne? But I thought..." before Jack could finish his sentence, he fell to his knees clutching his head.

"Agghh" Jack yelled in pain and collapsed to all fours. Thearon felt his forehead, which was fiery red and hot to touch. Thearon stayed over him to ensure he didn't hurt himself even more while he wasn't in control. Thearon turned his head as he heard a rustling behind him.

"Maddox!?" he shouted but no response, what was it? And where is Maddox. He couldn't see anything. So, he turned back to Jack but then had to spin to see a hound flying across the ruins and land on top of him. Thearon managed to hold the dog's jaw stopping it from biting at his neck. The dog was strong especially after catching Thearon off guard. Saliva from the dog's mouth was dripping onto Thearon's face. His hands slipped and his left forearm went in the dog's mouth. He couldn't shake it off, as its teeth ripped through the sleeve of his jacket. He could feel it getting tighter and tighter. His right arm, which was now free, felt around his leg. He finally managed to grab hold of his knife which he pushed through the hound's neck, killing it instantly. He pushed the dog off the top of him and looked at his arm. Luckily for Thearon he had an old but reliable shield covering his forearm, all scratched up now of course, the dog had a good go.

Thearon picked up Jack's sword and laid it next to him, he then turned to grab his sword hilt which was sheathed to his side. He buckled the belt with his sword attached, on his waist and went to find Maddox. Thearon's sword was something special. Beautifully crafted, it always had a gleam to it and the pattern thrown in the blade was created by the most talented craftsman in the land. It was a dragon-like creature crawling down towards the point.

Thearon stepped outside of the temple and saw Maddox being circled by six Dominion soldiers, like a group of crows waiting to strike its prey. It was Agent Lo's Gindar Squad. The Squad were so concentrated on

Maddox that they hadn't seen Thearon appear from the hole in the wall. He used this as an opportunity and reached for his bow. He pulled out an arrow and let it go. It flew at such a speed it took a soldier off his feet after crashing into his chest. They split the group. Thearon unsheathed his sword and matched every strike the Gindar soldiers threw at him with ease. Clash after clash of swords followed by Thearon spinning and sticking his blade through the stomach of one of the enemies. Then turning, pulling out his knife and splitting the other's throat. Maddox held one soldier above his head and had his hand around the other's neck. He then made very quick work of them by launching the one in his hand against the wall and the other. He dropped him back on the floor and then pushed his sword through the soldier's belly which turned his face from pure terror to nothing. The man against the wall collapsed as if every bone in his body had shattered. Thearon bent down to one of his victims and gave him a quick examination. He found a badge on the arm with a black circle and a dagger through the middle.

"He sent the Gindar Squad!" Thearon said,

Maddox gave him a confused look back. "Lo's either massively underestimated us or he is just playing with us, wait... there are only five bodies here, I counted six soldiers... the boy!" they both rushed straight back to the ruins, leaving the fallen soldiers behind. Thearon climbed through the hole first, lifting his head and greeted by a blade poking him in the throat.

"Drop your weapon! And you big man!" the soldier said in a slow but very confident voice, still holding the blade to Thearon's neck.

"Put it down son there's two of us one of you, the others are all dead." said Thearon.

"You seem to underestimate my position, old man... I will kill you both and take the boy back to Agent Lo and he will have no choice to promote me to his Knights of the Dominion, I can then say bye to this joke of a squad, those men you killed back there were weak, I'm not like them... time to di..." he got cut off by a black sword piercing through his chest. The soldier turned his head to see Jack behind him.

"Good story!" Jack pulled the blade out and swung round taking the man's head clean off his shoulders.

"Well done, Jack!" Thearon said tapping him on his shoulder as he passed him.

"Who are the Gindar Squad?" Jack asked.

"Trainee fighters." Thearon replied.

"They think they can beat us that easily?" Maddox shouted picking up the dead soldier and taking it away.

No, they don't, Jack it's an old trick to make us think they aren't as strong as they know they are. They want us to go after them."

"Well, we were going to, right?" Jack asked, as he started to question Thearon's plans. "We can't sit and be scared of them because you know what they are actually capable of!"

"Jack, we are going to go after them, we need to be careful and be mindful as unfortunately, we do know what they are capable of!"

JACK

The group had moved on from the temple and Jack started to want a few more answers from his new companions.

"So, who are you guys actually and how do you know my father?" asked Jack.

"We are Andos, like your father. Your father and I travelled around the world looking for and trying to help descendants of Androne which is how we know each other so well. In fact, I can remember him making that sword and shield you carry now." said Thearon.

"But I was taught that Androne was evil so why go looking for descendants to save?" asked Jack.

"Jack, there are a lot of things I know your father will want to tell you and there was a time I know he would have. I'm going to respect that and still give him that time to tell you, but your question on Androne, he wasn't evil. As you know there were two brothers, Androne and Typhone. They were in constant battle with each other, both leading huge armies and other followers. Androne wanted to protect his people and his land, but Typhone wanted more and went for the capital. He wanted to rule everything and everyone and unfortunately because Androne knew what he was trying to do he did what he could to stop him. But Typhone managed to use this to turn the government against Androne and declared him an enemy. Typhone got what he wanted and managed to dissolve the leadership and he took over. It of course finished in the great war that we know of now and they were both killed with Typhone been hailed as a hero and Androne as an evil villain. People like me and your father have been trying to clear his name for centuries. But I'm afraid there isn't many of us left now as many years after the war the followers of Typhone and his government created the Dominion. They then killed anybody who as little as mentioned Androne's name." Thearon took a deep breath as Jack walked silently beside him.

"I don't understand why he didn't tell me the truth!" said Jack, looking disappointed down towards the ground.

"To protect you, Jack. If anyone found out even your friendly neighbourhood of Beachdale, they would have killed your family. Your father would not have been able to join the Dale Guard and I know you wanted to do the same." Thearon replied. Jack nodded in quiet agreement.

In his mind he continued to see images of a warrior in battle. They were so clear when they were in the temple ruins. On his chest plates was the symbol that he saw on the stone back at the temple. He looked a fierce warrior, strong, respected by his followers. He assumed this must be his father during his Dale Guard days. But when he thought about it, the resemblance of his father was small. Was it him in the future? Or now? ever since Thearon's story of the war, was it Androne? It was his symbol after all. But why was he having these visions? He thought that hard Thearon had to pull him aside from a tree he was about to hit.

"Watch where you're going lad!" Maddox shouted. Jack replied with a smile. After finally shaking himself out of his thoughts and started to concentrate on the road ahead. Thearon stopped in front of them and gazed into the forest.

"There," he said, pointing at a little clearing in the trees, "We will rest there, Maddox get a fire started."

Maddox strode into the forest with a huge grin on his face picking up branches that he could set fire to.

Once the fire was lit Maddox reached into his shoulder bag and pulled out a blanket and threw it towards Jack. It wasn't much but at least it might keep him warmer than having a campfire alone. To Maddox's credit, it was giving out some heat and he was very proud by the way he was looking after it as the flames never fell below two feet tall.

A couple of hours passed, and Jack could not lay still. When he lay on his left side there was a stone and on his right a stick would poke him. Not to mention the heat coming from Maddox's fire that was still burning well with Maddox asleep. He stayed on his back and felt like he finally found his preferred position until this time he felt a few little itches on his shoulder. Before he knew it, he could feel it on his face, he waved his hand past his ear and picked up a spider.

In shock he threw the spider as far he could as quick as he could. Jack stood still realising how silly he would look to his new companions reacting like that to a spider. He lowered himself back down under his sheet and glared nervously into the fire.

Everything seemed to calm and maybe he could fall asleep.

"Aarggghhh!" Jack opened his eyes in a rush and in front of him he saw Maddox do the strangest of moves. It was almost like a choreographed dance, he then moved around the fire like he was performing a ritual, until Jack heard "get off, in the fire you go!" Maddox threw the spider into the fire.

Jack dropped himself back down to the floor before Maddox noticed that Jack had seen what he had been doing. Jack looked over at Thearon who was still sitting up against a rock. Exactly where he had first settled and had still not moved an inch despite Maddox's reaction to a small insect. He moved his eyes back towards Maddox who was back laying down, snoring. Had he dreamt that whole thing, either way he decided he was going to pretend he hadn't seen anything and that nothing had happened. So, he turned on to his left side and put up with the uncomfortable rock sticking into his side and tried to sleep.

Once again Jack was woken up, but this time there was no little insect, which meant there was no outburst from Maddox, so what was up this time? As he looked deeper into the forest there was a strange feel to the air. It somehow felt like it was pulling him into the darkness of the woods. Jack tried to concentrate on what was in front of him but could only see tree trunks and a black backdrop behind. Before Jack had realised, he had taken several steps into the forest. He looked behind him but could only see the glimmer of Maddox's fire through the trees. The sound of the wind got louder as he moved deeper and deeper into the forest. The sound of each gush wailed like a stampede of burtings charging towards him. Why was he still walking? He had to keep going as something was pulling him in. To Jack, it felt like the wind was carrying him, it was effortless and almost calming, yet it was chaotic.

It then alternated from blowing towards his face and then reversing. Blowing him forward as if the elements were having a strange game of tug of war using him as the rope. The path in front of him seemed to get darker, the only light he could see were little flickers of flame that seemed to be coming all the way from the bonfire. He felt no heat, just the cold and pure darkness. It was like his black out back at the temple except he could feel the stormy winds whooshing past him, but he couldn't see a thing.

"Death will come," travelled in a whisper around Jack, he tried to listen to where the voice came from, but it was like it came from every direction, but he couldn't move his body to find it "death will come .... to you." Jack tried his best to reply but words wouldn't come out of his mouth.

He listened for more, but the wind got stronger and then a hand touched his shoulder and he fell back. It was Thearon.

"Jack, you ok? it's me."

"Thearon, what happened?" said Jack in a state of shock trying to get back to his feet. The wind had gone, the only flames he saw were coming from Maddox's fire and the voice seemed like it was never there.

"You were sleepwalking, I reckon lad!" Maddox said, Thearon gave him a stern unimpressed kind of look.

"Sleepwalking? it was like what happened

at the temple except I felt everything and heard everything." said Jack.

"Heard everything? There was just wind, and the snapping of twigs under your feet." said Maddox. Thearon stood up beside Jack who was still a bit shook up.

"Get him up Maddox and let's get back to the camp." Thearon started walking back towards the camp lit up by the fire.

"OK, come on kid, we're doing this again, let's go." Maddox flung Jack over his shoulders and headed back to the camp.

JON

The cage Jon and Heena were locked in felt like it was getting smaller and smaller. To the normal eye they fit in quite comfortably. In fact, the guards wouldn't think twice about squeezing a couple more prisoners in there if they had to. But for Jon and especially Heena, they couldn't breathe. The conversation was not flowing between the two, not pleasantries anyway. Jon tried several times to comfort her, but he got pushed away each time. The night before they had had an argument about how they had ended up in the situation they were in, and it was mostly Heena telling Jon.

"You should never have encouraged Jack to fight, this is all your fault. If he hadn't have fought, he would be safe with another villager and only we would have been taken!" Jon did try to stick up for himself, but it never worked for him, so now he felt better when he ignored it.

There was a little hole at the back of the cage where the wooden planks hadn't met properly, or it had warped somewhat. It was an old transport after all. Heena had spent most of the time looking out of the hole hoping not to see Jack coming for them as he knew that would be putting him at risk. Jon could see Heena hadn't moved, and he knew that it was Jack that was on his mind.

"You know it's Thearon and Maddox who broke Jack out." said Jon trying his best to settle Heena's nerves.

"That doesn't fill me with confidence!" Heena replied.

"Thearon will keep him safe, he kept me alive when most would have killed me themselves." Jon tried to lighten the mood, but Heena wasn't taking it at all.

"You and Thearon went looking for trouble, you had no concern about the welfare of others. You weren't fighting against a group that overthrew a government."

"You have no idea what we fought for or who we fought against!" Jon said.

"Was it not Thearon's job? To keep you safe?"

"Well, I'm still here." Jon said.

"That is not the point Jon! He walked you into a war, more than once. That is exactly what he will do with Jack, this time he might not be so lucky to survive!"

Jon turned away to leave her to herself.

"If he's with Thearon then they will definitely come here as he will want to try and save you, I have come to terms with that now, I don't like his odds." said Heena.

"Thearon won't take on the Dominion with two men and a child. He knows it will be impossible to defeat Lo with the three of them. Its Jack who will be trying to come, he would take the world on to save us, not just me. Thearon won't allow him to leave his sight, he knows better, he learned that much from watching over me. I know Jack's actions at Beachdale were rash, but now he has had time to reflect and has Thearon to guide him he will do the right thing, he is some kid." Heena gave Jon a short smile.

"I know, but that's what worries me, he doesn't have any fear when it comes to battle. Especially if there is someone he cares about at risk," Heena sat down next to Jon a leaned against him "do you think they're going to kill us?" Heena asked.

"No, but if my directions are correct were on the way to Woodale and I imagine we will get sold to their boss." Jon replied.

"Will he kill us?"

"Well not straight away I don't think." they both smiled at each other and for the first time since leaving Beachdale. They were close to each other, and they felt calm, until the door swung open with a crash, it was Hi-Pec.

"My Lord!" Hi-Pec bundled into the room; Lo started to come down the stairs from his quarters.

"My Lord, the Gindar team, they have been killed" Agent Lo walked past giving out a weird chuckle.

"Sir?" said Hi-Pec in confused manner.

"Oh, come on Hi-Pec we knew this is what it would happen. Now they think they are invincible and will come searching for their leader," Lo replied gesturing towards Jon in a victorious kind of way. "This proves that if they were not going to come for Jon and his wife then they would have gone the other way and the Gindar squad would never have found them. not with one hound. I assume the dog is dead as well?" Lo asked like he already knew. Hi-Pec gave a slight nod towards Lo. "Shame, mind you some of these hounds are easier to train then that Gindar Squad, there was one with potential. Shame I had big plans for that team, anyway, must get on, Jon anything you want to tell me today?" Jon looked away, "Ha! ok." Agent Lo stood up and started to walk towards the steps up to his quarters when a guard stepped in.

"My Lord, apologies, our scout has spotted three men west of our position." Lo put a sharp grin on his face and turned to look at Jon.

"Three men Jon, the boy? And two noble rescuers." Lo said.

"There is no way you can be sure," Jon replied.

"You sent a squadron of rookies put against them, who's to say you scouting network are much better." Lo scowled at Jon.

"Precious Ando's, always think you are better than the others. Like Androne, your beloved leader. He thought he was better than Typhone who was far superior in power and wisdom. Androne's foolish actions and decisions killed them both and allowed the Dominion to rise in their place."

"The Dominion will fail Lo. You think you

have a grip on the whole planet when you haven't, we will push you back! like we have before." Jon said, without moving from up against the side of the cage.

"We will see." Lo ended the debate and turned back to Hi-Pec.

"Shall I rouse the men my Lord?" Hi-Pec suggested with urgency.

"No!" Lo snapped. "I don't want them involved." he paused "get everyone back on board, let's test out our latest creation, release the gushlow."

JACK

"So, Jack, you never told me what you saw in the forest. It's best for us to talk about it alone as Maddox will never understand." Asked Thearon as they were walking a few yards behind Maddox who was looking out for anything that could be of threat to them.

"I didn't see a lot, it was dark. The wind was strong, like it was surrounding me," Thearon nodded along like the news was not exactly new to him. "There was a shadow that was even darker than anything around me and it said, well I think it said, death will come to me, what do you think it was?" asked Jack, Thearon held back from saying anything straight away. "Thearon, I feel you know, please tell me." said Jack.

"OK, Jack you must understand that my travels with your father didn't always have a happy ending. We had to fight and upset people you don't want to upset, but it was our job that these people were threatening. And there was one man who killed someone very close to your father so, as your father was still very young, he had no fear and wanted revenge, so we went to take it. The man was a very powerful Mage of the Brewin. The Brewin are people who learn very special abilities that take a lot of practice and training. You can become very powerful, and you can achieve long life. But the rumour is that you don't get a choice about what happens to your soul at the end of your long life. It might rest in peace like everyone else or it might get cursed and you will never rest. It might be this Mage who you heard as after we defeated him years ago, your father told me about having similar visions ever since." A sense of slight fear sank into Jack.

"What happened to the Brewin?" asked Jack.

"Anybody can learn it if they have the right teacher and source material. In the early days of the Dominion, they hired a Mage of the Brewin. His name was Broxholme Watts. They wanted him to help them get rid of the

Androne followers and any other descendants. Watts was very powerful by the time we got caught up with him and the Dominion realised how powerful he was. They then felt the Brewin could be a threat to them and so they hunted them down."

"So, you killed this Brox... err Watts?" Jack asked.

"Oh god no, we were never going to be able to kill him, but we wounded him quite severely and we never saw him again." Thearon replied.

"So, he just gave up?"

"Some praised us saying he died from his wounds. Others say that he left because he wanted to be cursed to get his revenge. I didn't believe that, but your father continued telling me about his dreams and now you're having them too I'm starting to change my mind."

"Where can you learn these skills?" Jack asked. He wanted to know more about the Brewin and the powers they possess.

"Before the Dominion, there were underground schools teaching it, they weren't legal of course but the government at the time turned a blind eye. The Dominion came into power, and it all changed. After learning what Watts was capable of, they shut them all down and threatened to kill anybody practicing it." Said Thearon.

"So, you think it's him who I saw."

"Possibly," Thearon snapped back. "As were not sure it's best to try not to think on it now. Besides a dream can't hurt you. Plus, if he could hurt anybody the Dominion would be in big trouble I should think after what they did to the others."

"Thearon!" Maddox shouted, "The transport, I can see it in the distance!" Thearon jumped up onto the rocks that Maddox was on to look. It was way in the distance, but Thearon soon took his eyes off the transport as something else took his gaze.

"Get you swords out, we may be in a spot of bother." Thearon stepped back down off the rocks and pushed Jack back away. "Maddox come on with me!" he jumped down with a crash and joined Thearon and Jack.

"Jack, get your sword out!" said Thearon, he did as he was told and pulled his grey bladed Vendel sword out of its sheath.

"Thearon," said Jack in a whisper, "what is..." he didn't get to finish before a jaw full of teeth pushed through the bushes in front of them. It was followed by four huge feet with dirty grey skin.

"What is this creature?" Said Maddox trying to identify it. "Some sort of hound?" Thearon shook his head in disagreement.

"No, it's some sort of mutated beast, conjured up in a Dominion basement! A gushlow I believe they call them," Thearon said, "get ready Jack this isn't going to be easy." Jack tried to remember his fight with the burting and how he managed that, although they didn't have sharp teeth and claws like small knives. The three men lifted their swords ready for the attack. The beast leaped from standing position towards Jack. He couldn't move his sword quick enough and ended up swinging his arm, hitting the jaw of the gushlow knocking it to the floor, they stepped back.

"We need to attack it, put it on its back legs!" shouted Maddox.

"Wait!" Thearon shouted, holding his hand out, the gushlow circled them and they were now facing the opposite way to when they started. A rustling sound came from behind them, and two more gushlows stepped out of the overgrowth. "Ok Maddox looks like it's one on one so we will do it your way." said

Thearon. At once they jumped out at the gushlows. They all swung their swords towards the beasts, but they were quick, and every swing missed. Thearon teased the gushlow towards him and had to dodge a swing of one of its front legs, feeling the claws narrowly miss his face. Thearon swung his sword towards the other leg but instead of going through it like he had hoped, the blade got stuck in the skin.

"Your sword won't hurt it; their skin is too thick." Thearon shouted; he had no choice but to back off. The three of them found themselves up against rocks.

"Ok then, what's the plan now?" Jack asked with clear panic in his voice. "How do you kill something that your sword won't cut through?" The gushlows crawled closer to them with their teeth grinding together and saliva dripping from their jaws.

"Jack, yours is looking ready to pounce lad!" Maddox warned.

"They all look ready to pounce!" he replied, but before he could set himself the beast jumped at Jack who fell back. The gushlow fell flat on top of Jack. He opened his eyes thinking he would be scratched and torn up, but to his surprise the gushlow was lying flat out on top of him.

Jack managed to push him off and there was his Vendel blade poking out the back of the beast. As he pulled it out the other two took a couple of steps back.

"Oh no you're not going anywhere now." Jack ran out towards the gushlows swinging his sword like he was trying to put out a flame on the end. They were still too fast for Jack to hit them.

"Maddox, we need to distract them so he can hit them." Thearon started to climb to the top of the rock pile and lifted his bow with an arrow ready to fire. He let it go towards the gushlows, a turned its head towards Thearon growling.

"Jack now!" but the gushlow had focussed his attention back on Jack.

"Sorry Thearon, err try again!" Jack shouted back.

"Well, I haven't got many arrows, ok ready!" Thearon set another arrow. Jack stood ready as an arrow hit the other gushlow who flinched which gave Jack the chance to catch it below the jaw slitting its throat. Before the gushlow died it stumbled into the other one and Jack jumped, driving his blade into the back of the beast. As he pulled it out Thearon walked up next to him and took hold of the blade.

"My father told me Vendel is stronger than other metals, I didn't even think." said Jack.

"It's an amazing sword, your father was very proud of it and if he could see you now," Thearon put his arm around Jack. "Now we must move to catch up with your parents."

CHAPTER 3

ATTON

The walls of Woodale could be seen for some miles. But the oddest thing about it was they looked so new, that compared to the other buildings within the town. Lord Atton, as confident as he might come across too many people, was very fearful of attacks or people who he would consider unwelcome. For example, the town of Davenport down the road was very well known for its fighting sport. This attracted a lot of people from many places around the world which Atton would not entertain. Many fans of a particular fighter or fans of the sport would arrive at Woodale assuming it would be a cheaper option for them to stay. If riches were all that Atton cared about, he would be a lot more welcoming as drink, food and bed sales would go through the roof most weeks. He didn't want what he considered to be the low lives of society appearing in his town, so his answer was to build a wall and have the gate always manned.

The main hall of Woodale was very grand. Atton spent most of his time there as he very rarely went out of his way to see any of his townsfolk as he regarded them as low lives. The hall was where his top table sat or his throne as he called it, even though there was no royalty on the whole planet, yet alone in his little town. He did believe he was royalty and the stress that he had in his life revolved around people not giving him the royal respect he felt he deserved. In fact, there was not a lot of respect at all. The villagers paid their taxes and that was all they concerned themselves with as far as leadership. That was only because Atton would have his guards at their door if they didn't pay it. Twenty silver pennies a month was expected from each household.

This was, of course, the part of the currency used all around the world, which included bronze pennies, silver pennies, and gold trophies. They were not actual trophies, they were gold coins, but they were so rare years ago that they were considered a trophy if you had one. Woodale hadn't moved on much as economics go, so they were still a rare sight for the normal townsfolk. In fact, ninety eight percent of golden trophies in Woodale were in the 'royal vault', as Atton likes to call it. Although twenty silver pennies were a sizable tax, in the capital of Mitchler the tax payable was fifty silver pennies or one golden trophy a month.

On waking, Atton went about his day as he would, having his breakfast of eggs and bacon served at his throne. Bacon wasn't offered to anyone else, his Lords had only eggs and bread. Atton was a plump man who never cared for his appearance. You could tell this by his hair that fell down the side of his head. So thin and greasy it looked like a couple of black rat's tails hanging out of his hat which he put on his round head only to hide it.

His Lords' main role was to look after the town as Atton wasn't interested. They all put effort and care in their appearance and these men were the only thing that made the group look like any kind of responsible leadership.

Breakfast was a quiet affair, as nobody asked Atton questions about the town's affairs as they knew they wouldn't get an answer. So, they showed their faces, ate their pathetic breakfast, thanked their 'king' and left as quick as they could. Today's breakfast turned out to be not as straightforward as they are usually used to. For as they got interrupted by a heavy knock on the hall doors. Lord Patton who dealt with financial issues sat and waited with the other Lords for someone to answer and took it upon himself to stand and shout.

"Come..." but before he could finish the doors flew open and there stood a man in his twenties who outdid them all in self-respect. He was dressed in full armour of silver carrying his helm under his left arm and his sword sheathed on his right side.

"Ah Spence, what do I owe the pleasure?" said Atton in his low pompous voice. Spence was the only person in the town Atton had a little bit of respect for because he was the only soldier who he feared. Spence oversaw Woodale's army and defences.

"I'm delivering today's report my Lord as I do everyday sir," Spence waited for a nod from Atton. "Captain Cole and his men are on their way back from the South ridge. He is confident that Davenport's intentions of holding a tournament next month won't cause us any issue." said Spence.

"Thank you, Spence, erm would that be all then?" Atton replied.

"No, our scouts have spotted a Dominion marked transport headed this way."

"Oh excellent," Atton shouted louder than intended. This came as a shock to the Lords, as Lord Atton usually detested any kind of capital interference, Dominion, or pre-Dominion government.

"Set up a welcome party Spence would you, and when they arrive bring them to me here straight away, that will be all Spence."

Spence did a half bow and left the hall.

"Now Lord Gibbins," Atton said to a very tall thin man sitting down the table to his left. "Am I right in saying you will keep the townsfolk from making any unwanted interruptions during this visit?"

"Er...er yes, my Lord!" Gibbins replied and scurried off. He was the voice of the town, the only person willing to do it, for often, whilst making an appearance in the town he was stoned or had other things thrown at him. if he had not done what the townsfolk had asked of him. This wasn't through him not trying but down to the fact that his Lord didn't care. In each meeting, if he didn't speak up promptly after being asked, Atton would interrupt him with something he felt to be of more interest.

"Lord Sharp!" Who was a Lord because Atton, at a whim one day, decided to make him a Lord. Nobody knew his role within the town's leadership. "Go and organise the cells will you, we will be needing them, in fact for those of you who are unaware." which was all of them. "I received a crow yesterday from an Agent Lo of the Dominion telling me that he has something of interest to me and will deliver them to me this evening. He wants some information in return but that's minor, this news has pleased me and may end a very hard period for me and the great town of Woodale." He spoke with quite some excitement as nobody moved, until he turned his head towards Lord Sharp which made him jump up and run.

"Now then, let's get this hall ready for our guests." He stood, turned, and wobbled off. Of course, when he said we, he meant you, referring to the other Lords and servants he had dotted around the hall.

AGENT LO

The two doors at the front of the transport flung open and Lo stepped out onto a balcony like platform. He could see the walls surrounding Woodale, he wasn't impressed. The gates opened in front of them, and guards were led out by Spence. Agent Lo turned to go back inside and headed over to Jon and Heena. They both lifted their heads to see Lo standing in front of them.

"So, Jon, anything new you want to tell me today, I thought that as a couple of nights have passed you may have remembered something or had a change of heart?" his black eyes came closer and closer to Jon, "who took the boy?" Jon looked to the floor. "I know you know Jon, and I also know that they will continue to try and rescue you." Jon knew this was true, even if Thearon had other plans there is no way Jack would stay away.

"So, as I know that they will show up at some point, let's try something new. Who, were the Andos and who attacked Mitchler last month?"

"I don't know, I swear" Jon pleaded with Lo,

"Are you sure? Or... were you involved? Because from the intelligence that I have picked up before visiting Beachdale you have not been a part of the Dale Guard for some time Jon." Lo's interrogation intensified.

"I had no reason to go to Mitchler, I may consider myself an Ando, but I have had no contact with Ando for years."

"I believe you, although I still think you know who was likely to have been involved, do you know what damage they did? Well because of you, people create inaccurate conspiracy theories about the capital. They did damage worth more gold than you will ever see, even as Dale Guard Captain. Unfortunately for you, Beachdale was my first stop on finding out who was responsible, and it has opened some new opportunities for me." Lo turned and walked back towards the door.

"I assume you have figured out where we are, Lord Atton will be excited to see you." Lo looked pleased with himself slamming the door on his way out. "Hi-Pec, you come with me, leave my firsts in the chamber with the prisoners until I send you to fetch them." Hi-Pec nodded in agreement and followed Lo out of the transport.

As he stepped out on to the dusty ground, he looked up at the wall surrounding Woodale. twenty-five foot of stone circling the whole town.

"Looks like you're trying to keep something out Captain," Agent Lo shouted towards Spence and the other guards who had welcomed him. "Or someone." Spence walked up to greet Lo.

"Agent Lo sir, welcome to Woodale." said Spence along with a short bow.

"It's a pleasure Captain," Lo replied. "I'm sure your king is awaiting me."

"Il take you to him." said Spence as he turned and waved to the other guards to head into the gate. As the heavy wooden gates started to shut Lord Gibbins was walking ahead of the group ensuring there would be no unwanted spectators. Any villagers who had heard about the visit were already at their windows and behind their doors to get a glimpse of the visitor. The excitement within Woodale was high as they didn't get guests of any standing. They prefer towns like Davenport for the tournaments or Beachdale because of the docks.

For every person peeping out the window Gibbons threw a dirty look but that's all he could muster. Luckily for him, they had no intentions to hang around in the streets of Woodale. The buildings were made as cheap as they could, and the upkeep was non-existent, because most people were poor. One trader tried his luck shouting about his burting meat towards Agent Lo.

"A breast of burting only twenty silver pennies!" Lord Gibbins ran over waving his arms but before he could offer any kind of authority in the situation Hi-Pec already had his hand round the trader's neck.

"Hi-Pec put him down, that won't be necessary." Lo turned back to Spence who had about as much sympathy towards the trader as Lo did, so they continued.

"Ah yes, let that be an example to you all." Gibbins called, the trader threw his butcher knife in his direction which made Gibbins turn and scurry off at pace.

"I hear you have something for our King, Agent? Said Spence.

"Well, that depends completely on what your King has for me Captain," replied Lo. Spence raised his thin blonde eyebrow knowing full well Lo would be disappointed as he hadn't seen anything that Atton had got that Lo would be interested in. "I'm surprised your King hasn't greeted me at the gates Captain."

"He doesn't leave his great hall, Agent Lo." Spence replied. The hall came into their vision once they turned the last corner. It was an impressive building, with wooden beams running alongside neat brickwork and a slate roof topping the building.

"I can't blame him for staying inside." said Lo as they entered the hall.

"My lord," Spence shouted. Getting the attention of all the Lords who quickly lined themselves up behind Atton. "Agent Lo, Sir." Spence gave a small bow and moved aside with Hi-Pec as Lo stepped forward towards Atton.

"Lord Atton, thank you for allowing us into your home." Lo said, whilst giving what looked like a sarcastic bow.

"Welcome Agent Lo, Lords leave us. Come

take a seat my new friend we have a lot to talk about," Atton pointed in the direction of the chair that had been pulled out for him. "Agent, I have to admit that I feel a little uncomfortable about not seeing Jon Skies yet, where he is?" Agent Lo took a seat, picked up a cup of water and took a big gulp.

"Patience my new friend, he is safe on our transport. can assure you, if I get what I need, you will get what you desire," said Lo reassuringly. "But first a toast to Lord Atton and the new partnership between Woodale and Dominion." They both lifted their cups up into the air, Atton looking very smug like he'd had an incredible compliment.

"So, my Lord, Jon Skies, does he have a son?" Asked Lo. Lord Atton smirked, pimples pushing into his puffy cheeks.

"Yes, his name is Jack I believe, a good fighter I have been told." said Atton whilst gurgling on his drink.

"Yes, so I recall, so it is his son, interesting," Lo said.

He sat right back in his seat trying his best to keep a not so disgusted face with the sight of Atton watering himself.

"During our visit to Beachdale he was taken from under our nose, and I want to find out who took him."

"Agent Lo! Jon Skies has many enemies but also many friends who would give their lives to protect him, one being Thearon." Atton interrupted Lo but Lo's eyes met Atton's for the first time since he had entered the room.

"I've heard that name before." Lo said, he started to learn forward,

"You will have, he is an Androne descendant hunter. He didn't leave Jon's side throughout the war. And yes, the information you were looking for Agent Lo, they both attacked Mitchler with a group of soldiers from our town. But I can assure you they no longer reside here, but also Thearon is someone we are currently looking for so if you know where he is?"

"Well Lord Atton, our new friendship may do that. He has been following us with Jon's son. Now my Lord I am going to retire as the travelling has taken it out of me." Agent Lo started to get up and head towards the doors.

"Hold on for a second Lo, I want my prize. I have given you the information that you requested so you need to keep to your end of the bargain." shouted Atton as he rose from the table, Lo stopped and turned back to

Atton.

"Lord Atton, I can assure you that you will receive everything that you deserve, but in the morning, good night, Sir." Lo turned around with a swing of his cloak, and marched back towards the doors. He gestured over to Hi-Pec to follow him. "We may be holding someone a lot more important and the men following even more so, Atton thinks we're playing him so I'm going to try something new, come with me."

JACK

The trio had finally caught up with a stationary transport which seemed to have been left outside the great walls of Woodale. It was guarded by all the Firsts, which Agent Lo considered to be the best of the best of all the guards and other soldiers. Jack recognised them as he had fought against some in Beachdale.

"How do we get into that transport?" asked Jack.

"We don't, they have come here to trade with Atton, he wants information from the war, and your father will be his trade. So, we need to get him from inside the town before..." Thearon stopped talking and looked at Jack who was staring straight into his eyes waiting for him to finish his sentence. "We need to get into the town," Jack nodded but then looked up at the walls.

"Ok, so how do we get in," Jack asked.

"Don't worry kid." Thearon chuckled.

"You know a way in? because those guards are not going to let us stroll in."

"The walls may look nice and big, but it doesn't mean they actually work, this is Lord Atton's Wall, built on the cheap." Thearon said.

"So, you have done it before?"

"Of course! the rooms are cheaper here, I'm not going to pay Davenports prices during a tourney, ha!" Thearon and Maddox moved away crouching within bushes, but he struggled to keep his back from peeping out to top of the branches.

"So how do we do it?" Asked Jack.

"I have a friend who lives on the boundary. He has always helped me in the past, I haven't been back for a while but there is a way to climb the wall and land straight into his back room." They continued to sneak around through the overgrowth until like Thearon promised, the wall had a part that looked very rough. Perfect for climbing and a flat roof at the top.

"That's some climb though Thearon." Jack said as he looked up to the top of the wall.

The darkness of night made it an even harder prospect as he could not see where to put his hands and feet.

"It's fine Jack, come on before Atton's scouts come searching for us and also, they will be expecting us so be on your guard!" Thearon said. Jack finally started climbing the wall. Every part of the wall he grabbed didn't hold his weight and he had to maneuverer himself several times before reaching out for the next grab point. He realised he was almost halfway up but lost his concentration after looking down and seeing the ground. After stabilising himself he had held onto the ledge of a window. He hung there for a couple of minutes trying to figure out how he was going to move up without being seen.

"Come on lad let's go!" Maddox had now climbed past him and held his hand out to help Jack up. Jack tried reaching out with his left hand, but his left side was useless. He had no strength in it at all being right-handed, instead he shouted at Maddox to keep going and meet Thearon who had already made it to the top. After looking down at his feet he managed to push them against the wall which gave him some momentum to climb up some more. Until his head lifted above the window ledge, and he saw someone inside. She was beautiful, she had long brunette hair that covered her shoulders, but all else was covered with a long dark cloak. The room was very dark, the only light was coming from a small candle that lit her front. Jack leaned closer in to get a better look, she was reading a book, and there was a pile of books on the table next to her. Jack couldn't take his eyes off her. The girl closed the book, turned around and pushed the book into an empty space on a bookshelf.

As she stepped back the flame lit the wall showing bookshelves covering the wall like it was some sort of library. Jack's observation ended there as his hand slipped, pulling rubble down with it. They landed on the ledge startling the girl who blew out the flame, picked up the books and left.

"Jack, come on." Thearon urged in an angry whisper, he and Maddox had already made it to the top and started looking at how to get into his friend's house.

Jack finally made it to the top and pulled himself over onto the flat roof, Thearon and Maddox were nowhere to be seen. He crouched down behind a wall which gave him a little bit of space between the side of the first floor of a house and the wall of the town. Along the wall of the house there was a wooden door with a lock and an old rusting doorknob that looked like it wouldn't even turn if tried. Jack felt that was his only option, so he turned his sight towards the road to check if anyone was coming and edged towards it. As he got closer, he reached out to grab the knob but dropped to the floor as he heard two soldiers and their horses ride past. Jack was breathing heavily trying his best to keep as quiet as he could.

"Thearon where are you?" Jack whispered, the wooden door behind him swung open and Jack felt a hand grab him by the scruff of the neck pulling him inside. The door slammed shut leaving no light inside, "hello?! Thearon? Maddox?" Jack had his hands out feeling the walls as he was trying to find his way to the others. As he turned the corner, he saw a light which was being given out by three candles on a table which had three men standing around it. It was Thearon, Maddox and one other.

"Jack, this is Alekzander." said Thearon as Jack came walking over out of the darkness.

"Jack, it's nice to meet you finally. I served with your father during the war, oh and Thearon of course." Said Alekzander while holding out his hand for a shake to greet Jack. He was younger than Jon as he was only 18 when he went to war alongside the Woodale army.

"And you sir." Jack replied.

"Please don't call me sir, I am no Knight, Zander will do. Now, Atton has wanted your father's head since the war ended and as you lot are here and there is a Dominion transport out front. I'm guessing Jon is there somewhere?" Jack nodded back at Zander "the truth is Jack if Atton finds that you and Thearon are here, he will think it's a gift, so you can't be wandering the streets." Zander stood and turned to a draw in his wooden cabinet and pulled out a parchment.

"Now I haven't got much to offer you other than you can stay here as long as you need. I can go out and get food and other supplies if you have any coins, also you can have this," Zander handed Thearon the parchment. "it's a map of the town, so if you need to go at any time, you can study and use this to get where you need to go to." Jack's eyes moved to the map, held out his hand to have a look,

Thearon passed the map to Jack, and he studied it.

"Where are we now?" Jack asked. Zander hovered his finger over the map and then finally landed it on a small box outlined at the far right of the map. The map wasn't labelled well, other than 'main hall, front gate, butcher and Karla'. Jack didn't ask who Karla was, but he felt he didn't need to. He hoped that there would be a label on Zander's house so he could identify the room where he saw that girl and if there was any labelled prison.

"You won't be able to achieve anything while the Dominion are here. I suggest that you let them do their deal, leave and then I can help you break Jon and Heena out," said Zander. He downed the rest of his drink and placed the cup back on the table "right lets gets some rest eh."

Zander led Thearon into where he and Maddox would sleep. It was only a small room but there were cushions and a throw, so it's an upgrade to the past few days. For Jack who got a room to himself which also had some cushions and a throw. Although it wasn't a bedroom it was separated from the living area by a curtain which didn't even close fully. Jack lay down and tried to get comfortable, but he wasn't as tired as he thought. He couldn't help but think about how his mother and father were in a building in this same town, yet he was still unable to help them.

The night passed quickly considering his feelings and lack of sleep. Luckily for him sleeping with a roof above him gave him a lot less anxiety than he thought. To his pleasure he felt quite refreshed apart from his calves aching after his wall climb. He snuck out of his room and slowly pulled at the brown curtain closing off Thearon's room. Enough to see in and still laying on the floor were both Maddox and Thearon. Jack carried on into the entrance to the house and he saw Zander coming in through the door.

"Ah Jack, sleep well I assume?" Zander asked.

"Er yes, sir," Jack replied. "Alekzander, I'm thinking of going to get myself and the others some breakfast."

"What out there? Alone? I can't let you do that Jack." Zander said.

"No one in this town knows who I am, as long as I stay away from the main building and any of Agent Lo's men." said Jack.

"No, it's too dangerous."

"With all due respect sir, I'm going." Jack walked towards the door.

"Wait, wait, take this at least," Zander handed Jack a cloak. "Keep in the shadows and for god's sake don't go down Pevers Avenue, they will eat you up down there." Jack nodded and headed out the door.

The streets of Woodale seemed very strange to Jack. The buildings were very close, not like at Beachdale where the paths were wide and spacious. People were not interested in others, not a care in the world, which made the paths look very chaotic. Fast moving people trying to get on with their lives. Jack looked lost already, he stayed close to the wall determined not to get in anybody's way. Instead of staying on the main pathway he turned down an alley which ran down the side of Zander's House. He was looking up for windows or any other doors to get in. He wanted to find the room he saw the girl in, hoping to see her again but there didn't seem to be a way in. As he turned yet another corner he looked up and saw a damaged wall. It's like someone had dug through it. Jack had to look. He started climbing the wall which was made easier by there being a wooden framework going up and across the building. A different style of architecture unlike the smooth walls around the town. When he made it to the hole, he tried to peep in, but it was pitch black. He managed to lift himself into the gap and before he got to his feet he was pulled up and slammed against the wall.

"Who are you? You're spying on me I saw you yesterday." the voice said, all Jack could see was the shape of a hood and cloak.

"I wasn't spying, let me go." Jack retaliated trying to remove the strong fist from the scuff of his neck.

He reached down to his side and pulled out his sword and swung it towards the person, but a sword had already swung out to meet Jacks.

"Tell me who you are, and I will stand down." It then occurred to Jack that it was a girl's voice and she had spoken about yesterday so it must be her.

"I'm not here to hurt anyone!" Jack said, he lowered his sword and held his hand out upright. The girl sheathed her sword and turned back to the table where a book was open.

"What is this place?" Jack asked. The girl re lit the candle on the table and two candles that hung from the wall.

"This is where I come to get away from the world." the girl replied.

"It has no doors?" Jack said.

"It did have, once, a long time ago, until the plague, they called it the silent death. Two hundred years ago Woodale's people started falling and no-one knew why. But when they realised it got passed on from man to man this room became a dumping ground for bodies of those who had died of the disease." Jacks face dropped and edged back slowly. "It was then forgotten about until ten years ago when my friend was doing some work on the structure, he came across it and somehow cleared it all out."

"What happened to him?" Jack asked.

"He travelled a lot and brought back lots of books and turned it into a personal library, a year ago he got taken away by the Dominion as... because... I shouldn't tell you." The girl turned away to the table. Jack followed her and then when looking at the table he saw the title of the book "The Brewin – The History of the Mage."

"The Brewin? you are a Brewin?" Jack

stared in amazement. "How much do you know?" Jack got very excited.

"You can't tell anyone I'll get my father in so much trouble." the girl said to Jack looking very nervous.

"I won't, I'm Jack, what is your name?" the girl took down her hood to show her long brown hair, she had small thin brown eyes and a golden shy face.

"Sophia. I know some basics, when I first met Lynx, he was so clever, and talented, the things he could do amazed me. He taught me this, watch." Sophia waved her hand over the flame which then floated in her palm. Jack's face dropped and he knew at that moment he needed to learn some of this magic. Sophia closed her eyes, and the flame grew and started to burn bright green sparks started spitting from her palm. As she opened her eyes she lowered her hand back to the candle, the flame slipped back to the tip of the wick.

"That was amazing, can you teach me?" Jack asked Sophia.

"I can but it takes time and practice a lot of work, these books are all teachings from hundreds of years ago," said Sophia. She picked up the candle and took Jack to the back of the room and showed him the books that filled a bookcase.

"All these books are different teachings from different parts of the world." Jack pulled a couple of books off the shelf and opened one gently as the brown pages started to slip out.

"These are in bad shape, how are you going to read them?" Jack asked whilst juggling with pages.

"They are ancient, I have been working on something come see." Jack walked back over to the table with Sophia, she picked it up and stood in front of the window that Jack saw her through. it was only a small window, more like a gap but enough to be able to see out. She placed the book open on a shelf below the window and pulled her hood back up.

"When mastered, you can control small animals or insects. Now, I'm only learning remember so don't expect miracles." Sophia said. Jack stepped closer to Sophia to see what she was looking at, but the book was so old and battered he couldn't read it. Sophia looked out of the window for a second and then closed her eyes. Jack stayed silent and stared into her closed eyelids until a little bird landed on the shelf next to the book. Jack smiled at Sophia who opened her eyes letting out a little giggle.

"You shouldn't do it for long until you have mastered it as you can do damage to the animal," said Sophia. The little bird then hopped on to Sophia's finger, "I have only ever dared make them come to me, then I let them go as this skill can go dangerously wrong." She placed the bird back on the shelf and the walked back to the bookshelf "so, what's your story?"

"Er, I'm Jack," he then looked down knowing he had already told her that. "Err yeah, I'm travelling around, don't stay anywhere long" he looked around desperately trying to come up with a story that Sophia may believe. Then suddenly the shelf fell off the wall with a crash. Sophia ran to see and picked the book up but couldn't see the bird anywhere until she turned and looked under the table. There lay the bird in a heap, but it was now black as the night sky and twice the size.

"Oh no!" she stood back up straight "you need to help me get it out quick!" There was a sudden sound of terror in her voice, Jack tried to get down under the table to get the bird but before he knew it. The table had smashed in two and his face was in front of the bird, but it was now at least four foot tall.

"What's happened to it?" squealed Jack. The bird used its new long powerful neck to knock Jack out the way and it leapt towards Sophia knocking her to the floor. Its beak gave her a scratch down her cheek narrowly missing her eye. Sophia waved her arms down to her side trying to grab her sword, but it was painfully out of reach. Sophia braced as the bird leant back ready to strike again but then a sword sliced into its neck and with an extra bit of strength, Jack forced it all the way though chopping its head clean off. Jack held his hand out to Sophia and helped her up.

"Are you ok?" Jack asked. "What happened to it?"

"I told you it can go dangerously wrong," said Sophia. "I need to go home; my father will be wondering where I am."

"Wait I want to learn this stuff like you have." blurted Jack, Sophia turned back to him then looked at the bookshelf, she picked a book out.

"Here take this, it was the first book of the

Brewin I ever read. It is the first teachings from when they had schools, anyway enjoy, bye." Sophia slipped out of the hole in the wall onto the street and out of sight.

Jack returned to Zanders and Thearon was waiting for him with his hood up.

"Where have you been? if you get caught!"

"Look, I appreciate what you are doing but I'm not going to be a prisoner Thearon, I was in the room below us that's all, I won't go any further I swear."

SPENCE

"Ah Spence you're here!" Atton boomed as Spence walked into Atton's office, which was quite small considering the size of the other parts of Atton's quarters.

"You called for me my lord?" Spence replied.

"Yes, well you see Spence. I'm getting more and more concerned about Agent Lo's location. he hasn't been seen for some time and isn't at his transport. worst of all Spence I haven't seen Jon!" Atton scoured, "he was my prize Spence and I want him!"

Atton sat back down in his chair, he started looking through notes on parchments on his desk, but it only distracted him for a few seconds.

"Oh, Gibbins can sort this nonsense out, but you Spence you are going to get my prize for me."

"My King. Agent Lo is not around the transport, but it's still well guarded," breathed Spence. "I would need to take at least a dozen of our men with me, and I can't promise all of us would come back especially with Jon!"

"Spence, you see all these pictures on the wall," Atton held Spence on the shoulder and turned him to face the portraits. "These two, who are they?"

Spence knew he was about to be lectured on Atton's family history again as he gave a half eye roll when Atton couldn't see.

"This one is my brother." Atton pointed to portrait of a tall yet well-built man and then to the other. "And this my father, they were both betrayed by that Jon Skies. They went as allies to defend the land from the Dominion and they swore an oath together to protect Woodale as well as Beachdale. But what happened once Beachdale was cleared out of Dominion soldiers? They sold us out and left Woodale to be over run and that's when I lost them. We couldn't compete with the Dale Guard, but the Dominion has done the hard work for me so now they must pay, and you're going to go and get him for me!"

Atton turned and went back to his desk where he downed a small glass of whiskey. "Now go and see it done."

Spence gave a short bow and turned to leave Atton's office. He couldn't believe what he had been asked to do, well he could but now he had to go and try and achieve it. He made his way down towards the barracks to try and come up with some sort of plan.

As evening fell, Spence knew it was time and to his surprise he put together a plan. He recruited six of the archers and six of the soldiers, all from the Royal Guard. At first, he thought that he got too few men, but then decided to concentrate on stealth to avoid getting the attention of any of the townsfolk.

They all left together out of the barracks and snook out of a side door of the main hall. This brought them out behind a small marketplace that sat to the left of the entrance to the main hall. The archers crouched behind some market carts and hid in the shadows. Spence crouched with them to see what they were up against.

"Two guards on the door my Lord, no signs of any other patrols in the immediate area" the Head Archer told Spence.

"Great, but there will be a welcome party inside I suspect." Spence looked up towards the rooftops and made a signal by pointing his fingers towards the Dominion Guards. Two archers lifted their bows over the gritty brickwork of the hall and then shot arrows which flew silently through the air and with two simultaneous thuds, both guards fell lifeless to the floor. Two of the Woodale soldiers sprinted up and dragged the guards away past where Spence was crouching. With a nod of his head, Spence carefully moved towards the transport after waiting for his archers to join him. The door that faced Spence was held shut by a silver latch, but no lock.

"No lock my Lord, do you think it's a trap?" the soldier asked.

"Maybe, if it is a trap we die, if we go back without the prisoner we will die," lamented Spence. "So, let's go!"
Spence unclipped the latch, pulled the door open, and the archers ran in ready to fire at any soldiers inside. There were no soldiers, no more guards, they all stared into an empty shadow. Spence walked into the empty transport and looked around searching cautiously for the prisoners.

"At the back my Lord!" shouted an archer. Spence looked up and made his way to the back, he picked up a candle that was lit up on a table and took it with him. Until in front of him was thick, rusting metal bars and behind them lay two people.

Jon started to look tired and exhausted. His eyes looked like they were starting to sink into his skull and circled with dark shadows. Jon's eyes opened as Spence crouched down in front of the cell.

"Who are you?" Jon pained.

"That doesn't matter, but you're coming with me." Spence informed Jon. He pulled out his sword and placed it on the lock. "Step back."

Jon pushed his body along the floor closer to Heena who was sitting up against the back wall. Spence swung his sword and shattered the lock off the door of the cage. He entered the cage along with another soldier and picked both Jon and Heena up and carried them out of the transport.

"My Lord, we're still clear to go through the main door." the lead archer informed Spence.

"Get them gates open let's go."

As the gates opened Spence and the soldier carried their prisoners into the main hall leaving the other soldiers waiting outside.

"Ahh Spence, you have done me proud sir!" Atton boomed as he marched into the hall. The prisoner was dropped in the centre of the room.

"Jon Skies, we meet again, you have no idea how long I have waited to have you on your knees in front of me." Atton laughed as he paced up and down in front of Jon and Heena.

"He's going to kill you." Jon groaned. Atton laughed at him, "Agent Lo? Ha! you were my part of the deal he owed you to me, he will not be able to kill me if he tried."

"Don't do this please." Jon pleaded.

"You left my father and brother to die after failing to live up to promises Beachdale made to Woodale. We cleared your town of the enemy, and you didn't come to our aid when we needed it!" Atton pushed his round red face into Jon's.

"You're my prisoner now and you will pay for your crime, take him to his new cell." Atton shouted at Spence.

Spence picked Jon up by his arm to his feet and signalled to Heena to follow.

"No, leave her with me," said Atton as he held her by her arm. "We have things to discuss."

Spence walked with Jon down into the dungeon below the main hall where the prison cells were located. It was dark only lit by single candles on the walls spotted every ten feet or so.

"You got another one Spence," spat the gaol guard. "Ere put him in this one, Feroz could do with the company," the guard wasn't allowed out of the dungeon so you could say he was a prisoner himself. You could see this in him as he was a hunchbacked skeleton with black eyes. His skin was so white it lit up the cell. "Watch out for Feroz, he killed the last person he shared a room with."

Spence grabbed him and turned him to face him. "If he dies Bones, I won't be holding Feroz responsible," he dropped Bones to the floor and he scurried back to his desk. "Feed him some porridge."

"But my Lord this is all I have, it's mine." Bones begged.

"Feed him!" Spence ordered and started to walk away before Jon's voice made him turn back.

"You know he knew you were going to take us, why do you think it was so easy." said Jon.

"Where is he?"

"I don't know, in the town somewhere waiting, but he has eyes all around the main hall and especially his transport," he had got Spence's attention. "Those two guards on the door you killed, they weren't his men, they were Woodale townsfolk, from the pig farm. He promised them two golden trophies each to guard his transport and gave them some old armour. They jumped at the thought of two golden trophies like anyone in this town would." Jon's voice got quieter as it started to pain him to speak. Bones squeezed past to give Jon his porridge.

"Get him some water too." Spence ordered Bones, with a grunt and an eye roll he did as he was told.

"What's his plan now?" Spence asked Jon. Who waited for Bones, who had a face like thunder, to arrive with some water.

"Your men, who you left to guard the doors... will be dead before you make it back up."

"I warned him of this, stupid man." Spence sneered.

"You look a decent man, leave, you won't stand a chance against Lo, he's probably already taken three quarters of your town under Atton's nose. You won't survive going back up there."

"And I suppose you want me to free you for providing me with this information?"

"No, you will be found and killed, but if you do want to thank me, I have some friends out looking for me. Please find them and help keep them safe, you might be able to slip out, but it will be impossible with me as well," said Jon. "You need to go now." Spence hurried past Bones and up and out of the dungeon.

AGENT LO

"My Lord!" Hi-Pec beamed as he burst into the room. "News from the watch party."

"Go on." Lo returned curiously.

"They did exactly as you predicted sir. They broke in and took them." A victorious smile grew across Agent Los face as he stood up and attached his sword among other things, to his belt.

"Get the men ready, we must move." Hi-Pec bowed and turned to gather the troops. Lo's plan had worked to perfection, as they very often did which he knew all too well. For the first time since leaving Beachdale he dressed in his best golden armour that sat over his blue coat.

"Thank you for the hospitality you both have shown us. For that I shan't kill you." Agent Lo sneered, pulling some cloth out of two villagers' mouths. He allowed his guard to untie the rope that was wrapped around their wrists.

"I do sincerely apologise for the way we barged into your home. But it was quite necessary I assure you, for my safety and yours." said Lo.

The faces of the two didn't change as they got to their feet.

"In fact, if our mission proves unsuccessful, we may even return for supper, but don't get your hopes up."

The two villages took a gulp and together they said in a whisper "ye...yes sir."

Lo marched through the streets of Woodale with Hi-Pec by his side. The townsfolk were scared and stayed safely behind their doors and curtains. He had brought many troops, with every regiment marching behind him. Lo's smile stretched from ear to ear as the hall got nearer and nearer. Then as they got closer to the hall, they stopped. Lo made a signal with his fingers and two soldiers ran around the corner of the building and then stopped again.

"Get them!" a voice echoed from the distance and the men ran back to the ranks followed by Spence's archers and soldiers except, no Spence. They came to a sudden holt, and they soon looked terrified as arrows from behind Lo flew straight at them taking three of them out.

"Charge!" Shouted Lo as they all cleared through the Woodale forces and within thirty seconds the dust had settled, and they were no more.

"My Lord, a survivor." Hi-Pec said from across the square. He dragged him and dropped him in front of Lo.

"Are you prepared to tell my friend here where your barracks are? If you do, we will spare your life and the rest of your army." Lo reassured the archer.

"Yes… yes sir!"

"Excellent! Hi-Pec go sort this will you leave me with my guard I'm sure they will be sufficient. You can take the rest. Remember Hi-Pec, we don't want a bloodbath." Lo pushed the archers out the way and marched into the main hall where King Atton was sitting on his throne looking somewhat bemused.

"Where are my soldiers Lo?" said Atton in a dark croaky tone.

"The more important question, my lord, is where are my prisoners?" Lo responded in calm, low voice.

Atton pulled on a chain and Heena got to her feet.

"Ahh there's one, now I assume the others is in the dungeon, so if you don't mind us, I will go and collect him." Lo took a few strides towards the door that led to the dungeon before Atton got to his feet holding his sword out towards Lo.

"Lord Atton this is ill advised and definitely not a fight you are going to win." And in perfect timing both doors to the great hall flew open as Hi-Pec walked in being followed by Lo's army and most of Woodale's.

"What are you all doing?" cried Atton.

"Hi-Pec what are you doing?" Lo said mocking Atton.

"Well, my Lord most joined our ranks, some didn't so you know." Hi-Pec said.

Lo turned back to Atton whose sword arm had started to shake. Lo's guards circled Atton as Hi-Pec re-joined Agent Lo.

"My Lord we had a very good chance of something special and your lack of patience and overconfidence has destroyed it. I'm very disappointed, I'm sure you're now happy for me to go and get Jon?" Atton's arm continued to shiver even heavier, but he resisted by standing up to the guards surrounding him.

"Fool, kill him!" ordered Lo. Atton dropped his sword as the guard behind him kicked the back of his legs making him drop on to his knees. Hi-Pec held Atton under his chin and cut his throat with one stroke of his sword. Atton's body bowled to the floor hitting the bottom step before coming to rest in an ever-growing puddle of his blood.
Lo made his way to the dungeon where he came up to Bones.

"Who are you?" he cried whilst he was patting down his trouser pockets before pulling out a small dagger. Lo stopped in front of him and looked him up and down.

"Open the cage."

"Yes, my Lord." Bones ran over to his desk picked up his keys and after fumbling around for some time he finally got the key in the lock and opened it.

"It's your luck...oof!" Lo kicked Bones out the way and stood in front of Jon.

"Well, that was short lived wasn't it, come on." Lo turned and walked back up the steps and Hi-Pec along with another guard chained up Jon's wrists and led him back up the stairwell. As Lo got to the top, he was met with the Lords of Woodale. Lord Patten was at the front of the gathering.

"You had better prepare a coronation my Lord" Agent Lo smirked as he past them and continued to march through the doors of the hall.

"Where is the Princess?" Lord Gibbins asked Lord Patten.

"I'm here!" a beautiful figure stepped out of a door behind the throne, it was a very tearful Sophia.

"My lady," Patten rushed up the steps to try and comfort Sophia who was staring down at her father who had been moved into a more respectable position. Two maids were trying to clean up the blood left by Atton's body. "I'm sorry my Princess." Sophia made a sudden change from her teary state to pick-up Atton's crown from the throne as he never wore it because of his hat. She placed it on her head as the Lords bowed in front of her.

"I don't need a coronation; I just need revenge!" Sophia snarled in a surprisingly dark way.

"My Lady we don't have the forces to take on such an enemy." said Patten.

"Watch my throne, I will do it myself."

"My Lady please," Patten shouted in a desperate attempt to stop Sophia. "You are our Queen, our leader."

"Fine, then I lead you into war!"

CHAPTER 4

JACK

In the morning Jack and Thearon stood on the top of the wall behind Zander's House watching the main hall.

"The transport is still there," Jack said, "I want to see my father."

"Zander and Maddox were on watch last night and they saw your father being taken from the transport." Thearon said. Jack took a quick look at Thearon then back at the transport which they could see through the gaps between other buildings.

"So, are they taking him away? I thought he was being given up as a part of a trade deal?"

"So did we, and that wasn't the only thing they saw," Jack once again looked up towards Thearon. "The deal must have gone sour, they saw Woodale troops break your father out and then the Dominion troops being led by Lo, decimated the Woodale troops. They then headed into the hall, it didn't take long before they brought your father out," Thearon turned to Jack and leant over to him. "Listen something is happening, and we need to be careful. Lo must have found a reason to keep hold of your father. Zander does some trading with some of the families around the main hall, so he's going to try and find out any news."

Jack strolled away and entered the small room in which he had slept, he pulled the curtain shut and took the book from under his small pillow. Since being given the book by Sophia, he had anxiety about reading anything after the accident with the bird. He plucked up some courage and opened it at the first page. How did Sophia learn anything from this, the book seemed to be scribbles and nonsense? But then Jack remembered her telling him about her teacher, how can he find her? He didn't see her last night. He knew now he was going to need a teacher to understand the writings in the book. Having lost patience, he dropped the book and then fell onto his makeshift bed in frustration. The room went quiet as Jack closed his eyes, until he heard a whisper, which turned into more of a whimper. Jack lifted himself upright into a sitting position. He listened carefully but it was quiet again. He lay down again with his ear on the floor and he heard it again, it was then he realised where it was coming from, was it Sophia? He had to find out.

Jack managed to sneak away from the house and made it to the hole in the wall where the crying got clearer. He pushed his head through the gap and then saw Sophia. She was not what he remembered from the last time he saw her, she looked beautiful even though she was crying and really upset.

"Sophia," Jack whispered, she turned her head slowly and when her eyes met his, all he could see was a girl in pain. "what's up?" he asked.

"You shouldn't be here." Sophia said.

"Why? I thought you were going to help me?"

"I don't mean in this room I mean in this town," Sophia stood up and walked towards Jack. "I know who you are Jack, your Jon Skies' son, if Agent Lo knew you were here, he would kill you like he has my father!"

Jack looked closer at Sophia; she still wore her silver crown which held three black crystals on the front.

"Your father is King Atton?" Sophia turned her gaze away from Jack and started to move towards a bookshelf.

"He wanted to kill my father, if Lo killed the King, then that's why he took my father back into his transport." he stopped and looked sharply towards Sophia once more.

"Does this mean you're going to take me to Lo?" Jack asked.

"Luckily for you, I'm not my father. I have no issue with Beachdale, if my uncle and grandfather were anything like my father, they were never going to survive a war anyway."

"What is Lo doing now? His transport is still outside the hall." said Jack.

"He's still here?"

Jack nodded and grabbed her hand and took her to the top of the wall where he had been standing with Thearon. The transport, as Jack promised, was still in the same position.

"Princess Sophia?" a voice sounded at the bottom of the steps. They both turned to see who it was with nervous looks on their faces. Zander appeared at the top of the steps with

Thearon trailing behind him. "or should I say Queen Sophia?" Zander said with a small bow. She returned a bow, "I see you have met Jack, and this is Thearon of the Ando's."

"If you have come to negotiate Jon's release, I no longer have him, Agent Lo has him in his transport." Sophia replied.

"He has since returned to the hall your highness," Thearon said stepping in front of Zander. "His army has taken over, for your safety I suggest you come with us, it's no longer safe here for you." Sophia looked over the town where she had always called home and then lost the reign as quickly as she had inherited it and then she agreed with a nod. "We will not go far as we still need to save Jon but until we get a plan, we're in danger here, we should prepare to leave." Thearon turned and headed back down the steps with Zander leaving Jack and Sophia alone.

"Why is he doing this?" Sophia mumbled, "what did my father do to Lo for him to do this."

"Thearon told me that they saw Woodale troops break my father out of his transport." said Jack.

Sophia shook her head in disbelief, although deep down this wasn't a surprise to her.

"he's waiting for me too, the way he spoke to me when they took my father and then things Thearon is telling me. I'm guessing he is setting up camp here so he can keep eye on Beachdale and any other surrounding towns. I can't escape anywhere but he also knows I want my parents back."

Jack and Sophia joined the rest inside Zander's house. Zander was standing behind the table with some old clothes piled on it, they looked like cut up old rags that had been picked up off the street.

"My Lady you need to leave, but Lo has got guards surrounding the walls so the usual way in and out would look too suspicious." Zander said as he looked down.

Sophia's jaw dropped as she stared at the clothes and then realised Thearon and Maddox were now wearing similar style clothing.

"You're suggesting that I wear them?" Sophia said half disgusted.

"We're suggesting you both wear them," Thearon shot back. "If they see you leave, they will want to know why so you need to look like a normal Woodale citizen as will you Jack." Jack stepped forward and started looking through the clothes and picked out his preferred items, leaving what was left for Sophia. As they were walking on their way down to the town Sophia started trailing behind, they stopped, and Jack went to her.

"Come on, we've got to go." said Jack.

"Will it get easier? Leaving the town, you grew up in?" Sophia asked Jack.

"If it's for the right reasons, it will get easier." said Jack.

The streets were quiet, the only sounds that could be heard was the ringing of the blacksmiths making a boy's first sword or a knight's next armour. The rain was soaking the streets as Jack and Sophia made their way towards the gates which towered over the small market stalls that sat at the base of the walls. The atmosphere was eerie, they both continued walking with their hoods covering their heads. As they approached the gate a guard moved to stop them.

"Hold it!" the guard lifted his hand up towards the pair.

"Pull your hoods down, we need to see who is leaving the town."

"We can't do that" said Jack, the guard reached out and grabbed Sophia by the top of the hood. Before he could pull it all the way down Jack leaped forward pulling his sword out, holding it pointing into the soldier's throat.

"Let her go, now" said Jack sharply, slowly poking the sword point into the windpipe of the soldier.

"The Queen!" spat the second soldier "men get her!"

Jack quickly slit the soldier's throat before gashing the second across the chest.

"Come on, let's go" Jack said, pulling on her arm. A crowd of soldiers raced after them. Jack and Sophia had made it a hundred metres out of the gates before the guards very nearly caught up. They made it to the nearby forest, within the mass of trees, it was pitch black. The ground underneath their feet started to become sloppy and sticky and it made it impossible to move quickly. Suddenly they were surrounded by soldiers, they had nowhere to run. Their feet were sinking that deep into the mud they could barely see their shoes as the mud climbed upwards. Jack and Sophia had their backs against the trunk of a huge tree, but the soldiers encircled them. Jack pulled out his sword to stand up to them. Before he could swing it, Dominion soldiers started to fall at their feet as Thearon and Maddox had finally caught up with them. The Dominion soldiers' attention was now divided but Jack kept his sword out with one arm around Sophia trying his best to keep the soldiers away from her.

More soldiers fell, yet the pressure on them increased. The more they killed, the more arrived behind them.

"Thearon!" Jack yelled, "we can't keep this up for much longer!"

"Don't worry I have a plan, just hold on a few more minutes!" Thearon replied. Straining to keep soldiers at arm's length. The ground was becoming a mess, the sound of swords clashing and soldiers dying filled the dark surroundings. For now, it was only Dominion soldiers that had been killed but it felt like it wouldn't be long until their luck changed, and it was they who would feel the sharp end of the swords.

The Dominion soldiers finally had them all surrounded.

"Drop your weapons!" a man stepped forward from the group, his once shiny black boots now a dirty brown from stepping through the sludge of the forest. "Your Highness you need to come with me, the rest of you."

"She's not going anywhere!" Jack interrupted, with his sword out getting closer to Sergeant Hyde.

"You're surrounded boy, put the sword down, you won't win this fight, you're outnumbered ten to one." said Hyde.
Sophia closed her eyes and grabbed hold of Jacks hand.

"Sophia? Hey!" said Jack.

"Ha, closing your eyes won't save your friends your Highness!" Hyde remarked in a smarmy tone.

Sophia's grip intensified and her facial expressions pained her eyes. Sergeant Hyde's smile started to shrink as confusion started to hit everybody. Hyde looked down towards her feet as he saw a snake with a body the size of a small tree trunk slithering past her left foot. Its jaws opened showing its fangs.

"I don't know what this is, but a snake will not help you, you sort this snake out" he gestured to the soldier next to him who edged forward towards the snake. After taking two steps forward, Sophia's eyelids snapped open showing two completely black eyes like she had nothing there. The soldier turned his attention back to the snake.

Which grew three times its size with black vein-like lines running from its nostrils all the way to the tip of its tail. The snake flew forward and caught the soldier's neck within its jaw then continued to bite down, pushing the soldier to the floor.

Many of the soldiers fled leaving a handful including Sergeant Hyde. He swung his sword taking the snakes head clean off, leaving the soldier motionless on the floor with the snake still with his neck its mouth. Sophia fell to her knees blinking repeatedly as her eyes started to turn back to their usual brown colour. Jack tried to comfort her before the tip of a sword appeared in front of him.

"You are coming with me," said Hyde. He placed the sword under Jack's chin. "All of you."

Hyde turned around to his men who suddenly all fell to the floor with arrows pointing out of their bodies. Hyde jumped back as one hit him in the shoulder and he fell to the floor.

"You can tell Agent Lo..." said Jack as he started to lean over him, "we might be leaving his new town, but I'll be back for my father." He pulled the arrow out of Hyde's shoulder as he yelled in pain and started to crawl away. As Jack stood, a new group of soldiers stood in front of them.

"Spence!" Sophia called in relief as she finally made it back to her feet.

"Your Highness, when we spoke with Thearon and learned that you were alive, we felt it was our duty to protect you," said Spence giving a bow along with his soldiers. "We need to move now before they can track where we are."

THEARON

The morning sun rose over a rocky cliff where a small camp stood looking over Woodale now controlled by the Dominion. The once quiet streets had soldiers patrolling, carrying weapons making sure they knew who were in control. Thearon, who was finishing his watch knowing that it wouldn't be long until the Dominion would continue their pursuit of them.

A black bird caught Thearon's attention gliding past at some speed. He gazed with concentration as it approached. Its wings were outstretched as it landed on a rock next to Thearon. He placed his hand on the bird's head and reached out for a piece of parchment that was strapped onto the bird's left leg. No sooner had he moved his hand away, the bird took off and flew back towards the horizon. He inspected the note for a short time and then folded it back up and placed it into his chest pocket.

Thearon started to hear movement from within the camp and walked to join his rising companions. He noticed Jack and Sophia were sitting around a small pile of ash that was their fire from the night before. He joined them by sitting on a rock next to Jack.

"What can we do now?" asked Jack.

"We need to be careful; it won't be long until the Dominion come searching for us." Thearon replied.

"I don't want to go back, not yet." said Sophia.

"But they are your people now." said Jack.

"They won't accept me as their leader any more than they would Agent Lo, my father hardly gave our family a good reputation."

"We need to find a way to get into the town to get my father and drive Agent Lo and his men away, Thearon you have fought your whole life there must be a way?" said Jack.

"I can't do that." Thearon replied.

"Why?" Jack snapped back.

"My part in this mission is over."

"What!" Jack and Sophia gasped.

"My job was to get you out of harm's way.

My feelings towards your father blindsided me to continue but a new mission has been given to me which I have to complete."

"I don't understand, what job? I thought this was all for my father? not just a job?"

"I would die for your father, and I protected you because of the love for him, but I have been summoned for a job that I can't ignore!" Thearon stood up to meet Jack and Sophia who had already stood up in shock.

"What you choose to do now is up to you. I can't protect you forever." there was silence within the camp, Spence and his men were gathered behind Thearon, who had similar reactions on their faces as Jack.

"I'm a Androne descendant hunter. It's always been my job, one that I'm damn good at especially when I was with your father. I can't turn my back on my part in this war, a war that will only intensify as the Dominion gets stronger. All other Androne descendants will be killed if I don't continue my search." Thearon turned to Maddox who was waiting for him near the cliff face.

"Here take this," he lobbed a bag of supplies to Jack. "You will need them."

"They can stay with us, and we will protect them." said Spence as he did a small bow at

Thearon as he walked off towards the cliff.

It was a long walk for Thearon that evening, he couldn't shake away a constant feeling of guilt about leaving Jack. He had always helped young people by picking them up and travelling some distance and leaving them in a safe place, it was his job. He never built any kind of feelings towards them. Jack reminded him of his father a lot. As Jon was the same age as Jack when he started travelling with him. Although Jack had a lot more arrogance about him, but still, plenty of ability to go with it.

They managed to find a small cave in which to spend the night, Maddox had settled himself up against a wall and fell asleep. Thearon hadn't heard a word from Maddox since leaving Jack. Which was very unusual as he wasn't the kind to build relationships with anyone other than Thearon himself and that was only because of a life debt. What life debt? Let's just say Thearon got him out of a small predicament involving some bandits in the town of Brid. Maddox gambled on the sea games which involved very dangerous tasks and races off the coast which often involved a death before the end of it. He had put all his money plus more on the favourite, who lost and died in the last event allowing a rookie to take the winning spot of the whole games. As the bandits arrived to collect their money Thearon was in the right place at the right time to help Maddox escape the bandits. Who they killed later during a search for a descendant which made Maddox feel he owed Thearon his life.

The cave was cold, damp and the smell were as strong as if he was sitting in Mitchler's sewers. Clouds had covered up the last bit of light that the moon had to give, leaving the cave in complete darkness. Still Thearon couldn't find a way to close his eyes, yet alone fall asleep. He then resorted to rummaging through Maddox's bag to find his stash of Dale beer that he had taken from Zander's house.   Maybe the beer would help him sleep, he thought. Before he touched his lips with the bottle a faint light was glowing deeper in the cave. Thearon jumped to his feet clenching his sword hilt instantly thinking they were not alone. He moved cautiously deeper into the cave with his right hand holding his sword hilt and his left still clinging to his Dale beer. He followed the corner to an open space which had no covering. The moonlight shone through revealing a small pool of water which was topped with a blanket of fog rolling to the walls of the room. Thearon had found the source of the smell at least if nothing else.

At the back of the cave on the other side of the pool sat a stone very similar to a tombstone. The stone was mossy and cracked, but in the middle still stood a symbol that Thearon has seen many times before. It was made up of a circle with a phoenix inside with flames coming away from its body. This symbol was of the Brewin. Thearon stroked his hand over the front of the stone and in a flash two torches lit either side and the room filled with smoke. Thearon was lifted out of his body. He could see his body limp on the floor in front of his eyes as the smoke poured over the floor covering him in a sheet of ash like fog. The room began to change, the rock walls started to erode revealing fine walls carved out of stone. The fog disappeared, taking his body with it, leaving the pool. It was now clear water with carved sides, a fountain in the middle and plants placed around it. It was laid out and decorated like a Royal Palace, the stone around the pool had a golden shimmer to it which reflected the light in all directions when lit.

Thearon slowly lowered to the floor, his skin was almost completely transparent, but his body was nowhere to be seen. With a bang behind him four men ran in dressed in nothing but old rags. They were carrying something wrapped in black cloth. It was a body.

"Who are you? Who is that?" Thearon asked but they didn't look at him, yet alone answer him.

The man at the front of the group let go and opened a wooden door where the stone had sat before the transformation of the cave Thearon was once in. The four men lifted and placed the body inside the small compartment, and all took a step back. The black cloth fell off the front of the body revealing a middle-aged man with messy black hair and stubble chin. His eyes were closed and his body limp. Into the room stepped another cloaked figure, they removed their hood revealing their face, it was a woman, a woman Thearon didn't recognise. Her brunette hair was held up with many gold pins and her dress was light blue scattered with silver sequins.

"Goodbye my love" she said. She kissed the man on the lips and stepped back as the four servants shut the door and locked several locks. The lady stood and stared at the wooden door for a few seconds before pulling out a small book and placed it leaning up against the door. Before she stood up, she closed her eyes and muttered.

"Life of a Brewin, servant of a mage, vita continue." She rested her hand on the book for a few more seconds.

"My Lady are sure this is what he wanted for a tomb?" the servant asked.

"Yes, of course." the lady replied.

"But anyone could steal the gold and perhaps even burn his body if they found it." a sharp smile grew on the woman's face.

"Then they will be following his desires exactly." the woman rose to her feet and strode out of the cave, followed by her servants.

The smoke rose once again and Thearon collapsed back into his body and came round in the old cave once more, which was now back to its old, broken, smelly form. Thearon inspected the stone closely; now there was light from the torches that were still lit but he could not make out the carvings. He looked around him and could now see how the walls used to be and how time and nature had nearly destroyed them. He could even see the door that once closed in the body that was put in the hole but was now lay flat on the floor. He looked behind the stone and saw the book the lady had placed on the ground. There were no words on the cover, just symbols and shapes. Thearon picked up his Dale beer and started heading towards the way out until, for a moment, curiosity got the better of him. He turned back towards the stone and opened the book. Before he could inspect it, a black ball of dust shaped like an evil angry face flew towards him knocking him to his feet. Thearon managed to keep hold of the book and acting out of instinct he threw his beer at the burning torches. A huge explosion blowing Thearon out of the room, dispersing the dusty figure, and leaving a burnt smoky ruin in its wake. The blast left Thearon in pain after slamming into the wall before being lifted to his feet by Maddox.

"What happened?" Asked Maddox.

"I'm not sure, but I think I just found and possibly destroyed the resting place of the old Mage." Maddox looked at him in confusion.

"But I thought you and Jon destroyed him years ago." said Maddox.

"We never killed him Maddox, he left our battle wounded. What ever happened to him after that I don't know, but he was buried here, and I have just destroyed whatever nature hadn't."

"Was his body still there, Thearon?" Maddox asked.

"I'm not sure, the wooden door that sealed his body in was no longer attached. Somebody may have taken his body or attempted to. imagine they died trying, but he doesn't need his body anymore, I believe he is now roaming around as a shadow, cursed."

JACK

Jack and the others made it to Harpur's docks, which was the main supply entrance to Woodale. The only place that Woodale would call their own with grand architecture to the level of the main Palace of Lord Atton. The group held back away from the archway into the docks as the main hub was crowded with Dominion soldiers. They were socialising and enjoying the other thing Harpur's Docks was known for and that was drinks. The home of the Dale beer and the best place to buy it as on either side of the hub were two saloons which were also full of Dominion soldiers.

The summer evening was lit up by torches attached to the walls and being carried by the unlucky few soldiers who were on duty trying to keep a little order. The celebrations were for the successful taking of Woodale as it would have been a huge target for Dominion. So why not make the most of the docks, already known for drinking.

Spence found Jack and Sophia sitting behind a huge old oak tree as they looked on to the Docks.

"Your Highness, I'm sure you know her but let me introduce Deneen. She worked in the prison security team, back at Woodale but she left as we did after Agent Lo and his men took over." said Spence.

Sophia stood to welcome Daneen, and they gave each other a bow of respect. Daneen was dressed in a silver breastplate which had a red strap around it holding three medals that Daneen had earned working her way up the ranks.

"My Lady, I may have left but I will continue to fight for Woodale." said Daneen.

"I understand and appreciate your future efforts, Daneen." replied Sophia.

"You worked in the prison system?" asked Jack stepping forward with interest. "My father, is he still there?"

"Your father? You father is Jon Skies?" Daneen's face turned a flustered red and she quickly held the hilt of her sword, "my Lady! this boy is dangerous and the reason the Dominion are in our town, they were looking for him and his father!"

"No!" Sophia demanded. "He has helped me get out of Woodale and kept me safe." Spence held on to Daneen's shoulder to hold her back from Jack.

"His father helped me get away Daneen they are not enemies." said Spence.

"Your father saw him as an enemy and you should respect your father." Daneen began aiming at Sophia.

"My father was a coward; the Dominion were coming anyway as it was father who called for them. He smelt war and wanted to be with the most powerful team." Sophia replied with a fierce tone. "I will stay with the people who will fight with me." Sophia looked towards Jack who gave her a little nod of agreement. Daneen took a step back and looked towards Jack in a short look of distrust, but she stood down.

"Please Daneen, is my father safe?" Jack asked.

"He's alive." Daneen answered shortly, not giving anything away.

"I haven't got time for this; I need to get my

father out of that prison." said Jack barging past Daneen and Spence and heading back towards the woods. Jack stopped against a huge oak tree when realising he had to plan and now had no help. He fell on to his backside, sliding down the trunk of the huge oak as his face fell into his hands. He was by himself! Thearon and Maddox were gone; he may well have just lost Sophia to Daneen's influence. He couldn't break into Woodale alone, could he? What he would do to be back at Beachdale right now. He knew without a doubt he would have been accepted into the Dale guard by now, but he was now sitting under a tree, in the dark and on a damp, dirty, leafy floor.

"Jack!" a soft voice shouted from the distance; Jack turned his head in the way of the voice. He saw Sophia stepping carefully downhill towards him.

"Jack! Daneen will help us; she can give us information on your father."

"She trusts me now suddenly? what did you have to do?"

"I agreed that we will help them first." said Sophia.

"Oh Sophia, what does she want?" Jack said in annoyance.

"Do you want to get to your father or not." Sophia started to get frustrated with Jack making hard work of the situation.

"Of course, I do but I also don't want to get killed before I get the chance." said Jack.

"She will help us; I trust her as a Woodale citizen."

"Ok what is it she needs us to do?" Jack said impassively.

"There is a boat arriving at Harpur's dock soon with supplies from Mitchler to be taken to Woodale. What she wants to do is the right thing as we can't let Agent Lo get more supplies to cause more havoc." Sophia felt like she had convinced Jack until he turned away and looked out towards the dock.

"There must be a hundred if not more soldiers in the docks." Jack said.

"Yes, but she does have a plan and what have these soldiers been doing at the famous Harpur's Dock breweries?" Jack managed a quick smirk at Sophia who may have won him over.

The evening turned into night. Most soldiers retreated to their quarters that were conveniently positioned in two huge buildings alongside the saloons. Leaving a few stragglers sprawled around the main hub of the docks. The torches that lit the main street had been extinguished which signalled the end of the drinking and the saloons were now closed. Jack and Daneen watched on patiently from a distance waiting for their opportunity.

"So, what exactly are we doing, I can't see a boat anywhere, I thought you said it would be here by now?" Jack said.

"It will be here, my scouts saw it pass Stones Ridge an hour ago, it won't be long." Daneen replied. Jack didn't have the full trust of Daneen, but the feeling was very much mutual, but their goals were similar in that they wanted to slow down the Dominion.

"So, what's your plan" Jack asked.

"Behind each of the two saloons there are breweries, I have two explosives I stole from Woodale. We blow both breweries to cause a distraction and sail away on the boat with all the goods on board" Daneen said in a confident tone.

"As easy as that then ye?"

"If you have a better idea, then please share it." Daneen snapped back.

"Ye go straight to Woodale and save my

parents. If you take this boat and its goods, the Dominion will just send another it isn't going to change anything!" said Jack raising his voice to a level where the others started to hear him.

"Jack please!" said Sophia.

"it's not all about stopping them from having the supplies, we need them," Daneen said meeting Jacks volume. "If you haven't noticed we don't have big towns supplying us or armies at our disposal. In the time I have known you, you have already lost two of your fighters, we need all the help we can get." Jack knew he didn't have a comeback for that one, Thearon and Maddox did leave him. He had not thought about that. Intentionally or not, they started him on this journey and left him with no guidance. So maybe he needed to take the guidance from who was left and trust them.

"Spence, you and I will take one explosive behind the left saloon, an' Jack as Sophia seems to trust you take the other to the one on the right, take this too." Daneen handed Jack a small heavy wooden box and a small thin steel rod.

"You have to push that in and twist to ignite, you then have twenty seconds to move and get dockside. Follow our lead when you see ours blow ignite yours, when they are dealing with the flames wait for my signal and we hijack the boat." Jack seemed extremely unconvinced but before he could comment on the plan footsteps caught their attention.

"Who is it?" Sophia whispered to Jack.

"It looks like Dominion guards to me." he replied, eight heavily armoured soldiers marched through the main street towards the hub of Harpur's Dock. They each were carrying a lit torch surrounding them with a golden glow.

"Well, this complicates things." said Spence.

"What are they doing here." asked Jack leaning into Spence hoping for the answer.

"That's why there here." Sophia said with a nervous tongue. She was pointing towards the docks as six huge sails filled the skyline over the top of the buildings.

"It's here, let's go!" Daneen said jumping to her feet.

"Good luck" she shouted back as she ran off with Spence over to the over side of the street. Once again, they were left by themselves.

"This is insane, come on." Jack picked up the explosive case and started heading to the brewery. Harpur's Dock never felt quiet even though most of the soldiers had gone to their quarters there were still people about. so, they knew they had to keep quiet and out of sight.

The brewery building behind the saloon was overgrown, a shadow of the rest of the buildings on show. Jack and Sophia found a small area where they could place the explosive.

"Wait Jack, look!" Sophia pointed towards a wooden door at the foot of the wall of the brewery. "We should drop it in there, that's where the beer is kept in storage." Jack gave an approving smile before turning back to the crate. He placed the lighting rod in place.

"OK, we wait for their signal then I will light it if you get the hatch." They waited patiently for any sign of an explosion or panic that it would cause. Then the sky lit up and they could feel vibrations in the ground around them. Jack held on to the rod and twisted it, but nothing happened, he twisted again and again, nothing.

"Oh, come on." Jack pleaded.

"Wait Jack move." Sophia pushed Jack to

the side and placed her hand on the crate. She closed her eyes and muttered which to Jack sounded like gibberish. Her eyes turned to shadows and then she retreated, and the crate started to smoke.

"Quick, Sophia the hatch!" Jack shouted. Sophia lifted the hatch and Jack pushed the crate inside. Jack grabbed Sophia's hand and they ran. As they made it to the dock, the sky lit for the second time, except this time the whole saloon went up in flames. The front of the building went up like it wasn't there, filling the street with rubble. This upset Sophia.

"Jack what have I done, there would have been innocent people in there."

"No there wouldn't, innocent people would be far from here." Jack replied. Jack was trying to look out for Daneen and Spence but couldn't see anything as well as trying to keep out of sight. Dominion soldiers were panicked trying to pull other soldiers out of the inferno coming from the saloon. Jack however had his attention caught by the Dominion guards boarding the boat. It's like nothing had happened, they kept going on about their business.

"Where are they?" there was still no sign of

Daneen or Spence.

"Jack we're going to have to go on, I bet they are already on the boat." said Sophia in a confident voice which did not reflect her actual feelings.

Jack agreed, they both pulled out their swords and made their way onto the boat. With the soldiers just ahead, Jack stuck his sword through the back of one, quickly removing it to defend a strike from another. Sophia was defending herself blocking each strike in turn. Jack saw off the next by managing to slice his throat. He moved to help Sophia and managed to get a good blow to the soldier's head, knocking him out and then stabbing him in the chest. Two left... until other Dominion soldiers joined the fight.

"Jack we're not going to win this fight," said Sophia.

"The supplies will be better at the bottom of the river than in their hands." Jack agreed, he saw a cannon to his side.

He jumped over to it but before he landed an arrow hit his shoulder which took him off his feet.

"Jack!" screamed Sophia.

She continued to fight, killing another

soldier with ease. The remaining Dominion Guards picked Jack up. He was kicking as much as he could to get loose. He managed to kick his sword over to Sophia, who started fighting the soldiers with double blades, but still couldn't get close to Jack. One of the guards held Jack against the railing of the deck as the other pulled out his sword and placed it touching Jack's throat.

"NO!" Sophia screamed again but this time the flames of the torches lighting the deck of the boat lifted and the fire circled Sophia. Her eyes had gone again, and two black holes took the place of them. Fire balls left Sophia's side, forming the shape of phoenixes. Two of the soldiers were immediately engulfed, leaving the soldiers towards the back to flee, diving off into the river. Four other burning phoenixes went off in different directions, two went for the guards, they swung their swords, but it didn't do anything.

The other two fireballs went below deck hitting the supplies below causing a huge explosion. Sophia was hurled overboard, while the guards were ignited. But fell into Jack piercing his stomach with their blade before taking them all overboard. They all landed in the river as the boat slowly followed them all under the surface. The ship, now in two pieces, hit the bottom of the river causing it to shed planks of wood.

Sophia made it to shore, she was on the opposite side to the docks. She couldn't see Jack, not even a ripple in the river or evidence of him struggling. Now she really was alone, once again she had caused devastation and this time, she had killed the one person she needed to help keep her alive. She knew she needed to find him, dead or alive because if she didn't, she would be dead herself. As she made it closer to the river edge, she prepared to go in until a hand grabbed her face and pulled her away.

CHAPTER 5

AGENT LO

The river began to flow once again as the ship was no longer visible. The sun rose over Harpur's Dock creating shadows over the main street from the smoke rising from the other side. The soldiers who remained at the dock started clearing up rubble and moving the bodies of the deceased out of view. Agent Lo had arrived with his guards as they stopped what they were doing instantly to stand in line to welcome their leader. The hub, where all the ships would have docked to deliver the supplies, was like a warzone. The walls and any woodwork had burn damage from the phoenix flame let out by Sophia the night before. Two ships carrying soldiers were attempting to dock avoiding the wreckage of the vessel laying in front of the docks.

"What happened here Hi-Pec!" Lo asked his ever-present guard.

"The reports I have had my Lord are that it was the boy and the Queen of Woodale" he answered while pulling another guard to his side. "Where are they? You must have some trail of them?" Hi-Pec snarled at the nervous soldier.

"My Lord, we think the boy is dead, he got impaled before the ship went down."

"Dead!" Agent Lo shouted back before the soldier could finish, "I wanted the boy alive!" His face turned red, and his veins started to build on the surface of his skin.

"We haven't yet found his b... body yet s... sir." the soldier started to stand back upright "the girl has been spotted heading towards the woods but w... we need more men to search."

Agent Lo looked at the soldier and then at the approaching ships.

"Get them ships docked and up your search now." Hi-Pec threw the man to the floor in front of him and he scurried to his feet and ran towards the dock.

"Hi-Pec I need you to stay here and make sure they find them and then bring them back to Woodale. do not come back empty handed!" Lo turned away from Hi-Pec and headed back towards his grand transport that brought him to Harpur's Dock.

As he walked into his chamber, he was disturbed by a small thin shell of a man covered from shoulder to ankle in a black robe. His head looked like it was a skull with wafer thin skin laid on top.

"My Lady has a message for you Lo." he said in a low grunting voice, "it will not be wise to ignore her, Agent Lo."

"I have had enough messages from your Lady, I'm not interested and have my own mission to fulfil."

"You owe my Lady a debt," the man cried. Agent Lo stopped moving. "She is watching you, always." ice started to cover the walls filling the air with a sharp chill. Agent Lo turned back to the man glancing towards Jon and Heena who were still chained up in the cell staring back at Lo.

"The boy is still alive, he must be found," the man crackled. He then turned and started walking towards the door. "And Lo, she wants him alive."

Agent Lo nodded and watched him waddle to the door as he went out of sight.

"It's not just the Dominion that holds your leash then Agent Lo." Jon whispered loud enough that he could hear him.

"Nobody holds a leash for me Jon. In fact, the only person holding a leash here is me on you and soon the boy, I will find him." Agent Lo was angered by the lack of respect or fear from Jon. He had just been made a fool of in front of his prisoners. Agent Lo, feeling very undermined, ordered the transport to head for Woodale.

"You need to stop fighting this Jon." Lo said, approaching the cage. "Jack is out there, injured, to an extent my men figured he was dead. Now you just heard the old man and that he is still alive. perhaps now you will be more willing to help. Where will he go now? I don't want him dead Jon, do not be a fool, you have got to trust me."

"Trust you, why would I trust you? If you didn't catch us as quick as you did, most of Beachdale would be rubble and clearly any town that refuse to help will also suffer the same fate." said Jon, his voice pained him as he spoke as he felt weaker by the minute. Heena was sat curled up in the corner, silent. Agent Lo had notice how distant she was from Jon and himself. Lo hadn't asked any question of Heena, they were all aimed at Jon.

"You're very quiet Miss Heena." Lo said.

"Leave her out of this Lo." Jon snapped quickly as he rose to his feet using the bars for support.

"Steady Skies, were going back to Woodale and we will have a chat regarding your wife, I can't help feel she has more to tell me."

"What do you mean?" Jon asked.

"Yeah, more to tell both of us Jon" Lo and Jon looked at Heena, who couldn't look back at them. "she's hiding something Jon and for your sake and the boys, we need to know what it is, because I can't guarantee anyone's safety until I know."

"Whatever she does know, she's right not to tell you, the less the Dominion knows about us the better."

"Forget about the Dominion Jon, this is not about them" Lo leaned in as close to Jon's ear as he could and whispered.

"This is about you, me, and the boy, no one else. Forget the Dominion, they only pretend to be strong, they are a pawn in a much bigger mission. I must succeed."

SOPHIA

Sophia opened her eyes as morning broke, the last couple of hours were like a dream, had she passed out? She had woken up in the middle of a forest which looked like every other forest she had ever stepped into. Sophia got to her feet and moved towards the sound of movement a bit deeper into the forest. She heard the cracking of twigs and the rustling of dry brown leaves. She felt cold and nervous about who it might be but also driven by determination to find out who had grabbed her away from the riverbank. She hoped it was Jack and he was leaving her to rest to regain her strength, but she was not very confident. Was it Woodale soldiers or maybe Spence? where was Spence and Daneen? She hadn't seen them since the attack on Harpur's Dock.

Sophia was hoping they got split up and not been killed in the fighting. She walked closer to the cracking sounds, she moved. Branches out of her way to uncover a huge man. She quickly dropped to hide but then after seeing another figure getting closer, she realised it was Thearon and Maddox.

"Thearon!" she yelled. "You came back."

"Sophia, you're awake," said Thearon. "I shouldn't have left when I did and I'm sorry, I got summoned for a mission and it took me too long to realise I hadn't completed my last mission."

Sophia looked around hopeful that Jack would emerge from the shrubbery. Thearon pointed towards an opening of some overgrown bushes. She slowly edged into the dark opening to see Jack laying on his back with his eyes closed.

"He is alive but struggling with his wound," said Thearon. "We need to find a Corvon weed, it's the only way to stop his pain and heal his wound,"

"What does it look like?" Sophia asked.

"The root is what we need, the leaf is poisonous. Go into the woods and concentrate on the ground and look for a weed with dark green leaves and ruby hairs.

Now remember those hairs are poisonous and will paralyse you almost instantly. Use your sword and with one slash take the top off and dig the root out and bring it back to us, but Sophia, be careful!" Thearon knew that Woodale troops would still be looking for them.

Sophia looked back down at Jack. The stranger who she had only met back at Woodale, the town she should now be leading but now fleeing. Sophia ran her hand over Jack's head through his ever-growing curls. She then attached her sword to her waist and headed out towards the forest.

These parts of the forest were dark, gloomy. It's called Woodend Forest. No one just visits Woodend Forest. The Woodale people said that you only go there when you're dead, the forest of spirits. Sophia had never been afraid of the stories she got told whilst growing up in the self-proclaimed royal family of Woodale. There had never been any sightings or proof she told herself as she stepped deeper into the endless pool of trees. A thin mist seemed to cover the ground like a blanket. It circulated her ankles as she moved, making it harder to find a weed that she has never seen before.

She continued, concentrating on the ground but so far to no avail. Her head continued to be turned when she spotted dark green leaves poking out of the mist. But they were always missing the defining deadly hairs Thearon had warned her about.
Sophia started to get weary of how far away from Jack she was going, and it seemed like an age ago that she left him to start looking.

"How much longer do I have left?" she started to ask herself. She could no longer see any exit to the woods, only darkness surrounding her. She started to beg with herself to keep calm as she knew this could be her own downfall if her uncontrolled powers came out now.

"Breath, relax, keep going." She continued to tell herself, more and more wildlife than she had never seen before started to appear around her. A small bird which was red with black patches started to follow her tweeting every step she made. Sophia ignored it. She tried to not even look at it to ensure it didn't grow into another monster and try to kill her like the bird that attacked her and Jack back at Woodale. Sophia began to feel hopeless; she couldn't find anything in this darkness, she picked up a small branch off the floor and concentrated on the end of it.

"OK, come on Sophia stop being afraid of your power," she whispered to herself, "you are powerful, and you can do this!" Sophia closed her eyes and waved her hand over the tip of the branch which lit into flames.

"Yes!" she cheered, as the torch brightened the area surrounding her. Although her hope soon vanished as the light brought four men from out of the shadows.

"Ah your Majesty, the boss said we'd find you in ere." one man slurred, Sophia recognised the men, they were from Woodale. They were woodmen, whose job was to keep the town safe from threats from Woodend Forest, they were very good at their job. These men were not looked after by the town, and they very often let that be known to the King, but he had never listened. Sophia knew that if anyone would bow down to Agent Lo these guys would be the first.

"What are you doin' out here me Ladee?" asked one man with a round scarred face and missing half a dozen teeth,

"let's take you 'ome, keep you safe." he chuckled.

"I'm sure the boss won't mind us looking after you for a bit." they laughed together.

Sophia started to feel her blood boil within her body, she was no longer scared but angry.

"Come on me Lady, you're coming with us." another man said as he approached her. Sophia stepped back and now knew she needed to embrace her powers to survive. The man continued to get closer along with the others. Sophia stopped, closed her eyes, and blew into the flame of her torch. A fireball emerged crashing into one she then swung around hitting him round the side of the head knocking him out. She dropped the torch and pulled out her sword. The men matched her by pulling out their weapons in response. There was no more fear within Sophia as she made the first move taking out the first man, stabbing him in his stomach. The swords crashed together as the sound echoed through the trees. Sophia got stronger and stronger as the battle continued.

As one of the attackers swung for Sophia, she blocked him with her sword and held steady, she looked into his eyes as he glared back. Sophia's eyes once again turned black as the woodman stared. He was mesmerised, he froze which gave Sophia the time to swing her sword slicing his throat from side to side.

One left.

"You should have just come with me, me Lady," the man groaned. "I won't fall as easily as them."

A small smirk rose on Sophia's face, the attacks came faster and harder at Sophia but each time she blocked and hit back. She held her arm outstretch towards the man who froze for a second but that only held him momentarily. Sophia stepped back with annoyance, she tried again, nothing happened. The man swung his sword at Sophia who blocked it but then he kicked her so hard, she fell to the floor. Her head hit the floor hard, she was dazed as her eyes went back to their usual colour. As she blinked, she could see Jack dying next to Thearon. His eyes rolled upwards as they closed slowly.

"Jack!" she whispered. She regained full consciousness. The vision of Jack was replaced by dark green leaves hanging out of a light brown weed and the Ruby hairs as sharp as needles.

"Corvon weed!" She had finally found what she was looking for but as two hands grabbed around her neck, she forgot she was in a fight. She was lifted to her feet with the bald scarred woodman in front of her.

"you 'ave fought well me Lady, but it's over and you're coming with me."

"No, I'm not." she replied as she held her hand out once again but this time it pushed the man off her, he started to quiver as if his muscles were imploding. After holding him for some time Sophia made him fall to the floor with his face landing in the Corvon weed. Sophia still held her hand out towards him, holding him face first into the weed. The Ruby hairs grew, creating a web around his head. The points of the hairs started stabbing his skin, injecting him with poison. Sophia released the woodman and he jumped to his feet pulling half the weed with him, as the hairs were still attached to his face. Sophia took a few steps ensuring he didn't get close enough to her for the weed to attach to her. A few steps later the man fell to the floor lifeless. The ruby hairs and what leaves were left attached released from the body turned black and crumbled to the floor. Sophia looked at what was left of the weed, then pulled out her sword and chopped at the top of the weed. She made sure there weren't any hairs or leaves attached to the root and dug out the main body of the weed.

Sophia looked up at the sky and the trees around her trying to find her route back to the others. She couldn't see any recognisable sights to find her route. The events of the last couple of minutes and the realisation of being lost in a dark, frightening place took over her body. Tears started falling down her cheeks as she lowered to her knees. She felt helpless and hopeless. No one would be able to hear her and if they could find her, it would be impossible for someone who doesn't know the woods like the woodmen do. The twigs under her started twitching and the fog around her was swirling, it was the bird that she saw as she was entering the woods. It came closer to her and sat in her line of sight. Sophia moved her hand over the bird as it let her run a finger down its back. She closed her eyes and left her hand over it. The bird turned a bright red, it grew three times bigger and flew into the air and started gliding west. Sophia followed the bird, jogging to keep up and trying not to trip over anything on the floor covered by the sheet of fog.

Daylight started to seep through the thinning level of trees. Finally, Sophia stepped out of the woods into the field where she could see the opening in the bushes where Jack was lying. As she entered, she could see that Jack was still alive to her relief, although he was in a lot of pain. Thearon took the root from Sophia and placed it on a rock and crushed it with his blade. The root had cracked into two parts which Thearon placed in a small pan and held it over their campfire. As the root heated up a golden liquid ran out of it.

"That is what we need, right there" Thearon said pointing at the liquid. He looked toward Sophia noticing a cut on her forehead, "Are you ok?" he asked nodding towards her scar.

"Yes, I just bumped into some old friends." Sophia replied with a smile.

"You did well Sophia, you may well have just saved his life." Thearon looked back at the root in the pan which had shrivelled up, now floating in the golden liquid. "Grab his hand Sophia, this is going to hurt". Sophia held his hand with both of hers. Thearon hovered the pan over Jack and gently poured the liquid into his wound which caused Jack to scream and bend his body into an arch. Thearon pushed a small rag like cloth over

Jack's mouth to quiet the screaming. After a couple of minutes, the pain subsided, and Jack relaxed. The liquid had already thickened to fill the wound level with Jack's skin.

JACK

The pain and burning within the wound on Jack's stomach had become too much for him. The Corvon Weed contained a substance that would not only heal deadly wounds, but also there were stories of it sending the most intelligent people insane. Jack knew this and he did his best to keep his mind concentrated on where he was and who he was with. He could see Thearon and Maddox coming and going bringing water and dead squirrels, then cooking them on the campfire next to Jack. Of course, not leaving his side was Sophia, she hadn't let go of his hand since returning with the weed. Sophia very gently poured drops of water into Jack's mouth ensuring that he didn't choke.

"The woodman who attacked me in the woods, Agent Lo will have realised that hadn't returned, they will send more soon." Sophia said.

"We're well hidden, we can't move him too much, we have to give the medicine time to work," said Thearon. "Maddox will keep a look-out, he can move quickly you know." Thearon joked making a quick smile towards Sophia.

Jack started to feel very lightheaded, the pain had subdued greatly but he felt like he was starting to drift away. He kept his eyes closed to avoid seeing a trigger that might distract him into some sort of hallucination. Jack opened his eyes and behind the bushes he saw a symbol carved into a damaged stone, it was the symbol of Androne. It then occurred to him that he was laying in the ruins of an Androne temple. That's why Thearon brought him here. He lost his concentration at his mind went; all he could see then was white. Had he died? Or was it the Corvon Weed? Or maybe the temple giving him visions again like at the temple near Beachdale. Maybe all three. A silhouette appeared. It was shaped like a woman, she got closer, and features started to appear more definitive

"The past is your future," A soft voice

seemingly from the figure which vanished but Jack continued to hear.

"The past is your future; the past is your future." it went quieter and quieter like an echo.

Jack found himself laying on a sandy mound in the middle of nowhere. He didn't recognise any landmarks. He looked left and saw the horizon, he looked right, and he saw mountain ranges but no sign of life anywhere. He walked towards the mountain range, he figured he'd be more likely to find water and maybe some food there. As he continued towards the mountains, they didn't seem to get any closer. All that seemed to pass him was rocks and dry, brown patches of grass. Until he came up to a man kneeling in pain. Jack approached him cautiously.

"Hello?" Jack said but no reply. The man got himself off the floor, he had long dark brown straw like hair with a beard covering most of his face.

"This, is Androne, don't worry, he can't see or hear you," a voice said from behind him, "he is a brother at war."

"Androne?" Jack said in excitement, looking around, but all he could see was a shadow of light. As it came closer, he could see the prominent features of what looked like beautiful woman.

"Wait, who are you?" Jack asked.

"We're here to find out who you are, not me, I know my purpose, you do not." she replied.

"My purpose? Where are we? How are we finding my purpose in a desert?"

"Patience Jack, this is the desert of Typhone, named after Androne's brother, who he is fighting." Jack looked back at Androne who was crouched down looking at an ant which looked as though it was dying. He placed his hand next to it and closed his eyes. The ant grew, and quickly became five foot tall.

"He's a Brewin!" Jack gasped.

"Yes, their mother was the most powerful known Mage of the Brewin." said the figure in her calm, slow voice.

"She taught the brothers everything she knew; they became so powerful and skilled as a Brewin they couldn't defeat each other. Their battles over time resulted in slaughtering's of their followers, there was never a victor". Androne flung himself over the giant-sized ant which seemed to have got his strength back and galloped off into the distance. As he disappeared, everything around Jack dissolved and there was just darkness.

The calm didn't last long as from beneath them; mountains rose interlaced with waterfalls pouring down their sides. A thick fog rolled around the tops, leaving only small gaps for the blue sky to show through.

"Where are we now?" Jack asked.

"This is where you would now call Ando." the lady replied. Jack opened his mouth to ask his next question but was cut off by a loud high pitch sound. They looked far into the distance between two mountains as a swarm of black feathered birds were flew towards them. Jack recognised these as the same as the one he killed back at Woodale with Sophia. They were travelling so fast that before they could move, they were flying past them. Jack ducked down but the lady stood still. Jack followed them with his eyes and was once again amazed at what he saw as red feathered birds with gold breasts rose through the mist to meet them.

"What are these creatures?" Asked Jack still in amazement.

"They're not a type of species. They have

evolved and controlled by the power of a Brewin," the lady replied,

"The black feathered birds are Typhone's, and the Red are Androne's."

"Wait so, Androne and Typhone are controlling these," Jack's jaw dropped slowly whilst the flying beasts clashed in front of them.

"Look carefully Jack!" said the lady pointing towards the centre of the battle. Jack looked closer and saw riders on some creatures with bows and arrows firing at the others. While rider-less beasts were attacking each other with their claws and beaks. A pair got into a battle in front of Jack, the golden bird dug its claws into the others back and slammed them into the mountain side. Two birds chasing each other caught Jack's attention, one was ridden by Androne and the other by a man in black robes and had long black curly hair.

"Is that Typhone?"

"Yes, this was the last time they fought, the last time they saw each other as brothers, allies, or adversaries."

"If neither brother survived one team must have won?"

"They knew that the war could not end

with one alive. It was both or none. Typhone was happy living a life of power, but Androne could see his brother getting more support and other leaders turned to him. Androne knew what he had to do."

The mountains dissolved like the desert did and they reappeared in a grassy trench with a small stream running through it. Jack looked up to the mountain side where they stood which was now covered with dead birds.

"What happened to them?" asked Jack as he turned towards the lady standing to his left.

"Watch." she replied.

The two men came around the corner fighting with swords. Their style was identical, their ability was matched. Androne knew it was time. He placed his sword on the ground, giving Typhone the opportunity to attack, which he took, stabbing Androne through the chest. Not once but twice. Typhone held it there and stared Androne in the face.

"It's over brother! Finally, I will rule the world with no more little rebellions," Typhone whispered into Androne's ear. "I will now rule this world, and everyone will finally bow down to me." Androne looked up at Typhone's face.

"No" he whimpered.

Androne flung his arms around Typhone's body with the sword still Impaled in his chest. Androne was such a strong Brewin, he controlled the gravity to push down on their bodies. Androne's hold on Typhone was too strong for him to defend. The push back that he could muster created a shock wave as it clashed with the force of gravity. The pressure shook the mountain sides, cracks started to appear down the cliffs. The pressure started ripping the skin off both brothers. Typhone started to push back, he managed to loosen Androne's grip on him. Before he could escape a huge rock from the cliff face fell and landed on them both followed by many more boulders finishing the fight for good.

Once again, the mountains dissolved around Jack, he then appeared in a town. Two men stood in front of a group of soldiers and other townsfolk. The buildings were smoking, there had been a battle, but which of these men had been victorious?

"Where are we now?" he asked.

"We are about a mile from the battleground

and two years in the future" the lady replied, "those men are the sons of Androne, and this is the start of the Andos. They are now fighting for freedom against the followers of Typhone who had now taken over and created their own government, the Dominion."

The scene changed again to another man with a child in his hands celebrating another victory.

"This is Insley, grandson of Androne with his son Bane, great grandson of Androne." the scene continued to change showing different men and families.

"Harrod the Strong."

"Asbury the Mad."

and "Buxton the Sixth." it seemed to go on until a small box temple appeared in front of Jack. Stormy weather blew through the trees around him.

"These are all descendants of Androne and have continued his legacy and his battle against the rise of Typhone's followers and the Dominion." her soft voice waited for Jack's reply.

"Why are you showing me this?" the lady looked over Jack's shoulder. Jack turned to follow her gaze, standing there looking straight through him were two men, a woman, and a child.

"Father! mother!" he shouted but stopped as soon as he remembered that he wasn't with them. He saw the child holding on to his mother's leg, he realised that was him.

"I'm a descendant of Androne?" Jack said. As the realisation had not quite set in yet. He watched them enter the temple.

"That's why I have visions when I enter these ruins."

"Your father was trying to tell you this at this moment, but an enemy even stronger and more dangerous than the Dominion broke the connection." Jack looked at the lady in confusion until a clap of thunder made him turn to see where it came from. He saw the black figure that chased him all those years ago.

"Now you know your past Jack, you must make it your future." the lady disappeared in front of him.

"No wait please!" Jack shouted.
It was too late the temple; the trees and sky all fell around him. He fell with them into darkness. He opened his eyes with a gasp for air. It had felt like he hadn't breathed any oxygen for days. He breathed heavily,

struggling to settle his lungs. He saw the bushes around him and the temple ruins, and the feel of Sophia hand on his hand. He calmed almost instantly and was at ease.

THEARON

The thought of eating yet another squirrel made Thearon squirm.

"There must be more out here then damn squirrels. I'm ready to fight a king size burting if it meant eating well," Thearon said with a moan to Maddox. "We will keep looking, keep that just in case," he handed Maddox a stick with a couple of squirrels hanging from it. "I'm ready to see the open air again my friend, sick of these woods, cause us nothing but trouble, I'm tired of having an enemy hiding behind a bush ready to kill us."

"Try! Try to kill us!" said Maddox laughing. This made Thearon smile for the first time in a while.

"Do you think he'll live? The boy?" Maddox asked.

"Yes, I checked his wound, the medicine is working."

"Can he still fight?" Maddox interrupted.

"He'll be fine Maddox". Thearon had a lot of faith in the Corvon Weed medicine as he had used it many times throughout his life.

"Come on Maddox, let's go. Jack will have questions when he wakes up," Thearon shouted. He waited for Maddox to join before turning and headed back to the ruins. "That Corvon Weed can do some funny things to a kids mind." they both continued laughing back to camp.

As Thearon returned to Jack and Sophia, Jack was sitting up drinking some water, helped by Sophia.

"Ah you're awake, how are you feeling?" Thearon asked. "how's that wound?" Jack looked down at his stomach and lifted the cloth that was covering it. The wound had nearly gone, it now looked like a thin layer of skin covering the gash left by the blade that pierced him.

"I, I can't believe it!" Jack said he felt the skin but moaned as it was still very sensitive.

"You were out for some time, lad," Maddox said, giving him a nudge on his shoulder. "Be warned though, I'm not carrying you again!" that put a smile on Jack's face.

"Thearon, I had visions again." Thearon looked at Maddox and smirked raising his eyebrows.

"Let's take a walk kid," he grabbed Jack's arm and lifted him up, put his arm around him and headed back into the woods. "Maddox get that Squirrel cooking will ya, I'm starving." he shouted back before disappearing in the trees.

After they got deeper into the woods they stopped and sat on a fallen tree trunk.

"OK fire away kid," said Thearon. "What did you see?"

"Well, I saw many places, and a woman who was all white but all I could see was a silhouette which made out the shape of her and her features. You may have heard this story before do you know who she is?" asked Jack.

"Yes, every kid I have found and have been looking for have seen the same woman in visions. She is known as Lilah. No one knows who she is and why it's her they see but the description is always the same, she has a city named after her up north," Thearon replied. "What did she show you?"

"Androne and Typhone, it was their final battle. They both died and then we kept visiting his children," Thearon nodded and looked down like he knew what was coming next. "It finished with me Thearon, why didn't you tell me I was a descendant?" Thearon sighed and paused before answering.

"My job is to protect descendants, that vision you had just now. Your father wanted that years ago before you moved to Beachdale. That is how it is supposed to happen, I needed to take you to Ando but because of the way things have worked out it happened here."

"If you protect Androne descendants, what about Typhone descendants?"

"I don't think there are any, he didn't care for family like Androne did," Thearon knew he had to be honest but careful with what he told Jack. "There are rumours of a child. One rumour is that he had a son who died in battle, another rumour was a daughter who married away from the Dominion and forgotten about. The third rumour, now Jack, as you now know Androne and Typhone were powerful Brewin people. On Androne's side of the family you are the first in generations to use the Brewin power," Jack's face dropped slightly embarrassed. "Yes, I know and I'm not worried, you could be a powerful Brewin user. We might just need that help! Anyway, the rumour is that Typhone had a son who, when he became thirty years old, was found to be immortal. Which is the hardest power to learn, it hasn't been achieved before. Immortality isn't always learnt, there isn't an easy way to just learn it from what I know. Yet, something that I did read in a book is that a child of a strong Brewin can be born with a curse."

"How can immortality be a curse?" Jack interrupted.

"Imagine living for all those years, watching as loved ones died around you, watching war after war, destroying the places you call home. Even if you can't be killed, you can't protect everybody or everything, still, I don't believe any of them. I don't think he had any children." Thearon put his hand in his bag and pulled out a small book and handed it to Jack.

"You should have this, Jack." said Thearon, Jack took the book looking down and the cover.

"The first Mage," Jack read the title out

loud. "Thank you, Thearon."

"It was your father's, but he didn't want to learn and as you do, you might as well have it."

Thearon and Jack started to walk back to the temple when they heard a rustle in the bushes.

"Thearon! Someone is there!"

"Let's go, quick!" Jack picked up a rock and threw it as hard as he could towards the sound. A body shot up and ran away as fast as they could. Thearon pulled his bow from his back, attached an arrow, and shot it towards the fleeing man. He couldn't get the distance on the shot and the arrow just fell short.

"Ahh damn!" said Thearon.

"Who do you think it was." Jack asked.

"You might be sure it was someone from Woodale, one of Agent Lo's lot," replied Thearon. "let's go back, I guess we will be seeing more of them soon."

Jack and Thearon returned to the temple where Sophia and Maddox were waiting for them.

"You're back!" Sophia said welcomingly but was met with worried faces, "what's up?"

"We need to move Sophia," Jack said with

an impatient tone. "Woodale forces will be here soon." Jack started picking clothing, weapons and pans up trying to be able move away from the temple.

"What did you see Jack? Sophia asked.

"A Woodale scout, we think," Jack snapped back, "that's why we need to go."

"No Jack, in your vision!"

"I'm a descendant of Androne, Sophia," Jack stopped what he was doing and stared at Sophia in a very uncomfortable way. "I'm surprised you didn't know. Everyone else did."

"I'm sure it was for your safety, with the Dominion and all." said Sophia.

Jack went back to packing items of food into his backpack.

"I'm sorry Sophia I'm not annoyed with you, nor Thearon. But my father. Why did he run from the truth? I was shown that all our ancestors continued to fight, until one day they stopped, and I don't know why. They were all Brewin as well, but they stopped learning that too." Jack and Sophia were alone. waiting for Thearon to call them to leave.

"Jack, I'm sure your father made a choice to protect you and your mother, maybe he felt the Dominion is too strong to fight alone."

"No one is too weak to fight! We just need the courage, and we can defeat anyone, no one will fight alone." Sophia stepped closer to Jack, he looked up at her and stood up, their eyes met.

"I won't let you fight alone Jack," Sophia said softly looking into his eyes. "I'm not going to leave your side." Sophia placed her hand on Jacks cheek and moved her pouted lips towards Jacks, who closed his eyes and waited.

"Ah here you are," Maddox burst out from out of the shadows, making them both jump away from each other. "Come on, both of you, we need to move." Jack looked away awkwardly and tied up his bag flung it over his shoulder and followed Maddox after giving Sophia a small smile on his way.

Thearon, Maddox, Jack, and Sophia didn't make it far across the field before they turned to see the ruins of the temple slowly crumbling with flames eating the overgrowth surrounding it.

"They will burn any building down to find us, especially any link to Androne."

bemoaned Jack.

"We need to move on Jack," said Thearon. "We need to get you to Ando. we're not going to be able save your parents on our own and they might just be able to help us."

AGENT LO

"Still not found the boy. Agent Lo?" crackled the old man who had seemed to appear next to Lo who sat in King Atton's former throne. Agent Lo's eyebrow lifted along with the corner of his lips creating a curious grin.

"Oh, we know where he is, in fact," Lo stood up, throwing his parchment on to his desk. "We have a couple of new prisoners, Hi-Pec, bring them in." Three people walked into the hall from a side door, all had been stripped of any weapons and armour, leaving just cloth tops and trousers. "Who do we have then Hi-Pec?" Lo asked his Captain.

"Three deserters my Lord!" Hi-Pec replied. "They were found at Harpur's Dock, trying to blow the place up."

"Have they talked yet about the others?"

Agent Lo interrupted

"No, my Lord, they told me they didn't know them, but these three left not long after we arrived here." Agent Lo concentrated on one of the men brought in. He walked up close to him and looked him in the eyes.

"I didn't recognise you without your armour," Lo said in a calm arrogant tone. "Spence, isn't it? You welcomed me to Woodale, I didn't expect you to betray your King!"

"I didn't betray my King." Spence replied.

"Atton is dead, I'm now in charge and you betrayed me," Lo snapped back, "now what do we do with the two of you?"

"Ahem!" Lo stopped and looked towards Hi-Pec who had made the fake cough. "My Lord there's three of them." Hi-pec told him nervously. Agent Lo turned away with a smile on his face.

"You're right Hi-Pec, there is. However, Spence I have something I need you to do for me, which, of course like I said leaves me with two, what are their names?"

"I'm not sure my Lord, although I heard the girl answering to Daneen." Daneen looked up at Agent Lo, who stared at her.

"Send them to Mitchler, they wanted some testers," said Agent Lo as he waved his hand towards his guards who were standing by the main doors. "Hi-Pec take Spence to my new office and bring Jon up as well, I have some questions to ask them," Lo sat back down on his new throne. "In fact, cuff them in my office and bring Heena to me here first."

"Yes, my Lord." Hi-Pec pushed Spence through the door towards the cells.
Agent Lo looked back down at the parchments on his desk, forgetting the old man was still standing in front of him.

"So, what is your reply to my Lady, Agent Lo, will you get the boy or not, she is running out of patience." the old man leaning heavily on his stick, wobbled closer to Lo.
Lo lifted his eyes staring a cool glance at the man before once again getting to his feet

"It's time I give your Lady more than a message. Who is she?" Lo changed from being very calm to somewhat irritated.

"You don't need to know who she is; you need to answer her demands!"

"What if I no longer have any interest in her demands, and we should start looking more at my demands?"

"Your demands are irrelevant! my Lady

eclipses you in power and should you defy her, well, serious consequences I fear would be in line for you!" Agent Lo once again appeared to have a smile on his face.

"You see, I don't agree with you, I don't fear anything that won't confront me themselves. The only thing I know of your Lady is that she wants the boy as much as I do, but she has threats, rewards, and your ugly face."

"Watch your tongue, Lo!" Agent Lo steps closer and closer to the man.

"I might test this power you claim she has because I consider myself a powerful man, so yes I do have a reply for her."

"And what's that?"

"Oh no you don't need to take it for me, she can come and get it." Agent Lo pulled out his sword slicing the old man's head clean off his shoulders.

Later that evening, Agent Lo retired to his new quarters. This was King Atton's old bedroom; pictures of Atton's old family members had already been torn down by Lo's team. The bedroom was still very stylish, gold, with red sideboards and bed posts, the bed covered in silky sheets. Lo's attention was taken by a knock at the door.

"My Lord, I have the prisoner, she is in your office." a voice bellowed from the other side of the bedroom door.

"Oh yes, I forgot". Lo headed down the stone corridor and entered a small dark room which, just like the bedroom, all of Atton's family art or memories had been removed.

"Lady Heena, I thought you might appreciate some time out of your cell."

"You're up to your usual tricks again, killing innocent people." Heena replied quietly.

"Who? The old man," Lo chuckled. "It was necessary, he was nothing more than a pawn, sit down, please." Lo moved a chair away from his desk for Heena, but she stepped back.

"I will stand thank you."

"Suit yourself," Lo scowled. "I know where your boy is, but then I think you do too, but how when you haven't left my cell?" Lo let out a quiet chuckle again and picked a grape up out of a well-presented fruit bowl. "You have messengers don't you, I'm ashamed that I have only just seen it."

"I know your secret!" burst Heena.

"My secret? Well now I know yours. You

didn't walk through the main hall on your way here and I made sure my men left the old man to rot where he fell, yet you still knew he had died. So, who was the old man? An old friend? Or just a Woodale man that you paid to try and scare me?" Lo walked right up to Heena and looked straight into her eyes. "Now my Lady, I have no interest in killing the boy I need him. Now you can tell me where he is, I also now know he is a descendant of Androne which makes him even more important to me."

"Jon is a descendant take him." Heena said with tears in her eyes.

"Well, there is no love lost there then," Lo chuckled. "I don't want Jon; I don't want you."

"Let us go then!" Heena screamed.

"No, whilst I have you here, the boy will eventually make his way here. To be honest I'm not impressed about how easily you would give up someone you're supposed to have loved all your life. It's in your interest to stay here I can assure you."

"It's all his fault," Heena sobbed with tears running down her face. "My son didn't deserve this life and now evil people like you and the Dominion will hunt him down for the rest of his life." Heena's eyes were red, and Lo could see she was on the edge of breaking, but his face tensed as he turned back to her.

"I am not evil!" he yelled; this took Heena aback.

"Believe me, my Lady when I say do as I say, and you will all be back together unharmed. If I was evil, I would have just taken Jon and left you at Beachdale to die," Lo's voice became a whisper in Heena's ear. "Keep quiet and do as I command or that option will still very much be on the table," Agent Lo looked at Heena in her eyes for a few seconds... "take her back to her husband." Lo commanded; the guards held Heena by her arm a pulled her away.

CHAPTER 6

JACK

"What has happened here?" gasped Jack. Standing before him was a picturesque town with beautiful houses with wooden trims. Bunting hanging from one side to the other and flowers hanging from beams. Except the beauty was dying as it was being eaten by flames. The triangular bunting flags disappearing one by one, now hanging down the side of the buildings. There were people chasing after buckets of water to try and put flames out desperately before they spread further and further into the town.

"Do you think it was an accident, Thearon?" Sophia asked.

"I doubt it, I imagine the Dominion are involved and it probably has something to do with us." Thearon replied.

The villagers noticed the group standing looking at the flames and stared at them for a second, and then hurried out of sight.

"Where have they gone?" asked Jack.

"I don't think we're gonna be too welcome 'ere!" said Maddox. Thearon continued into the village looking around.

"Be careful and keep your eyes open, I think they fear that we are someone else." The flames around the buildings started to die as smoke surrounded the houses.

"Stop there, drop your weapons, and put your hands up!" half a dozen bows lifted with arrows locked in place ready to fire from balconies surrounding them.

"Stand down, my name is Thearon I am an Ando and looking for shelter and food" Thearon shouted to anyone who might come forward as a leader.

"Thearon? You mean the deserter," a voice shouted back but no one could see where from. "You call yourself an Ando, yet you leave a mission that was given to you."

"I already had a mission." Thearon replied. A man stepped out of the smoke, he had dark brown skin with messy black hair somewhat like a bird's nest, and a short beard pointing below his chin.

"You left a mission which meant us losing our leader, and left our town weak, now look at her," said the soldier waving his hand showing the burnt buildings. "Keep your arrows on him, drop your sword boy," Jack dropped his blade on the floor keeping his hands high above his head.

"Sergeant Serfarn!" Thearon bellowed. "The boy is Jack Skies, son of Jon Skies, descendant of Androne, leave him be!" Thearon warned.

"I don't care for your followers Thearon, I'm here to protect Caufton. Being a descendant means nothing here with me being in charge," Serfarn's attention left Thearon and Jack and moved on to Sophia. "Princess Sophia, or should I now call you Queen. Thinking about Woodale makes me feel so much better about Caufton. How can you run from a battle where your King, or even your father had been killed?"

"We needed help which is why we are travelling." said Sophia.

"You're heading to Ando, aren't you? they won't help you, where are they now? We're left alone to fight the Dominion, as they sent our leader to his death, fool!"

"What do you suggest we do then Serfarn?

being an all knowledgeable and competent leader, after all, the Dominion will be back. We will help you defend this place from the next attack if you let us rest here and eat." said Thearon.

Serfarn looked around at the damaged buildings and the crowds of people that had started to gather as the smoke started to clear.

"You know that they will be back, right?" Jack said to help convince Serfarn. He already looked defeated. The confident front he put on couldn't fool the villagers.

"Fine, I have lookouts in place, I'll show you where you can stay."

The damaged buildings lessened the further into the town they went until they arrived at the town centre and the real beauty of the town was evident. Each individual house had its own character with flowers hanging above each door. Serfarn led the group to a dark brown oak door. The carvings on the door resembled a tiger being hugged by a snake ready to squeeze. Serfarn placed his hand on the door and turned back to Thearon.

"You can stay here." they all stepped into a cosy front room; the wooden beams continued through the house as it did on the front.

"Very cosy." Jack said as he inspected the fireplace. The fire was just embers, like it had been abandoned.

"This house belongs to a very brave man and woman who gave their lives to protect this town," two small children brought a box of fruit, fruit juices in glass bottles. "Eat and rest but be ready."

"Thank you, Sergeant." Thearon gave a small bow and Serfarn turned and followed the children out of the house.

"Well, you three can fight over the second room as there are only two." said Sophia standing over the living area from the balcony of the first floor.

"You two have it I'll take the chair," said Jack as he moved two armchairs to face each other. He pushed a foot stool between to make a bed, then lay down and put his head in his hands. "Good night." he said sleepily. Thearon and Maddox picked up their bags and headed up the wooden steps to their bedroom.

A couple of hours passed, and Jack opened his eyes. It was still dark outside, and the window was being hammered by rain. The living room in which he was sleeping, was lit by two small flames just holding on after the wick having nearly burnt through. Jack's eyes were fixated on a tree that was blowing from side to side in the strong winds and rain. The rain came down heavier and the winds got stronger. The leaves were pulled from the branches leaving two thin tree trunks. Ice climbed up the trunks, the rain turned to hail. Cracks started to appear on the glass in front of Jack. He got up from his makeshift bed and got closer to the window and tried to concentrate on the tree. The cracks had got so bad he couldn't see anything through it.

"Jack," a slow dark voice whispered, "Jack." he heard it again.

Jack turned his head to his right and in front of him was the same black shadow that has haunted him since leaving Beachdale. Jack fell on to his back,
"No get away!" he scrambled back to his bag, where he grabbed his sword. "Get away!" he cried again, still laying on his back with his sword pointing up towards the figure.
"Jack!" the shadow repeated, again and again, getting louder and louder until.

"JACK!" the shadow held his hand out

towards Jack.

"No!" said Jack as he cowered away, closing his eyes. Jack was sweating, like he never had before. He could feel it running down his face. Everything went quiet.

"Jack." his name was spoken again but this time it was softer. Jack opened his eyes to see Sophia standing over him.

"Put your sword down Jack!" Sophia said. Jack dropped his sword on the floor and started breathing heavily.

"Sophia," Jack said realising he had been pointing his sword straight at her chest. "Sophia, I'm sorry."

"What happened Jack?" Sophia asked. Jack looked away from Sophia and stared straight out the window once again. It was still dark but there was no rain, no wind or cracks in the glass, and the tree was in one piece, still full of leaves. Jack looked back at Sophia.

"The shadow is back, he's still following me, he was here like you are now" Jack said as if he was very frightened.

"Who is the shadow?" Sophia asked.

"I'm not sure, Thearon said it's likely to be that Mage of the Brewin, Broxholme Watts."

"Watts? I've read about him. He was

supposed to be the most powerful Brewin in history."

"Yea one of, my father and Thearon defeated him, and he's now cursed to haunt me forever it would seem." said Jack.

"You still need to try and get some sleep, come on get up." Sophia pulled Jack up and led him back over to his bed.

"How come you were down here anyway?" Jack asked.

"Well, er you made a lot of noise fighting off your nightmares," Sophia replied with a smile but still rather awkwardly. She helped him on and laid the sheet over him up to his chin. "Sleep tight Jack." She moved in closer and kissed him on the lips, she kissed him again and laid her hand on his cheek. Jack wasn't sure what just happened and felt like he should call her back but just watched her walk back up the wooden staircase back to her bedroom. Jack felt some guilt from nearly stabbing Sophia, but something felt different from the other times he saw the Mage. This time it felt real, as if he was standing Infront of him.

SOPHIA

Thearon rose to a horn sounding that shook most buildings within Caufton.

"Bloody hell!" Maddox yelled as he rolled out of his bed. The horn was followed by a banging at the door.

"Thearon!" the visitor called. Thearon opened the door to find Serfarn staring back at him.

"What's happening?" Thearon asked.

"It's your turn to hold up your end of the deal my friend," Serfarn said. Thearon stepped out of the house and could already see a Dominion army marching towards the town. "Luckily for us I'm organised and ready for fight not like yourself," Serfarn teased. "ARCHERS! BOMBERS!" shutters were open all down the main street with arrows pointing out of them. The roof tops were now full of archers standing waiting for the order to fire.

After getting up and ready, Thearon, Jack, Maddox, and Sophia all made their way to join the army that had massed at the entrance of the town. As impressive as the army looked, it wasn't much in size compared to the Dominions.

"Captain Rantarn." Serfarn muttered under his breath.

"You know him?" Sophia said looking across to the sergeant.

"Oh yes," Serfarn replied. "We just came back from a battle with him, that's where we were before returning to Caufton."

"So, he's not one of Agent Lo's?" Asked Thearon.

"Oh no, not Lo's, he wants his transport back." Serfarn pointed to a gap between the houses at a bulky metal vehicle. It had a track underneath, but the metal exterior was battered.

"That's a transport?" Jack asked.

"Yea, the latest model from Mitchler, runs on oil, it's a good machine, not in great shape mind, I pushed it pretty hard to get here quickly".

The Dominion army stopped; the dust

started to settle around Caufton as both armies stared at each other.

"You really think you can get away that easily Serfarn!" a voice echoed out.

"Told you," Serfarn joked, turning to Sophia, "fire!" He ordered his archers, as arrows rained down on Rantarn's army.

"CHARGE!" screamed Rantarn, his whole army charged at once towards Caufton. The arrows coming from the rooftops, raining down taking out a dozen if not more at a time. Serfarn's army stood ready, swords pulled out of their sheaths. Before they reached them Serfarn put his fingers in his mouth and whistled up to the rooftops. Seconds later two huge explosions lifted the rear side of Rantarn's army up in the air in flashes of red, yellow, and black. The numbers advantage had turned significantly towards Serfarn.

"Let's finish them off!" the whole army moved to meet Rantarn and clashed with their swords. Serfarn's men were superior fighters compared to Rantarn and his soldiers. Jack continued fighting and with the others he was defeating man after man. He found himself in some space after killing his latest enemy and looked around.

"Sophia!" Jack couldn't see her anywhere. He headed back towards Caufton knocking men out of the way to get there until he saw her kneeling where they stood before they charged.

"What's going on, are you ok?" Asked Jack. Sophia looked up at him and her eyes were so black it looked like they were holes.

"Sophia what is going on?" Jack took steps back away from Sophia. A black dust started rising from Sophia, the dust then turned into a smoke and got thicker and thicker until it surrounded her. Jack was so shocked at what he was seeing he didn't spot a Dominion soldier running towards them. As he went to swing his sword at Sophia, she grabbed the blade mid swing, pulled it off him, and threw it back straight through the throat of the soldier.

Sophia's gaze never left Jack, he lifted his hands to try and calm her down. Her hand flew out and sent a force knocking Jack back a couple of feet.

"Sophia! no, let me help you." Jack still held his hands up to Sophia trying to stop her, but her face curled up like it was angry or in some sort of pain. Black vein-like lines started to grow up Sophia's cheeks that connected to the black holes where her eyes once were. Sophia looked down and shrieked in pain but then pushed out again with her hands sending Jack flying. The force even caught some of the army knocking them down.

"Hey Thearon, I thought she was on our side?" Serfarn shouted. Thearon tried to ignore this but couldn't help but agree. Thearon found Jack and helped him up, at this point Sophia was unrecognisable.

"Jack, you know this is not Sophia." Thearon asked. Jack nodded; a realisation hit Jack.

"I have seen signs of this Thearon, but I thought it was Brewin magic I didn't know it would lead to this."

"It is Brewin magic Jack, what scares me is whose Brewin magic it is?"
"Her eyes have disappeared before when something dark happens. Thearon, just last night I saw that shadow who you told me could be that Mage you fought, then when I came round Sophia was standing there, do you think-"

"Yes!" Thearon interrupted. "He has come back for one thing and that is to kill you, me, and your father!" Jack looked at Thearon and then back towards Sophia who was pushing soldiers away like they weren't there. "Jack, when he sees me, I promise he will come for me, I need you to get that book I gave you, do you still have it?"

"Err ye back at the house."

"Go get it, page eighty-three, there is a spell that can scare him off. But even with all my trying I couldn't learn it, but I have seen you practising in the evenings so you might be able to do it. Remember it's all in your mind, concentrate, now go!" Thearon pushed him away and got straight into Sophia's line of sight to give Jack the chance to slip away. Sophia's body was almost unrecognisable, she started walking over to where Thearon was standing. She held her hand out and the floor under Thearon crumbled like a small earthquake. The battle seemed to stop dead. The Dominion soldiers who were already losing, turned and ran the way they had come.

"Where are you going?" Rantarn screamed with clenched fists. Serfarn and his men gathered around Thearon and helped him back to his feet,

"Thearon, what is going on? Who is she?" Serfarn asked. "She is possessed by a very powerful Mage, Serfarn, you need to get your men away from here! I am a target because I tried to kill him a long time ago."

"Him? this is my town I will help protect it!" Serfarn stood strong next to Thearon and Maddox ready to defend themselves. One of his men threw a very frustrated Rantarn to his knees in front of Serfarn.

"You haven't won Serfarn. Agent Lo maybe messing around in his new home, but the Dominion are getting stronger. They will not forgive the Andos for their betrayal, they will head to Ando and destroy it, starting with the beloved Beachdale. It is too late they have already deployed the garrisons."

"We will deal with the Dominion in time, for now we have our own battle." said Thearon.

"I will help you destroy this enemy." Rantarn shouted as he turned to face Sophia whose face had now completely changed into Broxholme Watts. He had chiselled cheeks and a pointy chin, his face was a ghostly grey colour, and his eyes were black holes like two pebbles. His robe was made of smoke, surrounding his body like a small tornado. "Join the Dominion and together we can wipe the world clear of these traitors!" Rantarn walked towards Watts like a new best friend, he felt invincible.

"Yeah, that's helping us Rantarn!" said Serfarn.

"Dominion?" He snarled with a haunted whisper. Rantarn's confident walk turned into a slow nervous crawl. Watts was now full of anger; he held his hand out once again at Rantarn which made him fall to his knees. He couldn't move. Watts took a few more steps towards him pulling out a long black sword. He lifted the weapon which matched Jacks in design yet double the length. He swung it through the air leaving a trail of black dust behind it. In that one swing he took Rantarn's head clean off. Watts used his powers to hold Rantarn's head in one place, floating in the air. Watts looked back towards Thearon leaving the head to then drop to the floor.

"Come on Jack." Whispered Thearon, Watts continued towards them.

"Thearon you will pay, and the boy!" said Watts in the same deathly voice. Watts once again held his hand out to attack with another bit of magic, until a wall of fire appeared before him to separate them. Thearon looked round towards the centre of

Caufton, and Jack was walking up it. Jack looked different. This time there were now no pupils in his eyes, they were pure white.

Thearon lifted his arms from his side to push the rest of the soldiers away. The fire started acting as a shield that Watts couldn't pass, it circled around Watts, it grew taller purple smoke started lifting from the flames. Broxholme Watts spotted Jack getting closer, he clenched his sharp dirty teeth. Watts knew he couldn't pass through the flames, but he continued to try, he got pushed back each time. Jack started to tire, his arm that he held out started to shake but he held on. Watts knew the spell that Jack was performing and knew that Jack wasn't powerful enough to hold on for long. Watts pulled out his sword once again and started to strike through the flames, each strike knocked Jack back. The more Jack fell back the more nervous Thearon became; he ran over to him.

"Jack, you can do this, push!" Thearon said, trying to encourage Jack as much as he could. The strikes from his sword came quicker and faster.

"He will tire Jack; he hasn't gained his full strength yet." Jack continued to keep the flames rising and they got hotter turning the flames blue. Watts stopped swinging his sword and started to try and cover his face from the heat.

"Keep going Jack stronger come on." His confidence seemed to give him more strength; Jack lifted his other arm making the flames close in on Watts. Watts stopped struggling and stared at Jack, as if the connection was pulling him in. The black smoke surrounding Broxholme Watts rose and started shooting out in waves making everyone duck for cover. It then travelled back towards Watts like a vacuum and in a burst of black dust, he was gone. Jack fell to the floor as the fire extinguished, leaving a burnt circle of debris where Watts had stood.

"Sophia!" Jack screamed as he shot up after regaining consciousness, there was no sign of Sophia or Watts.   "Where is she? we need to find her, he'll kill her."

"Jack, he needs her body to survive. She is alive, but just dormant I have seen this before, I will help you get her back don't worry I promise. He will come to us, that is why he chose the cursed life, to get his revenge," Jack looked at Thearon and nodded. "If what Rantarn said is true we need to get to Beachdale."

"What about Lo and my parents?" asked Jack.

"I have a feeling that Lo will come to us."

JACK

After collecting all their personal items Thearon and Maddox waited outside the house in which they had spent the night. Jack was standing in the room that Sophia had slept in, her bag was still sitting in the corner of the room. As Jack picked Sophia's bag up a small book the size of a notepad fell out. The book was old and used, Jack looked through the book, it was full of writing which after a quick read he came to realise it was some sort of diary. Jack questioned himself on whether he should read it. But he thought it might help him understand what had happened to her, why Broxholme Watts had chosen her and how he got to her. It didn't take much of someone's intelligence to realise that Sophia was getting stronger with Brewin magic. She was an obvious choice for

Watts especially if he wanted to get to him and Thearon.

Jack read on in Sophia's diary and found recent entries. He recognised a chapter from when she first saw him,

'Whilst reading rare and extinct Brewin, I saw someone at the window, a young boy. First, I wondered how he found me and why was he there. This all came clearer to me later. My father was killed in cold blood by the Dominion that evening. After I witnessed his lifeless body in the great hall I returned to my chamber and cried. I felt angry but curious. I know who killed my father but what did the boy want in Woodale? I didn't return to the hall but went back to my library to read. A lot of darkness seemed to surround me. The atmosphere seemed cold and evil. My library was dark, and I didn't feel as excited as I normally did. After meeting Jack, the darkness grew deeper. I could feel it inside me yet around him it calmed. So, did Jack bring this shadow with him or is he, my cure? I need to find out.'

"I brought Watts to her?" Jack whispered to himself.

He started questioning himself whether he was a cure for Sophia or an invite to an early death. Jack packed Sophia belongings together and left to meet the others.

"Ah, Jack your here, finally." Maddox said taking Jacks bags and throwing them onto the transport.

"This is the Dominion transport?" Jack said unimpressed. "I thought you said you were fixing it." The metal shell was scratched, bent, burnt, and missing what Jack thought must have been important parts.

"I was, but she will get us to Beachdale, Jack." said Serfarn.

"She!" chuckled Jack in reply.

"Yea... Well, it's called a ground engine transport or G.E.T for short."

"Engine?" Jack questioned; he hadn't heard the word engine before.

"Yea, it's what they are working on in Mitchler, it powers the transport. So, we don't need them Bauley beasts anymore to pull them along! it runs on a fuel called Latimer one, Mitchler is full of it, underground I mean. Their making a right mess of that town trying to find it, but don't worry there's barrels of it in the back."

"And you know how to operate this thing?" Asked Jack.

"I'm learning on the job my friend; now get on board we need to go."

The bulky rear end of the G.E.T had a bench either side and one down the middle for passengers to sit and one seat at the front with leavers to drive it.

Once everyone was on board, Serfarn shut the door behind him, sat in his seat at the front and started the engine. Of course, this wasn't at the push of the button, he had to pull on a huge leaver three times to turn the engine over and on the third time it started with a roar.

"Serfarn, I want to get to Beachdale with my back in tacked!" Jack said holding on to the hull to keep still.

"Don't worry Jack my friend, once she gets going it will be as smooth as you like."
As he promised the road ahead was smooth.

"Is this as fast as she goes Serfarn!" Said Maddox,

"If you want to walk big man, there is the door!"

"I might do that Serfarn, I will get there

quicker!"

"Maddox sit down will you!" said Thearon. Maddox decided he needed to save his energy and sat drinking his last ale. Jack looked through his bag and picked out Sophia's diary. He didn't want anyone to see so he hid it at the bottom of his bag, then climbed up a ladder at the back of the hold which led to a seat on top of the G.E.T facing backwards. This seat would be used for archers if they were being chased by attackers and considering the damage it looked as though it had been used. The railings around the seat were scratched and some completely missing. Jack spent some time just sitting staring into the sky as the trees of the forest travelled past him in his peripherals. He held Sophia's diary in his hands and stared at it. He wanted to open it and read some more, but at the same time he didn't. He wished for a minute he had the rare and extinct Brewin book that she had mentioned. This intrigued Jack and would teach him some of the history of the magic.

The road was getting rougher. The G.E.T started hitting roots of trees that sent that side of the transport bouncing into the air along with whoever was on that side with it. Jack tried his best to get back to the ladder that led back inside but the next root caused such a bump that he lost his footing and fell through the broken railings and off the G.E.T onto the forest floor. The G.E.T engine made such a roar when fighting with the terrain, so any shout Jack tried was completely blocked out. The G.E.T soon moved out of sight, and after a short chase Jack fell to his knees breathing heavily. Jack was now in a forest alone and lost.

Jack had been walking in the direction the G.E.T had travelled, after following the trail of broken roots and squished vegetation it had left in its wake. A man's voice caught Jack's attention. He headed towards the voice and eventually came to the edge of a wide river and on the bank, there was a boat.

"Hello there!" a voice bellowed from under the canopy.   "You look friendly enough how do you fancy helping me?"

Jack started walking towards the boat.

"Here come on board, I'm Ben." he said to Jack keeping hold of his hand. Ben was a tall skinny man; he wore a navy-blue jacket which had a few medals on the front.

"Where are you heading young man?" Ben

asked.

"Err... Beachdale."

"Excellent, well, um that's a long walk through the forest and night fall is around the corner." Ben turned away and poured a cup of water for Jack. As he handed it to him his attention turned to the sword down by Jack's side and then his arm plate.

"Tell you what," Ben said followed by a pause and a deep stare into Jacks eyes, trying to prompt him to tell him his name, "hmm?"

"Oh, sorry I'm Jack." He realised what Ben was doing.

"Jack, excellent, right, I'll make you a deal as you look like you can look after yourself. If you travel with me to deliver these goods, I will take you straight to Beachdale, it's on the way!" Ben offered.

"Well, I need to find my friends' transport."

"Oh, you mean that Dominion G.E.T that went past a short while ago, sorry I didn't know you were a Dominion soldier."

"No, I'm not, my friends stole it from Mitchler, and we were using it to get to Beachdale before they attack it."

"Ah, that makes things simpler then, well let's get there as quick as we can." Ben returned to the rudder to control the boat down the river.

The sun gradually disappeared behind the trees, leaving a black shadow beneath the treetops. Jack and Ben hadn't spoken for some time. Ben was steering the boat while Jack was sitting at the front trying to see through the fog that had risen out of the river. The fog seemed to get thicker the further they travelled.

"Ben! We're not gonna be able to see soon if this gets any worse" Jack shouted.

"Don't worry lad just keep the torch lit and I will be fine, I have travelled these rivers many a time. I was once a member of the Dale Guard you know, never fought though I preferred sailing, that didn't sit very well with Skies, our leader." Jack looked up at Ben but chose not to say anything as he didn't recognise him as Jon's son.
Jack returned to the front of the boat. He held his hands out in front of him, he closed his eyes. The fog started to clear; waves of grey mist rolled onto the banks either side of the river clearing a path in front of him.

"That's the magic of the Malkav!" Ben said from behind Jack. "You want to watch what you're doing with that Brewin magic, the locals in this area don't take to kindly to it."

"What's the Malkav?" Jack asked.

"He is the old Lord of the damned Brewin; you must know the choices that are made when training in that magic? You either rest in peace or you're tortured for eternity." said Ben.

"I was told you don't get a choice?" Jack replied.

"It depends on what you believe but either way the Malkav will torture you, make you suffer. Others believe the Malkav uses these souls to create some sort of undead army and you get to choose your path, but I don't believe that nonsense. He runs the underworld in my opinion and once ya dead, you're dead, end of!"

Jack didn't know what to believe as he had only scraped the surface of Brewin magic. Would Ben change his mind if he had experienced Broxholme Watts return in Sophia's body, was he being tortured or being recruited in the Malkav's army. It all seemed too far-fetched for Jack, unbelievable as well, but it made questions for him to ask Thearon when they met back up.

As they continued to travel down the river,

the fog had now returned to coat the water as Jack decided to go along with Ben's warning. There was no longer any light apart from the small candle torch on the front of the boat to help them see ahead. A small rustle in the bushes on the bank of the river caught Jack's attention.

"Ben, I think there's something out there," Jack said. "Who are the locals that you were talking about?"

"Oh, the Guyler, yeah you don't want to be meeting them. Eat you alive they will, cannibals the lot of 'em," Ben replied. "don't matter how old you are, if they're hungry, they will eat ya!"

Jack looked back at Ben with a stern face.

"What? You're not scared are ya, that's why I brought you along, to help me protect the baggage from 'em."

Jack looked back at where he thought he noticed the rustling.

"What you seen Jack, not the Guyler?" Ben's tone suddenly changed. He jumped back up to his wheel and pumped the engine to speed up the best he could.

"Wait Ben!"

Ben peered his head back at Jack from behind his wheel.

"There is someone there!" Jack said leaning so far over he could fall in any minute. Ben joined him to have a look.

"A campfire, nah the Guyler are more subtle than that you will never find a Guyler camp," Ben said pulling Jack back into the boat. "Nah, sit tight, let's get to Beachdale." Jack continued looking towards the campfire. A shadow jumped past it.

"Wait Ben! a child, there is a child there, we need to warn them!"

"Nah, no children out here."

"Please, pull up so I can warn them at least, they must be unaware of these cannibals." Jack pleaded.

"OK, but any sight of Guyler and I'm gone, with or without ya!" Ben warned. Jack nodded and gathered his sword. Ben guided the boat as close to the bank as he could, giving Jack enough of a gap to jump over. Step by step, he moved on into the dark forest. The trees were silent, the only noise came from the fire as he got closer. Jack dropped to the floor as he saw the child run back across the fire.

"Father, I have the Corvon Weed!" the child shouted. Jack hadn't been seen but he knew what the Corvon Weed was. The same as had been used on himself. He now knew someone was in danger and potentially dying. Jack felt more like he had to help as he could get them to safety on the boat or at least get them to Beachdale. Jack stepped up closer to the shelter that had been made of fallen branches, stood up together with an old cloth covering all the gaps. Movement inside the shelter stopped as Jack got closer, he tried to be as quiet as he could, but he couldn't avoid the little twigs snapping under his feet. Jack felt nervous, why can't he forget it and go back to the boat and head to Beachdale? Someone could be dying, and he could help them. He stopped and took a deep breath before he opened the cloth covering the shelter. It was quiet.

"Just do it!" Jack continued to tell himself to build up his courage. The cloth crouched up in his hand as he held on to it to pull.

"We didn't do it! It wasn't our fault, I swear!" the young boy flew out of the shelter nearly knocking Jack over. "we found him like this, we're trying to help him."

"He's telling the truth, please don't harm us." a man said standing up. Jack leant forward to have a look whilst holding his hands up in reassurance. Then, his heart sank.

"Father?" he whispered. "NO!" Jack bent down to his knees next to Jon, his neck had been cut but just missing his windpipe, he was struggling to breathe. Jack looked at the rest of his body and found a stab wound in his stomach. The wound has the liquid of the Corvon Weed sitting on it to heal it as quickly as possible.

"He's your father?" the man asked. "We have tried our best but I'm not sure how much longer he will have."

"Father, can you walk? I have a boat on the river we can all get to Beachdale and get you healed" Jack asked to which Jon replied with a nod.

"The medicine won't work if we move him around." said the man who started picking up his belongings along with his son.

"We don't have time we need to move quickly." Jack warned.

"Why? We're safe here." the man said. Before Jack could answer an arrow pierced the cloth and slammed into a log that was the main part of the structure of the shelter making it shake viciously. They all looked at Jack.

"Move!" They grabbed their bags and left

the shelter as quickly as they could. Jack had his father's arm over his shoulder carrying most of his weight.

"Follow the light." Jack shouted pointing towards the small flame coming from the boat that was visible through the trees. Arrows started raining down around them, Luckily, the accuracy of the Guyler wasn't good at all. Jack could only watch as the others ran ahead nearing the boat, Jack was slowing, his father seemingly getting heavier.

"Jack, leave me, you won't make it." Jon said.

"No, we will make it together or not at all, I'm not losing you again." Jack replied, trying to keep Jon from giving up. The young boy had made it to the boat before turning back to see where Jack and Jon were, but it was so dark all he could see was the embers of his campfire. The arrows stopped, then a loud tribal call rang around the trees and skinny, long-haired men with paint on their faces appeared out of the shadows. They were not good fighters, Jack managed to dodge most of the Guylers' attacks. All they had for weapons were small machete style daggers. Jack kicked out, knocking some away. After kicking a couple into a bush, he grabbed hold of Jon and pressed on, then, the ambush came. One came swinging from a tree and kicked them both to the floor, Jack managed to pull his sword out and fought back protecting Jon from attacks. Archers rose from surrounding bushes, Jack fought for his life but got caught between two men and lost his sword. He wriggled free kicking one to the ground and smashed one in the face with his forcarm shield. He then stared straight at an archer; time stopped. Jack couldn't move, the arrow released. Time didn't go back to normal until Jack hit the floor, opened his eyes to see his father standing with the arrow in his chest.

"NO!" Jack screamed with a tear pushing its way from his eye. Jack grabbed hold of his sword and slaughtered one after another. his muscles started to increase in size, his face was red with the veins becoming more visible. No Guyler then stuck around, and they fled. Jack picked his father up and carried him once again towards the boat.

"Help me!" Jack shouted as they approached the boat the man jumped out and lifted Jon over the side.

"Captain Jon?" Ben said in disbelief.

His face filled with shock as he saw Jack trying to help and calling him father, he froze.

"Let's go Ben!" Jack screamed at him several times before he snapped out of it and pushed the lever to get the engine moving.

"Jack, you... must... find... your mother." Jon said in pain. He started to struggle to get words out.

"I will, I will I promise, father please, did Agent Lo do this?"

"Agent Lo... is... not... your... en... e... my... des... cen... ty... ph-" Jon's eyes closed.

"No, father please, come back, I can't do this without you. I have so many questions, I need you, father, I can't do this alone." tears now uncontrollably rolled down his face. His father had gone.

AGENT LO

The door to the main hall of Woodale shot open as Agent Lo walked through being followed by Spence. The chattering around the table of Lords stopped, there was now silence, and all eyes were on Lo.

"Where are they," he asked. "One of you must be responsible for their escape."

"My Lord, the cells were empty as well as the prison block, the guard wasn't there either." Lord Gibbins replied in his usual nervous voice.

"Lord Gibbins, I'm assuming you have already searched the town thoroughly, including all the houses and any hidden spaces." Lo asked.

"Err no, my Lord I shall get on it right away."

"Fool! Two people in this whole town I needed you to keep in, yet you can't manage it!" Shouted Lo as his fist slammed into the table. "They will be long gone by now; I want to know how they escaped and where they are now. Bring any accomplices to me, as the prisoners have been aided in escape before." Lo gave Spence a sharp look.

"My Lord I give my life to what you're trying to achieve and beyond, no aid was given by me." Spence assured.

Lo started pacing around the room as a very frustrated leader. Occasionally he stopped next to one of the Lords making them tremble with anxiety.

"I will have to do it myself; Spence get the men together were going out."

"My Lord we could be searching for days, let the scouts do their job." said Spence trying to calm Lo down.

"The scouts have failed repeatedly; I will do I -" Lo was interrupted by the main hall doors banging open. In stepped a bloody scout, he was struggling to walk, both his legs were very badly burnt, and he had gashes going across both arms.

"Spence who is this?" Lo asked.

"Scout my lord, one of the last groups we sent out."

"Help him, I want to hear what he has to say." said Lo.

Spence helped the scout to the table and sat him on an empty chair.

"My lord, the Andos were at Caufton." he said painfully.

"Good at least we know where to go now Spence, get the men ready."

"Wait, my lord. Captain Rantarn from Mitchler was chasing a group back to Caufton. They had a battle and the Andos were involved." the man continued as a nurse dropped a pain relief potion into the wounds of the scout and instantly, he relaxed. "It didn't last long as a shadow took over the body of the Woodale princess."

Agent Lo sat next to the man and looked at him in his eyes.

"A shadow? What is Rantarn up to?" Lo questioned.

"Nothing my Lord he's dead, this shadow killed him."

"And the others?" asked Spence.

"They fought him, well that Jack fought him and used magic of some sort that somehow scared him off." the scout said as he took a few sips of the water he had in front of him. The Lords around the table started talking amongst themselves, making more noise than a daily Woodale town protest.

"Shut up!" the table went quiet and stared at Lo, "thank you, now then where did they go then?"

"Rantarn warned the Andos that the Dominion would destroy Ando, starting with Beachdale on their way."

"Spence, change of plan we need to head back to Beachdale, that's where they will be going. It's not going to be pretty if Jack is learning Brewin magic." he stopped and looked back at the scout, "and what happened to you?"

"The shadow fled, yet we met him on the way back here, the men I was with just burned to nothing, I escaped."

"Get to the ward, and get recovered," Lo told him before turning to Spence, "do you have a library or some sort of old bookstore here."

"You want to read now." Spence looked confused.

"I think I know who this shadow is, but I need to be sure and know what we're up against."

Spence takes Lo away from the town centre arriving at a dead end.

"Where are you taking me Spence?"

"Trust me, I saw the Princess taking books in and out of this place, she was definitely up to something." said Spence. He moved a wooden ladder from down the street and placed it against the wall where the hole was that Sophia used to enter her library. They both climbed up and were amazed at the number of books she had. Lo started to look carefully down the rows of books.

"Hmm, Mages of Power," Lo said, pulling a green ripped and dusty book from the shelf. "This may give me some answers." He spent a minute or two scanning through pages.

"It's him."

"Who?" Spence asked.

"Well, this little battle at Beachdale may have just got exciting." Spence shrugged his shoulders not knowing what Lo was talking about.

"Broxholme Watts was an old Mage of the Brewin, one of the best. Now cutting a long story short Dominion hired him to kill a certain Ando, Jon Skies. He failed and ended up being killed himself, but before that the Dominion wiped out all the Brewin schools. So, if our scout is correct and it is Watts, think about it the Dominion are going to Beachdale. Jack Skies, the son of Jon is heading to Beachdale, Broxholme Watts will be able to get his revenge in one place. We need to get to Jack, and Jon, Spence before Watts and whichever unfortunate Dominion captain is on their way."

"I'll make sure the men are ready, my Lord." said Spence.

"No, just Hi-Pec and my guards. I have an idea, leave me I need to check something, I think there is more to Jon's wife than we think."

Spence bowed and made his way out of the library. Lo started looking through the books on the shelves, his finger running past each book.

"Are you looking for this Lo?" a voice crackled from the corner of the room. "Why else would you be in a library of Brewin magic books? You know you can't learn it, yes, I know your secret." Agent Lo stepped closer to see the old man who he left in the main hall, dead.

"I killed you, I left you in the hall and my men burned your body." Lo replied.

"Did they?" he crackled. "You will find that there was no body to be burned, ha! I am what they call a walker of death, pulled from the afterlife on command of the Malkav. My

Lady isn't finished with you, and she wants the boy."

"The book." said Lo, holding his hand out.

"You don't need to know who I answer to, yet you will find out in time especially if you don't find the boy." The table that the walker was sitting at started to cover with a sheet of ice.

"I know 'your Lady' has pleaded with the Malkav for help and I know who your Lady is, and her actions could cause me issues."

"Why do you care about her actions Maraj Lo? I know your past and who you really are, so why do you fight against my Lady. Just help find the Androne descendants, find the boy!"

"You may think you know everything, but you do not and neither does your leader."

"Careful Lo, we can kill you know!" Lo pulled his sword out and once again sliced the man's head off.

"I won't get bored of killing you." said Lo as he looked down at the walker. The book was still on the table. It was titled 'The Magic of Death'. Agent Lo wasn't looking for spells or power because the walker was right, he couldn't do Brewin magic. He had tried when he was younger but failed over and over. He turned the pages quickly until he found what he was looking for.

Malkav wish

Lord of the dead, will save a soul, from the blood that will be alive he must take from a life,
Walkers of death will be your servants, blood is taken to start the resurgence,
Follow the steps to receive the power, help from the Lord in their final hour.

He closed the book and went to leave.
"She will be more powerful than you could possibly imagine, now she has given the Malkav the blood he needs."
"The blood that he needs. She's killed him!" the walker didn't answer, with a clean swing of his sword, Lo once again cut his head off and left the library.

It was now midnight, and the moon lit the stables with a blue light.
"We're not taking the transport my Lord?" Spence asked. Agent Lo stood by his horse, whose muscles were like they were made of steel.
"I've had many horses in my time Spence.

Knight here has never let me down; I have had him since he was born. He's as strong as the Dominions new engines and as fast as the winds over the sea, he and his brothers will take us to Beachdale. They won't know were coming." Spence was never a keen horseman, in his training he had many accidents and even trampled by them many times.

"Did you find what you were looking for my Lord? I heard voices in there with you."

"Yes, they were no bother, things may have turned more complicated than I thought," Lo replied. "let's go."

They left the stables to meet Hi-Pec and the guards who were already on their horses ready to leave.

Agent Lo remained quiet for a long time. He believed he knew who the lady was but what he could only guess whose blood had been given. If he was right, his mission had now taken a turn for the worse.

THEARON

As the G.E.T came to a halt, Thearon opened the door to see Beachdale under the midday sun. It had cleared of smoke from the Dominion attack, but the repairs were still on going. Serfarn started looking around his machine at the damages it had picked up adding to the wrecked state he had found it in at Caufton. Thearon was a stranger to Beachdale, as his last visit was very short after picking Jack up, other than the damage, it hadn't changed. He found the closest merchant store and noticed the morale of the villagers was very low. The Dominion soldiers had taken everything that had belonged to these people. Leaving sellers with very little to sell and villagers very little money to buy anything. Before they took another step, six guards surrounded them.

"Stop there, Dominion scum!" the leader warned. They instantly raised their hands to show that they were not a threat.

"We're not Dominion, we're friends of Beachdale." Thearon told them.

"That is a Dominion transport!" the guards pulled their swords out and pointed them at Thearon and Maddox. Behind them two other guards pushed Serfarn to his knees.

"Please, we need to speak to your leader, he needs warning of a Dominion attack," Thearon kept his hands above his head. "You can walk with me, take me to him, we are on your side."

"Our leader?" the guard smirked. "Put your swords down men, I'll take him to our leader, follow behind me with the others, but don't leave them alone." said the captain and he pushed Thearon towards the town centre.

Before long, the impressive town hall building was in front of Thearon. He knew the leader of Beachdale but the reaction he got from the Dale Guard made him question who he would find in front of him. They walked through the heavy wooden doors of the hall, in front of him was a long wooden table stretching from one end of the hall to the other.

"Are you the leader of this town?" Thearon asked a man sitting at the end of the table, he got no response. "Excuse me." the man lifted his head and looked at Thearon for a few seconds.

"No, he's not here." the man told Thearon. Thearon looked at the guard who was still standing with him.

"Well, where can I find him?" but again he got no answer from the guard or the man as he lowered his head once again.

"You won't find him, well alive that is," a voice grumbled from behind Thearon. He turned to face where the voice came from. Out of the shadow walked a soldier full of armour and scars covering his face including one straight across his left eye leaving him only his right with vision.

"I'm Morton, captain of the Dale Guard."

"Captain, I wasn't sure any of you got out alive after the Dominion attacked." said Thearon as they shook hands.

"You're Thearon, Jon spoke about you, great things actually, guards, you can leave us, you rescued Jack?"

"Yes, although he's not with us, on the journey here we got separated and I need any help I can get to find him?" Morton sighed and shook his head.

"It's not something I can offer Thearon, many of the guards died on the day of the attack, most injured, including myself, we're working a bit thin." said Morton. He wasn't proud to admit it as Jack's family was close with Morton and helping Thearon would have been something Morton would have been proud to do.

"Did you go after Lo?" Morton asked.

"Yes, we couldn't get to Jon and Heena, but the journey led us back here with bad news. the Dominion will be back, but this isn't Agent Lo, he seems to have his own agenda."

"Why, what more can they possibly want with Beachdale?" Morton said with a concerned look on his face.

"They are heading to Ando, but they will destroy any town that supports Androne on their way, first stop, Beachdale." Morton sat down at the table, listening to Thearon.

"I don't know how we will survive another attack, Thearon; can Ando help at all?"

"I can't see how they will get here before Dominion. If the information is correct, they are already on their way," Thearon sat next to Morton. "Where is your Councillor? Biggs, is it?"

"Much good he was, he left a couple of days after the attack, fled in fear. I had to try my best to get the town back together." said Morton.

"Fear of what? has anyone looked for him?" asked Thearon.

"Yes, they found him, hung in a tree in the forest, we thought he went looking for Heena, them being family an' all. But he went crazy Thearon, went on about being chased by death walkers. In the end he hung himself to end it," Morton looked deflated, out of ideas. "Thearon, we're leaderless, no army to fight with, yet alone defend ourselves."

"We will help you, but I need to find Jack, he may well be the answer to our problems."

"Where are you going to start looking, what do you need?" Morton asked trying to offer any support he could.

"A boat, there was a river running along the path we took, we knew it led us here, so we followed it."

"You know who live in the forests that way on don't you Thearon?"

"Don't worry about me, just make sure your guards let Serfarn and Maddox go and get as many people together who can fight, I won't be long."

"I have a boat you can use," Morton said as they headed back out. Waiting for them outside were Maddox and Serfarn surrounded by guards.

"Release them!" ordered Morton. The guards lowered their swords and placed them back in their sheaths. "Men, we have work to do, Dominion are on their way I want any able man and boy of age to fight, you will be training them, let's get to work."

Morton rallied his men to get the villagers ready to fight a battle they were not born for. For some of the young boys, a battle that they dreamed of but coming years too soon.

"Maddox help these guards out will you, and Serfarn, get that G.E.T ready for a battle, we're going to need it," Thearon said. "I'll be back soon."

The Beachdale docks were untouched by the Dominion when they attacked. They approached by land and had passed the docks before they started their destruction. Roped up to the dock, were two huge ships. They were still loaded with wood and tools that had been ordered shortly after the attacks against Beachdale.

"We're going to have to move these boats before the Dominion turn up." stressed Morton.

"They might come in useful Morton," Thearon replied.

"What happened here anyway why has it not been rebuilt, the townsfolk are still here, aren't they?"

"Yes, they are, but when Biggs started having his moments, the townsfolk kept their distance and made sure families were safe from the crazy man. That's what the children started calling him, I managed to get some back working again. But keeping morale up is tough," Morton exhaled in disappointment or maybe a bit of embarrassment. "Some roofing work was being done, behind you there. As you can see its not to our usual standard. When Biggs had went mad, he started shaking the frames that the roofers were standing on. Then climbed up taking a hammer and a saw, fell off, how he didn't break a bone or cut his hand off I don't know. After that, those working had had enough they left and the work all around the town stopped completely."

The town was a mess, it needed major

repairs, work those women and children were unable to do on their own. Most of the men who were still in the working were farmers, sailors, or butchers. The majority had been convinced to join the Dale Guard who had to lower their expectations and standards so they could fill their ranks. This meant more experienced soldiers got rewarded with higher ranks for their help training and teaching them how to fight.

Thearon found a small boat with oars bobbing up and down between the two huge ships.

"Morton I'm taking this to find Jack. I will be back to help defend the town." said Thearon as he shook Morton's hand. He stepped into the boat which wobbled on the current. He started questioning his decision to take the river, but deep down he knew it was his best shot at finding Jack. Finally, after clutching on to the oars and steadying the boat. he sat down and started to row.

"Thearon, wait! Another boat is coming in.," shouted Morton. Thearon climbed on to the stone dock side and climbed up to his feet. He then saw the boat stop next to the dock and tie up.

"Identify yourself sailor." Morton

requested.

"It's Ben, my Lord, just dropping off a friend." he said stepping off the boat.

"Well, I never thought I would see you again, still sailing I see, not done the right thing and picked up a sword?" Morton teased.

"The water is where I belong my Lord, or Captain is it I see. obvious choice I suppose after Jon stepped down, huge shoes to fill. not sure I like what you've done to the place." Ben looked towards the damaged buildings.

"Well, if I had the help I needed, instead of soldiers running off to the water. I have a lot of respect for Jon Skies, it's boots I'm proud to fill." said Morton.

"Well, if you respect him that much maybe you'd stay and help us here." said Ben in a much lower, saddened tone. Jack and Sam carried a body wrapped in a cloth out of the cabin.

"Jack! You're alive!" Shouted Thearon as he rushed towards the boat. As he saw the body, he stopped then looked at Jack who had tears building in his eyes.

"Jack, who is that?" he didn't get a reply. Jack, Sam, and Morton lifted the body out and lowered it gently onto the floor. "Jack"

Thearon repeated, Jack looked up at Thearon, then lowered his head as he pulled back on the cloth revealing Jon's face. Thearon took a step back before freezing for a couple of seconds.

"Oh no" he gasped. Thearon kneeled next to Jon and ran his hand around the side of his face.

"Goodbye, my friend." Thearon closed his eyes and then got up and put his hands around Jack and walked him away. Morton stood and saluted his old leader then covered him back up and helped Sam and Ben carry him away.

Thearon and Jack sat at the end of the long table at the town hall. There was silence for some time before finally Thearon spoke.

"What happened Jack?" Jack told Thearon very slowly about finding Ben, Sam and then his father, then how he fought to protect his father but failed. "You didn't fail Jack, he sacrificed himself to save you, and don't underestimate the last moment he got to spend with you. He's your father and he got to see you again. Ever since you were born it was his job to protect you and, in that moment, he gave his life to do that. So, you didn't fail, he was doing his job, and he would be proud that his was able to do that, he would want to know that you were proud of what he did."

In Jacks head he knew that Thearon was right although in his heart he already missed him dearly and now he was gone.

"That Agent Lo will pay for this." Morton said breaking the short silence.

"He's up to something, but I don't think it's in line with the Dominion." said Thearon.

"He took Jon and Heena, it's his fault, he did this!" Morton said, his voice getting louder as if he was about to argue with someone.

"No," Jack said.

All the people around the table looked at him, they waited for him to continue staring. "My father told me before he died," Jack had to stop before emotion took over.

"Lo isn't my enemy, that's what said."

"I don't understand, why did he take him? Why is he now dead?!" Morton continued shouting.

"I don't think it's Lo's plan for them to be killed, he's not on our side but I don't think he wanted them dead." said Jack.

"It was a shock to me to see him dead,"

Thearon added.

"I always thought he would be too valuable to Lo as a descendant for him to kill Jon."

"He told me I need to find my mother."

"Lo must still have her." said Morton.

"No, Jon wouldn't have left without her, something doesn't add up," said Thearon. "And they didn't leave together because she would have been with Jon when Jack found him."

"Then we need to find her." Maddox said.

"No, I think she will come here, we need to defend this town. Dominion isn't looking for her at the moment and   Jon said Lo isn't their enemy so we should stay here and wait for her." said Thearon.

Jack nodded and one after another they started to leave the table and return to the jobs that had been were given to them.

"Thearon, my father had this in his hand when he died, I think he wanted to give it to me." Thearon took a note out of Jack's hand and read it.

"Hold on to this Jack, and then after we deal with the Dominion, you know what you have to do next."

"What about Sophia?" Asked Jack.

"She won't be far away from you, and it's

only you who can save her. The spell that you did at Caufton, you need to perfect it, use your emotion." said Thearon. He placed his hand on Jack's shoulder. Jack nodded to Thearon, and they headed out of the hall.

Beachdale as a town had always shown its support to Androne. Many of its townsfolk had travelled there from Ando, not knowing that a member of the Dale Guard was a descendant of Androne himself. The early travellers from Ando who arrived at Beachdale two hundred years ago built a temple for the people to pray in and meditate. It was though, ransacked and partly destroyed during the attack by the Dominion. Beachdale also had people who had not sided with either of the brothers during their war, they stayed out of the war completely. The families of the original Beachdale residence, who lived happily before the arrival of the Andos, sometimes get frustrated with the amount of support Androne got and they felt it caused trouble. Because of this the temple has always been the victim to vandalism by Typhone sympathisers who won't join a side to fight. An attack by the Dominion only strengthened their beliefs. So, repairs to the temple weren't going to be easy, which is why the damaged, smoking building still a ruin.

Thearon did his best to show support to Jack after the passing of Jon. After all it was his father and Jack was important to the survival of Beachdale, yet not alone the Andos. But behind the supportive face of Thearon, a big part of Thearon's life had now died. Thearon picked Jon up as a child, he trained him until he came of age. He knew he had to grieve as well. He decided that he needed to visit the Androne temple by himself was what he decided he needed to do to be able to say his personal goodbye.

On entering the temple, he could then see the real damage, all the wooden benches were broken and burnt. Huge pieces of stone were scattered around him from the walls and roof. He made it to the front of the temple, where he found a table that had survived the torching. A new cloth had been placed on it by someone who had tried to clean up the mess. Near the table were unused candles, left by whoever it was making the effort to restore the building. Thearon placed a candle in a holder he found by the table and lit it with the matches he carried with him. After clearing debris from around him he rested on his knees and closed his eyes. There was complete silence. A sole tear slowly ran down his cheek, falling to the floor after dropping from his solemn face. He hadn't just lost his friend but his brother.

Memories of past adventures and battles that he had experienced alongside Jon flew through his mind. From when he first rescued a young boy from a smoking orphanage to being held up against a temple wall by his neck only for Jon to break him out. killing ten other soldiers on their escape. He knew Jon was special, and that any children he had would also be special. Thearon made it his job to look after the family, even after Jon had requested that he be sure Jacks safety was above that of his own. After a long friendship moving his attention towards another was painful. He closed his eyes and his feelings brought him back to the day Jon and Heena were taken.

'On their way back from a mission for Ando, Thearon and Maddox were heading back towards Beachdale to continue keeping the promise he had made years ago. The heat was intense, the road was dusty, Beachdale was surrounded by smoke. The journey was long and tiring, yet nothing stopped Maddox from commenting on an achievement he made during the mission.

"The look on that soldier's face, Thearon... Thearon?" said Maddox.

"Yes, Maddox you did well." Thearon replied in a very sarcastic tone.

"You were being held up against that wall and I bust you free while holding off three other soldiers... Thearon?" Thearon had stopped as they had got to the outskirts of Beachdale.

"Maddox wait, somethings wrong." said Thearon as he held his arm out stopping Maddox from passing him. They both crept slowly behind a barn from where they could see the town centre where a gathering of people was forming. A group of soldiers caught Thearon's eye; they were being led by a woman who was moving very uncomfortably.

"Maddox, who is that?" Thearon asked, he tried to move the branches of a small tree out of his way to get a better look, but they had disappeared.

"She didn't look like a soldier or Dominion." Maddox replied.

"No but the soldiers following definitely were, come on let's get closer." Thearon and Maddox snook through the small pathways in-between the buildings and reached a ladder that took them to the roof tops.

"Stay low Maddox, come on." Maddox threw a look of sarcasm at Thearon knowing that to remain unseen at his size wasn't going to be easy. They stopped at a balcony and looked over the town centre where the soldiers had gathered.

"Agent Lo." Thearon whispered, "they have come for Jon."

"There is that woman again." Maddox said, pointing to the side of the square.

"There's Jon," said Thearon interrupting Maddox. "why's he next to… wait, that's Heena, and Jack is captured too."

"But why was Heena with the Dominion soldiers, she wasn't exactly running from them." said Maddox.
They both sat and watched as Agent Lo tormented Jack.

"What changed to require that Heena be chained up?" Thearon said.

Before Maddox answered, they both saw

Hi-Pec pulling back an arrow.

"Too late, let's go!" Thearon shouted.... before opening his eyes again, finding himself still in the abandoned temple staring at an extinguished candle.

After leaving the temple, Thearon went to the part of town where he had seen Heena enter it, followed by the Dominion soldiers. Heena wasn't a traitor, was she? Thearon questioned himself, but he had known her for years. It must be a misunderstanding. He entered the door and to his surprise it did not lead into a house but a stairwell going underground. Thearon pulled out his sword and used his matches to light a torch, illuminating the dark staircase. At the bottom of the staircase, Thearon came to an old wooden door, he opened it with a shove of his shoulder. The door swung open with a bang as it slammed into the wall, taking Thearon along with it. Dust filled the air making Thearon swing his torch around to try and clear it, but it seemed to just make it worse.

"Stop my Lady," scowled an old voice. "Wait a minute you're not her, who are you?"

Out of the shadows stepped a pale, gaunt

man. He was covered with a black cloak which barely covered his body.

"Who are you? And what are you doing down here?" the man crackled.

"I would like to ask you the same questions," Thearon replied. pulling out his sword and pointing it towards the man. "Who is your Lady?"

"Ha! I will never answer to you, you think you can walk in here and give me orders." Thearon continued to point his sword at him.

"You're a walker sent by the Malkav, yes, I've come across your lot before, who summoned you?" asked Thearon. The walker chuckled again.

"You didn't hear me the first time did you, I'm not going to answer to you human."

"Well, I'll just pray to the Malkav and get you to do my willing as well." said Thearon.

"Ha! It's not that easy, you need to have something to offer the Lord, you need to be powerful."

"Your leader isn't powerful; in fact, she's imprisoned as we speak."

"Wrong again human, she is walking free, with the walkers of the Malkav as her servants!"

"Why?" Thearon snapped at the walker,

whose smile grew closer to his ears. "What is it she seeks, what does she want?"

"I'm not allowed to say, even if I wanted to."

The walker continued to walk from one side of the room to the other, not doing anything constructive, just waiting. Waiting for his Master and Lady to return. Thearon tried to look around the room for any kind of clue to prove or confirm his suspicions. This accusation would be very damaging. Heena? She couldn't be, could she? To be able to make the Malkav wish you need to learn magic of the Brewin and she had never shown signs of that learning. She was always very negative towards the idea.

Later that evening they returned to transport.

"Ah Thearon, I have saved this bunk for you." Maddox called. Thearon arrives at the G.E.T that Maddox and Serfarn had managed to create a makeshift sleeping quarters inside.

"Do you like what we have done with the place Thearon?" Serfarn shouted in the direction of Thearon as they all got settled in their temporary beds.

"As long as it can still fight when the Dominion get here, I don't care, Serfarn." replied Thearon.
He turned over on to his other side away from the others.

The next day Beachdale was mourning as a whole town, a former leader was being put to rest. The streets were lined with villagers, some who were standing proud and others keeping their tears in. Jon had kept this town safe for many years whilst in the role of Captain of the Guard, at home and abroad. A hero in most of the villagers' eyes, a Captain to remember. A new Governor had been chosen for the town and had granted the permission for the funeral to be held in the town square. Which was the last place in Beachdale that he had been seen alive, albeit captured. Benches had been put out in the square, chairs, and even stools that local people had brought out from their houses to be able to sit to witness the service.

Thearon joined Maddox in finding a bench close to the front of the rows of seating.

"I hope you have brought your tissue with you Maddox." said Thearon turning towards Maddox.

"I have" Maddox replied with a smile on his face.

He pulled it out of his small bag that he carried around his waist. With quick reflexes Thearon snatched the tissue and kept it for himself blocking any attempts from Maddox to take it back.

"Hello there, fellas." a voice said as they both turned their heads.

"Zander, you made it," Thearon stood up to shake his hand, "I'm glad you got my message."

"I'm glad you sent it my friend, I'm sorry for your loss," said Zander.

He attempted to comfort Thearon as he nodded back to him. "How's the boy?"

Thearon looked down to the floor and then up to a teary Maddox who had a tired look on his face.

"Don't tell me the boy as well?" Zander added.

"No, no, Jack is fine, he is here, well with his father actually." said Thearon.

The sound of a trumpet made the congregation turned to look behind them and then find their seats. Thearon remained standing momentarily to see the local priest lead a wooden coffin that was dark brown with a ruby shine. It was being carried by Jack, Morton and five other official ranked members of the Dale Guard. As they entered the walkway down the centre of the rows of seats, people began to stand and watched as they made their way to the front. Zander looked around the crowd with a very confused look on his face and then back at the coffin that had now reached the front. His face looked as though he had a burning question but couldn't ask it. The men put Jon's coffin on a large finely carved stone, bowed and headed to the back. Jack and Morton took their seats at the front next to Thearon. Zander placed his hand on Jack's shoulder and gave him a supportive wink. Jack gave a small smile in return as they lowered down to their bench and looked back to the priest. He had now stood at the front and started to welcome everybody.

"Welcome, we gather here today to celebrate the life of Jon Skies," he said in an old wobbly voice. "Husband, father, friend and leader."

The service didn't last long. After the priest had finished his speech he once again bowed to the coffin and then left. Many left behind him apart from the people who wanted to say their own goodbyes and so they made a line along front of the seating. It consisted mainly of retired soldiers who had fought for Jon. Ben and the current soldiers who had respect for his career and achievements and were still told of his battles today. Jack waited by the side of Jon as people passed by, ending with Thearon, Maddox and Zander who all gave Jack a sympathetic bow. Zander placed his arm around Jack, and they left together.

JACK

The next afternoon felt very strange to Jack. He walked through the centre of the town and the market stalls were all open, people did their shopping as they did any other day. Just yesterday they were all sad and mourning yet when the sun came up it was business as usual. What made him feel even more uncomfortable was that when people looked at him, they gave a sympathetic smile and quickly turned their head away. He felt like a stranger in his own town, even standing outside his house trying to find the courage to go in every night to just sleep.

Jack's attention was drawn towards the sound of crates banging and sails blowing in the wind. Many, locals it seemed, were packing up their boats and hoping to leave.

Amongst those boats Jack recognised one to be Ben's.

"Your leaving Ben?" asked Jack.

"Ah Jack I was hoping to see you, er you know, Matthew here can't stay. I know what's coming and it's no place for a child." Ben replied. Jack looked towards Matthew who looked purely miserable.

"He looks glad to be leaving Ben," said Jack. "That boat at the end is going to be transporting children and a parent to safety I'm sure he would be fine on there."

"Oh, you know kids Jack, he knows this boat, he's comfortable."

"I want to stay Jack, tell him I can stay," Matthew shouted jumping towards Jack.

"Ben is right, you won't be safe here."

"But I want to learn to fight and become strong like you." Mathew said interrupting Jack, looking disappointed.

"Matthew you are young and have a lot to of time to become strong and powerful, here," Jack handed some parchments with spells written on them. "These are basic simple Brewin spells, practice, don't tell your father and definitely don't tell Ben. I will find you to see how you're getting on." said Jack.

"Do you promise?" said Matthew, moving

his blond fringe away from his eyes.

"I promise," replied Jack. "Take care of yourself Gregory and little one," Gregory nodded back at Jack. "And thank you for what you did for my father, you gave me those extra minutes with him. I will be forever grateful for that." Jack turned back to Ben who looked back down to the floor.

"Look Jack, I'm no fighter, if I was, I would still be in the Guard, I can't help you here" Ben said.

"Look after Gregory and Matthew, please, and thank you for bringing me home." Jack held his hand out which Ben took with a tight grip and pulled Jack in for a hug.

"Good luck Jack, I hope we find each other again." Ben said. releasing Jack. Work had stopped around the dock, people just staring at Ben and Jack.

"You need to go." Jack said, slightly embarrassed as he stepped off the boat back on the stone dock. They started to leave; Jack watched as they headed towards the open sea. A pop came from the boat, followed by a grey cloud of smoke. Matthew's head appeared bright red with a smile from ear to ear.

"My boy! Jack taught you that didn't he!"

Ben shouted but sounded like a whisper from the distance. Jack smiled to himself and headed back to town.

Later that day a meeting in the town hall had been called by Frank Stone, the new Governor of Beachdale. The large, polished meeting table was headed by Stone with people he considered useful for the upcoming threats.

"I need to know exactly what we are up against, and how we are going to fight back." Stone questioned.

"The Dominion are heading to Ando, they won't be looking to stay, so I'm expecting them to push their army through, hoping for little resistance." Thearon said.

"Surely they know we won't just lay down for them." said Stone slight offended.

"They think we are weak. After Lo came and made it look so easy, but only the Dale Guard who were stationed here at the time fought. We have more out at the borders we will call them in," said Morton.

"We will need more," said Jack. "We don't have Woodale to help even though Atton is dead, Davenport has a tournament on so they won't help, the villagers will need to rise and help fight back."

"The villagers?" gasped Stone. "They are still petrified since the last attack; you tell them that the Dominion are coming back they will run to the hills."

"They will fight for their home and their freedom I'm sure of it." said Jack.

"Jacks right," Thearon agreed. "In fact, we should take the fight to them."

"What?" screamed Stone. "You want us, with the little that we have to go out to meet the Dominion, it's suicide."

"Listen to me," Thearon said calmly. "Send all who can't fight to a safe place that is not on the route to Ando and we fill what boats we have with the ones who can fight and meet them. They won't be expecting it and won't be prepared."

"I'm with Thearon." Jack said thumping the table with his fist closed causing Stone to give him a shocked yet stern glare.

"Me to." echoed from the other members of the meeting.

"Fine, fine, fine!" said Stone. "I will leave this to you to arrange, as I'm too old to fight, but I will make sure the others who can't are safe. We will head north, where there is a stronghold led by a long-time friend, we will be safe there until we can return home."

Thearon nodded in acceptance.

"Maddox and I will round up the villagers who will fight and train them the best we can."

"I will train the younger fighters." said Jack. This caused looks from around the whole table.

"We will keep them with the other villagers Jack." replied Thearon.

"They will need different training to the men and women. My father wouldn't let me fight because of my age, now look at what I have achieved. Thearon, I know what I'm doing."

Stone shot Thearon a concerned look, but Thearon didn't make eye contact and kept his gaze on Jack.

"Jack, this is going to be a long hard battle, they will be safer with the older fighters." Thearon continued to talk Jack down from his idea.

"Give him a chance Thearon," said Zander. "He has been trained by his father from a young age, any man here would have died for the honour."

Stone continued to look from side to side and waited, until his patience ran out.

"Fine Jack, I'm with Aleczander. I trust

you with the younger fighters," Jack gave a smile in appreciation.

"Morton, the Guard can stay with you, Maddox take the men and woman, Zander, I want you to be the final line at the town hall with my personal guards. I will take the civilians to Marsh Hall until it is safe to return. Now we must move with haste, so we are ready, good luck to you all." they all stood giving Stone a respectful bow and went their separate ways to prepare.

The next day many villagers gathered in front of the town hall as Stone announced the call for fighters and gave instructions. Jack looked out to the sea of people thinking that not that long ago there were benches lined up for his father's funeral in front of him. Now they have been replaced by people gathered to find out their fate. The news didn't go down well. The villagers were scared, knowing that they hadn't yet recovered from the last attack and now just waiting for the Dominion to come again. Stone finished his speech and guided the people to their leaders. Jack, Morton, and Thearon, joined by Maddox of course, separated to be joined by the people who they would be training. Jack decided to use his parents' farm as his base. He thought that it worked so well for him growing up, that it may well work the same for the others.

His home had deteriorated somewhat, having been abandoned since no one was living in it. The burtings had all been stolen and the sheds and wooden fencing around the house were damaged beyond repair. But Jack didn't let this bother him. The open area in which he had quite often fought against his father, would be perfect for the training sessions to take place.

The first job Jack had to do was decide which fighters were suitable for a battle and those who were not. Those standing in front of him for his first session didn't fill him with much confidence. The hope that Jack had when suggesting taking this group was that he would have youngsters who were perhaps sixteen and over. This was not the case. The Burditts orphanage which was positioned not far from Jacks house had recently closed due to the death of the owner Mickey Burditt. It seemed that the orphans had followed the eldest who wanted to fight. Which added twenty children to the ranks with the ages ranging from eleven to sixteen. Jack knew he didn't have time to give up, so he went with it.

"Here you go Jack, you're going to need these." said Zander.

He arrived at the yard with a bag over his shoulder accompanied by a member of the Dale Guard equipped with the traditional golden armour.

"Well, if this is all we have to work with then I'll do my best I suppose" said Jack looking down at the old wooden swords inside the bag. The children's excitement from seeing the weapons completely outweighed Jack's disappointment. Jack handed a sword out to each fighter before making his way to the front of the group, how do you start? Jack could feel the eyes staring at him with high expectations. Jack started showing how to hold a sword which he thought would be easier than it turned out.

The evening arrived as the sun had set leaving a dim light over the yard. Jack had challenged the group to try and hit him, but all had failed, for some, Jack didn't need to block with his sword. The last in line was a small, thin, ragged boy. He had come with the group from the orphanage, which was clear from his ripped clothes and his hair was all scruffy.

"Last one, what is your name kid?" Jack said in a tired, unimpressed voice.

"Kaiden." he replied in a low whisper and lifted his sword. Jack lifted his sword to meet Kaiden's and nodded to encourage an attack from Kaiden. Kaiden swung his sword menacingly towards Jack who beat each attack away, one by one, but struggled to push Kaiden back.

"Not bad, let's go again." said Jack as he went on the offensive but couldn't find a way past him. Kaiden blocked hit after hit and a small grin appeared on Kaiden's pale face. Jack felt frustration flowing through him making his blows faster, stronger, and more deadly. A final blow eventually knocked Kaiden to the floor. Jack was blinded by his frustration, forgetting what he was doing but just continued swinging until he stopped suddenly. Jack didn't understand as his sword was stuck in mid-air, he couldn't move it, he couldn't move his hands or arms. He looked down at Kaiden who was laying on the floor with fear showing on his face. But it was his hand that was being held out towards Jack that made him understand what was happening.

"Kaiden, it's OK," said Jack. "I'm going to put down the sword. You need to lower you hand, Kaiden." Kaiden finally lowered his hand releasing Jack from what felt like chains wrapped around his wrists, clamping him into one place. Jack held his hand out to lift Kaiden up. The group behind them had slowly petered out during the short duel.

"Wait, our lesson hasn't finished!" shouted Jack but then gave up as no one turned back. Only Kaiden and five others were left. Jack felt deflated, he looked into the eyes of the boys who stared back and then to Kaiden who was still brushing himself down. Jack wanted to talk but no words came out.

"Same time tomorrow, drop your swords here for me," said Zander. Before putting his arm around Jack, "Jack, not everyone has the ability that you possess, and wooden swords and any teacher won't give them that." Zanders calming voice helped Jack clear most of the doubt from his mind.

"It was a foolish aim Zander," Jack said. "They are too young, I thought if they had the fire in them to fight back, they would be an asset."

"They could still be an asset Jack, you were thrown into battle, with a sword and shield by your father, you have thrived. You had the ability; you just needed the weapon. Find their ability and give them their weapon," Zander gave Jack another tap on his shoulder. "Remember not all weapons are swords and spears." he said and then left. Jack started to collect the swords together when he saw Kaiden still standing there.

"Hey, er Kaiden," said Jack surprised. "When did you learn how to do that, to hold my attack like that?"

"I don't know, I read something at the orphanage about magic, because my parents were fighters in the Dale Guard, but they got taken. I saw it happen in my house, they used magic on them and took them and I haven't seen them since," he said. "So, as there is a library at the orphanage, I wanted to learn more about it and I found a book with some spells in, very interesting actually."

"Can you bring this book with you tomorrow?" asked Jack.

"Yes, I will." Kaiden replied with a smile from ear to ear.

The next morning Jack was thinking about what Zander had suggested, but how does he find out their abilities and weapons, what did he mean? It was easy for Jack as he just picked up a sword, but they had proved useless with weapons. He still couldn't believe the strength of the Brewin magic that Kaiden had used on him. It reminded him a lot of Sophia, who he had not really thought about since his father died. This upset him. Sophia had been possessed by Broxholme Watts, whilst trying to attack him. But he wondered now that his father was dead, whether he was still going to come after him, or maybe just Thearon. Thearon was confident Watts would still come for him, but if he stayed away, would he ever see Sophia again? Jack started to feel like the longer he stayed here the more he was letting her down.

Jack spent the rest of the day thinking what to do for the training session that evening, that's if anybody bothers turning up. He saw that several of the boys who came yesterday had already boarded an evacuation boat and some had asked to leave with Governor Stone. He wanted to make use of the advice Zander gave to him, but he still couldn't figure out the way that he could do it.

"Give them their weapon," he repeated to himself. "Give them their weapon." He hoped that the more he repeated it to himself the more it would make sense or something obvious would fly across the room at him. "Find their abilities" he went on, but it was no good, what was he missing? Maybe he should go speak to Zander again? Or was it obvious which was why Zander only dropped the hint.

It was time for the session. This time Jack already had the swords laid out on the floor ready for the students to start. He hoped to see if any of them would instantly pick them up and maybe show that they did have some ability with a weapon. Five students had returned on time, but Jack had noticed that Kaiden wasn't among them.

"Where is Kaiden?" Jack asked.
But the responses that he received were only the shrugging of shoulders and the shaking of their heads. Disappointed, Jack started the session.

"OK pick up your swords, you all have

abilities, some different to others but they are there, and we need to find them. So, let's start with you Louie." Louie was another shy boy. He had long blond hair down to his shoulders, and bushy eyebrows that hid his eyes unless he looked up at you. Then Louie with his sword in hand stepped forward to attack Jack whose attention was taken by Kaiden running around the gate of the yard. His sword hit Jack square in the chest. It knocked him back and then fell to his knees.

"Oh sir, I, I'm sorry" Louie said trying to aid Jack.

"I'm OK, I'm fine honest, that was a good strike Louie, I'm impressed." after taking a deep breath he got back to his feet. He welcomed Kaiden back into the group. The session ended late into the evening and Jack felt he had made great progress.

"Here Jack, I have bought the book that I found!" said Kaiden. Jack eyed the book that was handed to him. It looked like the old books in Sophia's library. It had an old cover, a leather finish in a dark green. It was titled 'Schools of the Brewin'.

"Wow, I will look through this tonight Kaiden, now get yourself back and rest ready for tomorrow." Kaiden scuttled off away from the yard and out of sight. Thearon arrived after the students had gone.

"Well, the villagers are ready for a fight." said Thearon.

"Are they ready or do they just think they are?" Jack asked with slight sarcasm.

"They were never going to be members of the Guard Jack, but we have got what we have got, how are the young ones getting on?" Thearon asked. Jack shook his head. "That well, eh?" Thearon teased. "Well Jack it isn't getting any easier." Thearon handed Jack a letter.

Dominion boats just past, they will be with you at dusk tomorrow, good luck.

"We don't have enough time, these young children will need to leave with Stone, or they won't stand a chance." Thearon nodded to Jack.

"You can join us in a boat as we go out to meet them."

"That's still the plan, is it?" Jack said surprised. "Stone hasn't got everyone running yet then."

Jack didn't know whether to feel disappointed or pleased with the news that the students won't finish the training. The enthusiasm he grown at the end of the last session although they wouldn't stand a chance. Jack didn't realise he was still holding on to the book Kaiden had handed him. Now he was alone he flicked through it, then he looked very carefully at the front cover.

"Schools of the Brewin."

Jack can remember Thearon talking about the schools that were set up at Mitchler and then wiped out by the Dominion. He then began to wonder if anyone had set up any more schools or maybe they were too scared of the Dominion. It was a shame, he thought, because Kaiden's Brewin ability had huge potential, wait-

"Kaiden's ability, that's it!" he said to himself. He then sat down in his sitting room in his parents' house and started to plan, "find their ability and give them a weapon." Jack was over the moon with his new idea. Was this the beginning of his own school of Brewin magic? But did he know enough to be able to teach? Questions and uncertainties flew through Jacks head, knocking his confidence.

Morning came round quickly. Jack felt like he hadn't slept at all but the excitement of what he planned to do gave him such a boost he decided to round up the students early so they could practise. The Burditt's orphanage was cold and dark. All the adults who were looking after the kids had either been killed or had fled along with most of the orphans the previous day. There was no light at all, not even a candle waiting to be lit. The windows were so small they wouldn't allow enough sunlight to enter, not to mention the sheets hanging down in front of them. It didn't look like it had closed for an evacuation, more like it had been abandoned for weeks. Jack closed his eyes and his fist and muttered to himself, and when he opened his palm, a flame appeared and lit up the room.

"Hello!" he shouted. "Kaiden!" no answer. "Kaiden, anyone" still no answer.

He went up some steps on to the first floor, it had a haunted feel to it, cobwebs clung to the walls, shimmering in the light from his flame. Jack began to fear for Kaiden and the other boys who were only at his class yesterday. Until a thin slither of light surrounded a door at the end of the corridor.

"Kaiden?" it was more of a whisper than a shout. His arm that was free felt for his sword, but he hadn't bought it with him, it was still at his house. Nerves had now kicked in, he had no weapon, no defence. He approached the door slowly, trying his best to avoid any floorboards that squeaked. He held the rusty round doorknob and twisted. The door opened slowly making a mouse-like squeak. Jack stepped over the threshold holding his flame out in front of him. Before he could dodge a bright white bolt hit him in the cheek, Jack summoned a shield of flame in front of him lighting up the whole room. Little bolts continued to hit the flames but just dissolved as they passed through. With a swing of his arm the flames burnt away sending a shockwave, blowing away anything in its path. Jack relit his flame in his palm to see six boys on the floor. They were alive but injured.

"Kaiden!" shouted Jack running to his aid. Kaiden's face was bright red, but he was OK.

"Jack, we're sorry, we didn't know who it was, nobody ever comes here, all the workers are gone." said Kaiden apologetically.

All the boys started to get to their feet. Scattered on the wooden floor were sharp pieces of metal all different sizes.

"What are you guys doing in here?" asked Jack.

Kaiden just shyly looked around at the others and to the floor.

"We wanted to help; we were practising Brewin magic! The library is full of books on different types of spells, come see." Kaiden grabbed Jacks arm and pulled him out of the room and down the corridor until they reached a door that looked like it had been broken into. The bolt had been shattered, there were pieces of metal and wood on the floor surrounding the door.

"Did you do this? Asked Jack.

"Yes, we didn't think it would do this, it was a spell from the book I gave you. We heard a rumour that there were books in here, they never let us come in so, when they all left, we tried but it was locked. When we all read that book. We practised and learnt lots of spells, it took all seven of us to destroy it. I'm sure when we have practised ore, we could do it on our own," said Kaiden talking very fast. "Look!" Kaiden pushed Jack into the room nearly tripping over a pile of books left on the floor.

"It's a dump," Jack said. "All the books are

damaged, and the shelves are empty." It was a small room but most of the walls had bookcases up against them, but they were all empty, only holding a dozen each maximum.

"Yes, we were disappointed as well, until we found this." Kaiden led Jack to a bookcase in the back corner of the room. It had a metal cage that had been completely blown off its hinges that was now on the floor.

"Let me guess you did this as well?" said Jack sarcastically. Kaiden nodded.

"It only took three of us though this time." Jack shook his head with a smile and turned back to the bookcase. It was full, there were old books with non-existent covers and books that looked like new.

"I want to ask if this is the restricted section, but I suppose the whole room was open to you anyway?" asked Jack as he started to pull books from the shelves.

"We saw that there were more books in there, and it looked restricted which made us think it would be of more use."

"They are all Brewin spell books, and history books," Jack said as he pushed some to the side to look for more. "This is brilliant."

Kaiden was thrilled.

"Will you teach us more and in our sessions? we can learn Brewin magic, we will work harder with the swords as well, we have a name, the Brewin Knights! nobody will dare fight us, magic, swords, and you leading us, we would be unbeatable."

Jack surprised himself that he hadn't already discarded the idea.

"Find their abilities and give them their weapons." no that was too obvious surely Zander didn't mean literally give kids swords. But still Jack liked the idea.

"Look, the Dominion are coming, tomorrow evening, they will be here, I can't teach you enough myself to take out the Dominion army, but I have a plan."

Dusk came earlier than anybody had wanted it to. Jack was still in his yard with the kids, their weapons had been thrown aside and as much magic training that they could possibly do had been done.

"OK training is over, I want you to rest, have some food and water, then we will be defending this town, now go." the boys ran to Jack's house where he had left food on the kitchen side.

Jack continued walking past them and into

his room where his sword and forearm shield that belonged to his father both sat waiting for him to pick up. Before he did so he didn't know why but he found himself heading into his parents' bedroom. Above their bed was a painting of all three of them. Jack was only ten years old at this point and his father had the most amazing armour on. It was a bright silver and had ruby red down the side and around the neck. He wondered whether maybe the armour was here somewhere as he had never seen another member of the Dale Guard wear it. Thoughts flew through his head on where it could be, and one place instantly came to mind.

"The cellar". He rushed back towards the kitchen and opened the door that was still damaged from when he broke through it and headed into the dark cobweb ridden basement. Now where could it be? There were lots of boxes and cases around the floor, but they were not big enough to hold armour, he didn't think so anyway. He thought the best idea was to look at the larger areas first. Then his eyebrows raised when saw a wooden cupboard, it was huge, almost seven foot in height. He pulled at the handles but clearly his father didn't want to risk him seeing it as even though he always locked the cellar door he had put three locks on the doors one of which being the size of his fist. He had decided this was it, but how to get in, well, it was obvious. He had spent most of the day with the boys practising Brewin magic, one of which shattered locks. He held his hand out in front of the lock and then it broke apart. He repeated it on the smaller locks and then opened the doors. Dust emerged from inside, forcing Jack to cover his face, but seconds later, he lowered his hands, there it was, in all its beauty. His memory of when Jon gave him his forearm shield came back to him and he had said.

"That is for another time Jack." well, what better time to wear it, in his honour, whilst protecting the town, as his father done before.

The armour was too big for him initially; however, he found a way to remove parts to make the important plates far more comfortable. Once the armour was all fitted, he went back into the house where the children were all eating, until they saw him, and they froze in amazement. He finally felt like he was receiving the respect his father had done during his time in the Dale Guard.

THEARON

The bells atop the town hall of Beachdale rang with fury. Civilians who had missed the evacuation hurried into basements and any other stronghold where they felt safe. At the docks Thearon looked out to sea, but mist and rain clouded his vision.

"They're here." Morton whispered to him as boats started to pierce the blanket of fog and come into sight.

"Let's get aboard." said Thearon and he shook Morton's hand as they went their separate ways. Thearon boarded the Wonder. It was not as big as Beachdale's lead ship, but it was very heavily armoured. Ten cannons lined each side, each one manned ready to fire at the oncoming Dominion attackers. It was quiet, the Dominion ships continued towards them, as they sailed out.

"Are they waiting for us?" a young sailor asked.

"I don't know." Thearon replied. The Dominion pierced the port's waters like a knife, travelling quickly.

"They're not slowing down, SHOOT THEM!"

The Beachdale ships turned as quickly as they could to face their cannons out towards the Dominion. It seemed a lifetime until they were in range and all at once the cannons fired. Splinters smashed from the hulls of the ships; smoke bellowed from all directions. Thick black smoke now filled the port, visibility was zero.

"Can you see them, Thearon? I think we've done it." the sailor said.

The guns stopped. Thearon looked for sinking sails and listened for the screams and yells from the drowning crewmen. To his horror, the bows emerged from the smoke, closer and faster.

"Keep shooting, aim low, sink them!" Thearon yelled.
The cannons continued but the Dominion were now no more than a hundred yards away.

"they're not going to stop, abandon ship!"

Thearon shouted.

He threw the young sailor over the side of the ship and followed him with a jump and splash. The Dominion ships collided into the Beachdale fleet causing an explosion so big it caught every ship, Dominion and Beachdale.

Thearon made it to shore along with the sailor he had saved.

"Thearon, here let me help you." Maddox helped him up on to the dock.

"Maddox, you're, ok?"

"Yea, just about, had to jump and swim back." he said.

They looked at the wrecked boats slowly sinking into the shallow waters. All you could see was damaged sterns angled out of the water and broken masts hanging over the edges of the sunken ships.

"They were abandoned," Thearon said. "it's very clever on their part, they must have set the course and jumped ship. Although they must have known our plan, and now our ships have sunk along with many fighters, I don't know who has survived."

"Morton is alive, he's back on shore sorting the Guard out" Maddox added.

"Thearon!" yelled a voice approaching them. "The Dominion, look!" Jack stopped next to them pointing out past the destruction. More Dominion ships had arrived, with no defence in place they sailed casually past the ship graveyard.

"You father's armour!" Thearon said in admiration. Almost ignoring the approaching Dominion that Jack had pointed out to him, "it suits you Jack," Jack nodded in appreciation. "let's spread out back in the town centre and try and pick them off, it's already half destroyed a little more damage won't hurt."

Thearon led them back to the town and with the help from Morton and the Guard. People were stationed strategically around the centre waiting for the attack.

"Here they are." said Thearon. The sound of symmetrical footsteps, marched into the town centre. Rows of Dominion soldiers went all the way back to the dock. Banner men were holding the Dominion symbol high, ensuring everyone knew who were upon them.

"Stay low, we wait for them to get into the middle." Thearon ordered.

He, Maddox and six other soldiers sat quietly and patiently at the top of Beachdale's clock tower that protruded from the town hall. A towering red brick building fronted with rectangular windows and a huge white clock. The bells hung metres above their heads.

Captain Galen, an old leader from within the Dominion, was leading the assault. He had led many campaigns which the Dominion had won in the past against Ando supporters. He stepped into the town centre of Beachdale followed by his ranks. Lines of soldiers stood awaiting his orders, all wearing the same dark, charcoal coloured armour. Galen had his own silver armour, which made him stand out but that is how he wanted it, he was a bold warrior. He was proud of the scars that ran up his bronze skin and over where his hair once sat.

"Morton!" Galen shouted. "I know you're here and I know you can see and hear me, if you are planning on jumping us, I wouldn't bother. I have legions awaiting my orders in the docks, you don't stand a chance, although," he paused. "You could save a lot of lives, stand down and walk with us to Ando and no more civilians will be harmed."

"Morton won't do it." Thearon whispered to Maddox; the sound of footsteps could be heard to where they were sitting. It was

Morton.

"Thearon, have you seen how many they have, we won't win this fight."

"Then we die fighting Morton."

"Morton, I will give you to the count of ten, then we will find you and destroy the town along with all that call it home."

"Did the evacuations get completed?" Thearon asked to which Morton nodded. "I don't want to see the end of Beachdale, but I also don't want to let them walk through Ando without a fight",

"Then we will fight and take as many of them with us."

"Six, five, four," Galen shouted getting louder after each number. "Come on Morton, three, two, one, fine you have made you choice." Galen held his hand up ready to signal to his men to search but stopped suddenly. As a figure stepped out of the shadows, they wore a musky white robe down to their bare feet. Nobody could see a face. A hood fell halfway down the face, cloaking it in darkness. The robe lay tight around the waist resembling a woman, as she slowly strolled to the centre to face Galen.

"Who are you?" he blasted. "Is this a part of

your plan Morton, heh? send a wench out to distract us? ha! move aside sweetheart I will have plenty of time for you after I take over the town," she didn't say anything, she didn't move a muscle. Just stood there. "Move or we will move you ourselves," Galen added, but nothing happened. "You are there!" Galen shouted at a group of soldiers to his left. "move her and lock her away in the town hall until I'm ready for her."

The group marched forward towards the woman however, as they neared, they froze. It was as if an invisible being was holding them still. That is what it looked like to Galen.

"What are you doing? Arrest her!" Galen shouted, but they couldn't move. Thick black smoke started to appear around the trapped soldiers, it merged, getting thicker and darker. The hold on the prisoners got stronger, making them struggle to catch their breath. One started choking uncontrollably. The smoke became figures. Then in front of the Dominion army stood four walkers, all looking very similar but very different. They all had white, gaunt faces and black sunken eyes, wearing black ripped robes. Once they were fully formed, they released their prisoners as they fell in a heap to the floor.

"What is this? who are you witch?"

"No one calls our Lady as a witch," the tallest of the walkers cackled. "She has promised us souls to take to the afterlife."

"You will have to come and claim them then" Galen said releasing his sword, followed by the rest of his army. A walker, casually walked towards Galen who swung viciously at the walker, slicing his head clean off. The fallen body turned to smoke temporarily and within seconds a fully formed walker stood before Galen.

"No, it can't be." whispered Galen.
He struck again, turning him to smoke but once again he reformed.

"Get your weapons out." the walker croaked.
Immediately all four walkers had metal chains in their hands.

"You won't kill us with chains." said Galen.

"We will kill you with chains and take you to death in them!" a walker replied.

"Enough of this, we kill the witch, they then won't exist!" shouted Galen but the soldiers didn't move. "Fine!"
Galen charged forward and in seconds he

had sliced the four walkers turning them to smoke, he then swung for the woman. His sword flew through the figure, but nothing happened. In shock he waved his hand where the woman stood and all he was doing was moving smoke from side to side.

"What is this?" as he turned around the walkers had doubled in quantity and started swinging their chains at the soldiers. Every hit seemed to strike the soul from the body. Galen could only stand and watch his soldiers fall to the floor after being struck by the chains from the walkers. Galen couldn't just stand and do nothing, so he ran and tried his best to fight back. He took one walker out but as he looked up his men had retreated to the docks and scattered around the town.

"COWARDS!" the tired Captain shouted at his men fighting to try and get aboard the boats.

Grey thunderous clouds rolled in above as if a volcano that had sat dormant for thousands of years erupted.
Beachdale town was now surrounded by dark cloud. Galen stood with walkers one side and his fleeing soldiers the other. The hatches of

the cannons opened and all at once they fired towards the town causing buildings to collapse. Before they could fire the second round, tornadoes emerged from the clouds smashing into the ground a few feet in front of Galen. A figure stepped out from the powerful whirlwind of smoke and dust.

"Who are you?" Galen asked nervously. A gaunt, pointed nose figure stood in front of him.

"I have the pleasure of the Dominion I see, who are you soldier?" the figure said in his low almost breathless voice.

"I am Captain Galen, now if you don't m... m... mind I need to get to my ship." Galen shook as he spoke.

"You're retreating with them worms, well the Dominion has dropped its standards haven't they," another round of fire flew straight past them. "I didn't come for the Dominion this time, but a small bit of revenge won't hurt."

He held his hand up towards the ships, which then started to collapse within themselves until the heavily armed ships exploded taking each ship out one by one. Galen stood completely deflated. The tallest of the walkers approached him from behind, wrapped their chain around his neck and pulled him to the ground, dead.

"It's our time to go, come on, Maddox bring the explosives." Thearon said as they all picked up their bags and began to leave the clock tower.

"Thearon, he's here!" Jack said with determination.

"And what are you going to do Jack, just walk out and greet him, we need to reorganise ourselves, this is a different battle now."

The group moved quickly to find other members of the Guard, but all they found standing in front of them was Spence, Agent Lo and his number two, Hi-pec.

"Spence, we thought we lost you, we didn't think you would betray us for them!" said Maddox.

"I have betrayed no one." Spence replied calmly.

"We're not here to fight you" Lo said, stepping forward but instantly pulled back by Hi-Pec.

"What!" he yelled. "Then why are we here? They are enemies of the Dominion, so they are our enemies!"

"Hi-Pec, you have been a loyal member of my team but you're clearly not with us!" Lo said as he swung his sword out at Hi-Pec, but he easily blocked it.

"You're a traitor Agent Lo!" screamed Hi-pec. "I thought you were just losing your bottle, but you have proven to be a dirty traitor."

They clashed swords, throwing shots at each other but failing to strike a deciding blow. Spence pulled Jack to the side.

"We need to get back to the town centre and I'll explain."

"Go Jack, we will hold the fort here!" Thearon shouted. "Remember, you know how to beat him, you have done it before."

Thearon rushed back to the battle, but Hi-pec started to get the upper hand and caught Maddox on the chest with his blade cutting through his armour. Staggering, Maddox struggled back to his feet as Hi-pec retreated into a nearby barn. Thearon, Lo, Maddox and six guards crept inside, it was silent. A small goat jumped out and scurried out past them as they entered.

"We need to split up," said Thearon. "Maddox take one and head up the steps, Lo you can stay with me."

"We may not be enemies at the moment, but you don't give me orders I'm here for the boy." Lo snarled.

"That's fine, you're still staying with me."

Maddox pulled a guard with him and started to head up to the higher level. The first floor hung out to the middle of the barn like a balcony with the animal pens directly underneath. The goats and pigs sat like statues like they were waiting for an inspection.

"Do you think he left?" Thearon asked Lo in a whisper.

"No, he's good but we would have heard him," said Lo. Instantly after Lo finished an arrow flew past Lo's ear hitting a guard straight in the chest throwing him into a wall. "Upstairs!" Lo yelled.

"No!" Maddox called. "Get out of here."

Thearon had a look of disbelief as all he could do was watch Maddox and a single guard run at a shadow which they assumed must be Hi-Pec. The guard was easily defeated by Hi-Pec leaving Maddox alone.

"What are you waiting for, go!" Maddox yelled again but still they could only stand and watch. Thearon moved to get up to Maddox, but Lo grabbed and stopped him.

Maddox and Hi-pec clashed swords again and again until they both struck damaging blows to each other, and they both fell to their knees. Maddox looked around at Thearon and nodded picking up his belt of explosives.

"NO, Maddox!" Thearon yelled as he saw what he had planned.

"Let's go old man." Lo pushed Thearon towards the door with help from the guards. Maddox climbed to his feet, threw his sword to the floor, and started to charge at Hi-Pec. Hi-Pec who also had to somehow get back to his feet reacted to Maddox the only way he knew and pointed his sword at the oncoming Maddox. The floor started to shake, dust and chippings of wood fell from the ceiling like snow. Maddox jumped at Hi-Pec and held him.

Hi-Pec's sword tip dripped red from Maddox's back.

"You have failed," Hi-Pec said with a sharp smile. "And next, your friends will fail also!"

"No... they... wont." Maddox whispered as smoke raised from between them.

"No, No!" Hi-Pec screamed but Maddox would not let go of his grip and then a blast so big blew the side of the barn to pieces all that was left was fire, smoke, and ash.

JACK

"I can't defeat Watts, Spence." Jack said as they hurried down a short alley.

"You can," Spence replied stopping dead. "Remember it's not just about defeating him, he has Sophia, you know she is still alive". Jack nodded still looking at the ground,

"let's go!" finally they walked out of the alley into the open town square where six walkers stood.

"Ah finally," one crackled. "he's come to face his death."

"Where is Watts?" asked Jack.

"Oh, he'll be back I'm sure, but in the meantime, we're owed a soul, and you will do nicely," Jack raised his sword. "Foolish boy!"

The walker pulled out his chain and approached Jack who acted first and sliced the head off the walker who turned instantly to smoke. However, he did not reform.

"Who are you boy? and where did you get that sword?" the taller walker asked.

"What is it to you?"

"Well, that must be Vendel as my friend hasn't returned, you clearly are unaware of the power you hold in your hand," Jack held on to the sword tighter and raised it once again. "Careful boy, it's still doesn't make this an easy fight, you know."

The five remaining walkers, with their chains in their grip started to walk towards Jack, "your friends can't help you now!"

"Wait!" a scream echoed around the open town centre. The hooded woman returned, but this time she was there, no longer made of smoke and vapour.

"You are not to harm the boy!" she ordered the walkers in a voice Jack had heard before. He lowered his sword and stared at the woman to try and see her or anything that would help him recognise who she was and why the voice was so familiar to him.

"You owe us a soul, my Lady!" the tall walker said.

"You have taken plenty of soldiers, you have had enough to fulfil the debt." the lady replied.

"They were weak, we want a Brewin, a powerful Brewin." as the walkers once again started to approach Jack, smoke circled then and gathered in the centre and Watts was once again standing among them.

"You again, what do you want?" the walker asked irritated.

"The same thing as you it would seem" Watts' low, scarred voice was enough to make Jack raise his sword again and scuffled backwards slightly.

"If you want a soul take his." the lady said to the walkers.

"No!" one snapped back. "He is contaminated the Lord has no interest in it, for now, we want the boy."

"Why me? what is going on here?" Jacks voice wobbled with confusion and some terror.

"Let me help you" Watts raised a hand towards the woman and instantly, her hood flew down, Jack dropped his sword and stumbled.

"Mother!"

"Well, isn't this fun," Watts almost broke into laughter. "You didn't know she was a Brewin user did you boy, no? quite a powerful one as well it would seem, but that isn't the biggest secret of them all is it," Jack was conflicted.

He wanted to go and hug his mother, but something was holding him back, he feared her, but why?

"I wanted to get my revenge on your father who had to, cowardly I would add, catch me unaware to defeat me. But to my surprise and slight disappointment, the job was already done for me, by her!"
Watts crooked finger was pointed at Heena leaving Jack in shock and he could barely stand up he was shaking that much.

"Mother he's lying, tell me he's lying, please!" tears were starting to roll down his face. Thearon, Spence, and Lo stepped out behind him, Thearon placing his hand on his shoulder.

"I, I had too, it got too much, this Androne religion," Heena said holding tears in. "it's true he didn't know I studied Brewin, and It, it's true I left him to die. I needed to save you from all this, he had too many enemies, and I thought if he wasn't around, you would be safe, but it was too late." Jack didn't know how to feel, but for definite, the excitement of seeing his mother had gone.

"Enough of this nonsense, I have things to do." Watts croaked.

The walkers retreated to surround and protect Heena which created a standoff between the three parties.

The centre of town had filled with darkness. Hate and revenge poured out from each person within the standoff. Jack knew there was no happy ending from this fight.

Jack, who had the others with him, knew that they couldn't help. But also knew that the walkers who were on his mother's side wanted his soul. Several minutes passed by with them staring at each other, until Watts sent a beam of light so powerful it pushed Jack backwards, closer to Heena. Making a walker jump in the way to take the hit from the beam of energy which turned him to ash, then instantly reappearing once more.

"We want our payment, let us take the boy, and you can go about your business."

"By all means." Watts said in a bored tone.

The walkers all started towards Jack swinging their chains.

"No, you can't," Heena screamed. "It was in the deal to protect him not take him for yourselves."

"The deal has ended as the payment hasn't

been given. So, we now take what we deserve." Jack prepared himself along with the others.

"Wait, wait take..." said Heena before disappearing in a cloud of smoke and a second later reappearing with Lo, holding her dagger to his throat. "You know who he Is, he is more valuable than Jack, please!"

"By title he holds a similar value true, however, the last year has shown the boy to be more powerful which makes him more attractive to our Lord." the walkers continued towards Jack.

"No!" Heena screamed pulling the knife away and thrusting it in Lo's side in anger, then she threw it hitting the closest walker to Jack in the side of the head.

"My Lady, you are stopping us from collecting our payment." the walker repeated.

"The deal was to protect my son, so in which case it is over." Heena said, breathing heavily.

"Over? Well, my Lady you have wasted our time, so me and my friends will return to our home and our Lord. however, being summoned to your world doesn't happen very often, so, I think we should take a soul with us anyway." said the tallest walker.

They looked at each other and then at Heena.

"The most powerful one will be best," said another.

They then approached Heena, Jack ran to help but Watts threw Jack and the others into the wall of the bakery with just a wave of his hand.

"No, I'm enjoying this." Watts said as they crashed through the bricks of the bakery wall. The walkers surrounded Heena who had lost all hope and seemed to allow them to take her. As Jack lifted his head, he just saw the tall walker wrap his chain around his mother's neck and all at once, she vanished.

"Shame, just you and me now boy," said Watts. "Your mother has practically done all my work for me, just you are now."

Jack lay staring into the remained dust and ash floating around in the space his mother stood. Watts was right. It was him left.

"I won't be that easy, I have lost too much to let you win!" Jack warned as he spoke a new incantation and a power blow hit Watts square in the chest knocking him off his feet. His beady eyes constricted, he pulled out a large black sword as he stood up. Jack looked down at his, then back at Watts, it was identical.

"I killed the person who helped your father create his sword," said Watts. "After I made him make me one. Your father may have stopped me from taking over this world but all he has done really has slowed me down. You're a powerful Brewin Jack, together we can rebuild the Brewin religion and we can take down the Dominion together."

"Just because we don't like the Dominion, it doesn't make us the same. What I have learned about the Brewin was to help the world against the Dominion and protect my family."

"And then what?" Watts interrupted. "Your family are gone. I didn't kill them, your mother killed your father, your mother foolishly made a deal with the Malkav and his walkers. When you destroy the Dominion and if you manage to destroy me, what then? You live happily ever after? No, you're human, you will desire power. You have already started training children to fight for you, you're halfway there Jack. You want to lead, let's destroy the Dominion together and rule the world."

"You're forgetting something Watts, you may not have killed my parents, but you have taken someone from me that I want back. I will get her back, and maybe I will want more power, but I won't kill innocent people like you have."

Jack gripped his sword and could feel the anger that was building in him.

"You won't get her back, by the time I'm finished with her, she will be dead," smoke started to raise up around Watts. "I have given you your chance to live Jack, so I will have to kill you."

Watts disappeared within the mass of smoke as if he had just gone up in flames. The smoke flew at Jack who jumped to the side to avoid it but as he turned around Watts was standing above him. His tall figure blocked the sunlight leaving his face all in shadow. He swung his sword down at Jack like a guillotine. Jack blocked it with his shield on his arm and pushed Watts away using a spell.

"You're weak Watts," said Jack as he got back to his feet. "You challenged me too early after returning."

"You have guts boy, but this isn't over yet" once again he flew at Jack. They each threw shots at each other, but nobody managed to hit a good enough blow. Jack used another spell and swung Watts over his head into a group of the Dale Guards. They stood ready to fight Watts, but he pushed them aside with ease using Brewin magic.

"Jack, you need to use the spell I told you about, it's the only way to get him out of Sophia's body. Even if you could kill him now, you would also kill Sophia!" shouted Thearon.

"Ah now what do you do Jack, you can't kill me because you will kill that girl you care so much about. You only got rid of me last time because I was weak and only just returned but now, well you can't touch me."

"I'm twice as powerful since the last time we met Watts." Jack replied through gritted teeth.

He threw his hands forward and shouted an incantation which hit Watts who froze and started to yell in pain.

"Agghh, it's not that easy boy," Watts screamed.

He broke out by throwing a spell back at Jack knocking him over. Jack got back up and shouted another incantation which hit Watts holding his arms in place like he was chained to each side of the square. He then hit Watts with the incantation again, this time Watts couldn't move, guards surrounded him.

"No move away." Thearon shouted, most of them got away but one guard got surrounded by smoke. Now the guard and Watts were both engulfed. Jack was concentrating so hard he was tiring fast, until he gave up and fell to his knees.

The smoke finally faded away and from it lay Sophia. She didn't move. Jack and Thearon ran over to her.

"She's alive Jack." said Thearon.

"Where's Watts?" Jack asked.

As they looked around, they saw the guard rolling on the floor in agony. His face was unrecognisable, he no longer looked as he did, but he didn't look like Watts either. He was grotesque. His eyes were no longer symmetrical, his head was completely misshapen.

"Jack, he has possessed whatever he could once you forced him out of Sophia. He will be weaker; you need to keep doing the same thing. Every time he transfers, he will weaken, and he will no longer be able to," said Thearon. "I will stay with Sophia."

Jack faced the guard, who was still in a lot of pain and started to recreate his spell. But before he could the guard stood up, his face merely resembled Watts but still very disfigured.

"No Jack," he struggled in a very tired voice. "You won't win!"

At once he flew at Jack in a cloud of black smoke and took him up into the air like a depressing firework and soared over the buildings away from town.

Jack could feel Watts with him yet couldn't touch him, he couldn't touch anything. It was as if he was free falling at such speed until he hit the floor and he and Watts rolled apart. They were in the forest where Jack had found his father.

"Why here?" Jack asked. "Do you even know where we are?"

"It doesn't matter, we're alone now and my power is still great enough to defeat you." said Watts sounding out of breath.

"We're not alone Watts, not here, you shouldn't have brought me with you, you should have fled alone."

"No, I can't let you get more powerful I need to finish you!"

Watts attempted to attack Jack with a

spell, but I didn't work, Jack pushed it away. Jack used his power to hold Watts and lift him up.

"Now there is no one for you to possess, agghh." Jack yelled as an arrow pierced his arm, and all around them Guyler appeared from the surrounding bushes and trees.

"Ha ha you're finished now Jack" Watts shouted as Jack lay in front of him. The Guyler left Jack and jumped on Watts. They tied a rope around his neck and hung him up in the tree above.

The familiar smoke started to appear around him, and the body stopped moving. One of the Guyler standing nearby had then become disfigured in the same way as the guard. But this time, he could barely walk, and his facial features were barely visible. This angered the Guyler as they hated anything they didn't consider to be normal. They jumped on him and hung him next to the guard. At this point Jack who had managed to hide behind a rock, watched and waited for the next victim to be possessed but it never came.

Jack however couldn't hide forever as he clumsily snapped twigs under his feet.

The Guyler, on seeing him flee, chased after

him. He didn't know where he was running, it seemed like an endless forest. Then he saw it, the river he had sailed down. He dived in and tried to stay under as long as he could. He held his breath, holding on to a root to keep him from floating up to the surface.

After a minute he gave up, hoping they had gone, he surfaced back to get some oxygen. It was dark, the water was grey and covered in plant life. The smell was horrendous, but the Guyler had gone.

Jack rested on the bank trying to think how to get back to Beachdale, but his sense of direction had been lost. He decided to follow the river hoping that it would lead him to a settlement and then he could get back to Beachdale from there. The river felt endless. More river just kept appearing out of the blackness ahead. Until a light appeared, Jack didn't have the energy to swim so he just waited, prepared to accept his fate, whatever that may entail.

"Hello there me boy." a voice echoed from behind the light.

Then a recognisable boat came into view.

"Ben?" Jack wasn't even sure if it was him. Maybe it was a hallucination, or he had fallen asleep and was just dreaming. But then two hands grabbed him and pulled him aboard and in front of him was Ben, Gregory, and young Matthew.

Jack opened his eyes; he was looking up at a stone ceiling. Completely disoriented, he sat up to have a look around. He was in a small room and there were six beds up against the walls. Five of the beds were freshly made but the one next to him wasn't. The quilt looked like it had been thrown off in a hurry. The room had a little bit of light coming through a small window which was next to Jack's bed. He then realised he was in a ward at the town's hospital.

"Oh, Jack you're awake, how are you feeling?" a tall skinny woman walked in very quickly taking very little steps.

"I'm OK thank you, how long have I been here?" he asked.

"A week, you were exhausted when you were brought in, I wasn't sure you were ever going to wake up," she said in her high slow voice. "I see miss Sophia has gotten out of bed again, I swear she will never get better."

"Sophia?" he jerked. "she's, OK?".

"Oh, I suspect she must be feeling better, but like you, for a while she showed little improvement. she didn't say a word when she woke up, that is until they brought you here, anyway, let me get you some water" she scurried off out of the ward picking up an empty jug. Jack was still lacking in energy, so he lay back down and closed his eyes.

"Well look at you," Jack jolted back upright again. "Easy Jack, it's just me," said Thearon putting his hand on Jacks shoulder gently pushing him back down. "How are you feeling?"

"I'm OK, I suppose, where's Sophia?"

"She's at the store, helping them stock back up, I'm sure she will be back here once she knows you're awake, she has been through a lot, you both have. Madame Hines has done a great job looking after you and all the others who were injured."

"How are the others, Thearon?" Thearon looked around the room and anxiously tapped his fingers on the wooden frame of Jacks bed.

"Yea, I'm sure you will be out soon. Back to normal."

"Thearon, come on."

"We lost Maddox." he said.

"I'm sorry Thearon."

"He sacrificed him-self, a brave man

Maddox. It wasn't his fight really, but he felt he owed me some sort of debt. Sad really, but we will remember him as a hero, the part he played was an important one."

"What about Lo? Where is he?" Jack asked.

"Madame Hines tried her best to save him, but his wound was too deep, and he lost a lot of blood." Thearon replied.

"I don't understand Thearon, what was he trying to do?" Jack asked but Thearon didn't get chance to answer.

"Good morning, Jack."

"Spence you're OK!" Jack said with a smile.

"Your appearance is quite opportune actually Spence, you can answer Jack's question better than me." Thearon added.

"OK, it's very complicated and I don't know exactly why he did what he did, but he was part of the Dominion but a kind of double agent. I suppose, he came to take you and your family to keep you out of harm's way. But acted alone until he found me, none of his soldiers knew, he never said why. He then got caught in some agreement with a witch and harassed by walkers to find you. Which turned out to be your mother. He figured it out once they escaped, it turned out they wanted the same thing, to keep you all safe."

"The walker who was with my mother? he described Lo as equal in title with me what did he mean?"

"We don't know yet Jack," Thearon said. "It must have a link to why he was looking for you and your parents. Possibly you are Androne descendants, but he couldn't have been one for Ando would have known by now. They spot them early you see, and Lo hasn't exactly been in hiding recently, and didn't work for Ando otherwise I would have been told. But I promise we will investigate."

"Oh, you have returned then young lady, I say maybe one day someone will do as they are told." Madame Hines said as Sophia walked into the ward.

"Jack, we will see you soon." Thearon said and left the room with Spence.

"Hi Jack." Sophia said in her soft tone.

"Hi." Jack replied awkwardly. It had been a couple of months now since he had seen her face and he did feel quite unprepared for it. Sophia sat beside Jack and held his hand.

"You saved my life Jack."

"Well I... you know I wouldn't want to leave you with him. How are you feeling?"

"OK I guess, I still feel something inside

that I can't seem to get rid of, it's like he took a part of me or a part of him is still holding on." Sophia said.
They paused for a minute and looked into each other's eyes. Sophia leant in and they kissed.

Later that day, Sophia and Jack had both been let out by Madame Hines and instantly called at the town hall. Zander stood at the top of the table, next to a rather large round man who had pale white skin, sunken dark eyes and a top hat.

"Some more news has come in this morning," said Zander. "The refugees have returned in the last hour. However, Governor Stone- has been killed, as described by a small group of children who called themselves the Brewin Knights." Zander looked at Jack who turned light red and looked down.

"They have told me that he sacrificed his life as they got attacked by a fleeing group of Dominion soldiers. The other refugees have confirmed this and added that it was these Brewin Knights who were key to killing the attackers."

Zander was now smiling at Jack, who also

lifted his head with a smile.

"So, Jack I suggest these Brewin Knights, are to continue their training as they could be the saviour of this town."

The man standing next to him winced at that as though someone had poked him in the eye. "So, moving on, we have a new Governor who has now been here in Beachdale for a long time and worked very closely with Mr Stone and that is, Governor Lediam."

Zander bowed and stepped backwards to give Lediam space to head the meeting.

"Thank you er, Zander," Lediam said in his low gruff voice. "We need to rebuild, I cannot promise that there will be no more Dominion attacks, however I promise I will do all in my power to keep us safe and fight back."

Jack and Thearon were never much for town meetings and were relieved to be outside the town hall.

"So where do you go now, Thearon?" Jack asked.

"I'm sure Ando will let me know in due course; they usually do. Look Jack I'm sure you agree that you no longer need me, even if you needed me in the first place, you know the truth about your family. But just because you're a descendant of Androne it doesn't mean you need to fight in this war." said Thearon looking down at the piece of parchment Jack held in his hands.

"Oh this," Jack replied. "My father gave it me when he died, I can't read it all though, it got smudged at some point, all I can read is "head to _ and find Dartnell House." Jack looked again carefully but then shook his head to Thearon.

"Well, you know what you need to do then Jack, find Dartnell House."

Sophia, Spence, and Zander joined them.

"So, my Lady." Thearon bowed. Jack also bowed rather awkwardly making Sophia punch him to stop.

"I'm not taking that role, it's not for me to rule a city. So, Zander and Spence will return to Woodale and pass the message on to the Lords so they can start the process of finding a new ruler. After my father's rule I don't think they would want me anyway and besides I know where I need to go as I have questions."

"You're going with Jack, aren't you?" Thearon said with a smile. "Well, you will both find answers where you're going, I'm sure of it."

DESCENDANT OF THE OTHER

To the side of the hospital ward, a little further down a darkened corridor sat another room. Beachdale's mortuary. It was only lit by torches hanging from the wall and every little noise echoed around the room. The workers had just left, leaving one body laying still. Both of Maraj Los' eyes were closed. His skin was pale, and blood had soaked a cloth bandage that was wrapped around his stomach. His body was left out by instruction of Madame Hines. Officials wanted to look closer into his life and history before getting rid of his body. He was to be cremated along with the many civilians and soldiers lost during the fight. Madame Hines strolled into the room, along with a young girl who also wore a white blouse and long white skirt.

"Now then Dani we need to look a lot closer into the death of Agent Lo because, well Mr Lediam has requested us too," Madame Hines said frustrated. "Maybe the fat oaf can come and have a look himself, but oh no he's running the town now, ugh I don't know dear." She unravelled the cloth bandage from around his waist, "now then Dani the" she froze, still as the body that lay before her.

"What's the matter mother?" Dani asked. She tried to edge around to see what it was that Madame Hines had seen.

"I thought you said he had been stabbed?"

"He had, look there is blood but, but no wound," confusion and fear flooded Madame Hines. "No this isn't right Dani, it was definitely on his right, let me just check his left to be certain," she scurried around and pushed Dani aside. "No, no wound."

"Is this magic mother?" Dani asked. Sounding more excited than the fear that her mother had building up inside her.

"I don't know dear, but s.... something is wrong. He must not be human, maybe, I don't know, in all my years that I have healed and laid the dead to rest I have never come across a self-healing dead person." Madame Hines voice started to become so high pitch it sounded more like a whistle.

"Dani dear, please go to the town hall and fetch me Mr Lediam, please," asked Madame Hines. She frantically started to open the little wooden hatches that held bodies that were awaiting cremation. Holding her nose and checking their wounds. "Sword, arrow, sword again, head wound and burns, they are all still there, so," she made sure the doors were all shut and turned back to Lo. "So, Agent L, Lo, where are your stab wounds gone," she then stopped realising what she was doing. "Talking to the dead, Bridges told me it would drive me mad doing this job but my mother, ah mother, said do something proper, a job that will help the community." Madame sat down at her small desk that she had at the corner of the room, "a proper job, peh." she grumbled as she started writing notes on a blank parchment.

When she looked up from her desk, she was sure she saw a finger move.

"No, it's all in your head," she said. "it's just a muscle spasm, that is all."

She went back to her notes, the finger moved again. This time Madame Hines stood and edged round her table and closer to Lo, she was trembling. She felt his wrist to find a pulse, nothing. She then leant over him and placed her ear above his chest, no obvious heartbeat. The fear that was already building inside Madame Hines started to cause her to shake.

"Dani, are you coming." she shouted with a wobble.

She needed to be brave she thought and walked back over to the body and looked closely, then let out a deafening scream as Agent Lo's eyes slowly opened.

Printed in Great Britain
by Amazon